Team building takes on a whole new meaning—when work is the last thing on your mind...

The Illinois wilderness should be a relaxing change of pace for advertising superstar Ben Stitzer. But he has one goal during this company retreat: proving to his boss how far he'll go to succeed. Even if it means having to team up with the uber competitive, exasperatingly attractive, woman who has tried to undermine him at every turn...

Being in the great outdoors is Avery Scottam's biggest nightmare. And hard as she tries, she can't even hide her fear from Ben. When one of her especially huge freak-outs gets them lost, they'll have to rely on each other to survive wild animals, sketchy campers, and their mutual distrust. Yet somewhere between a malevolent crow and a surprising confession, they just might end up something more than friends...

Will returning to civilization make them forget how truly wild they can be together?

Also by Lindy Zart

The Map to You

Love Without a Compass

A Least Likely Romance

Lindy Zart

USA Today Bestselling Author

LYRICAL SHINE
Kensington Publishing Corp.
www.kensingtonbooks.com

First Electronic Edition: September 2018
eISBN-13: 978-1-5161-0581-6
eISBN-10: 1-5161-0581-8

First Print Edition: September 2018
ISBN-13: 978-1-5161-0583-0
ISBN-10: 1-5161-0583-4

Printed in the United States of America

To Logan and Dexter:
Remember to always be true to you, and never give up.

1
BEN

Extreme Retreat's goal for us is to reach our destination by nightfall. My personal goal is for us to make it there without first killing each other. I tell myself I can do it. I can endure Avery Scottam for the next however many hours. Haven't I dealt with her for the last six months? Not well, I admit, but I've managed. There's just something about her that—

A tree limb whacks me in the face. My eyes snap to my coworker. Avery looks back, innocence etched into her features. I rub my stinging cheek. "What the hell, Avery?"

"Whoops." Avery shrugs. "I didn't realize you were so close."

That. That's the something about her. She's a menace disguised in sensuous woman.

I shift my jaw back and forth, tighten my grip on the straps of the backpack to keep my fingers from finding her pale, slim neck, and stride past her. Her grapefruit scent teases my senses and I breathe shallowly, fighting my reaction to the pleasant smell.

"I'll lead," I announce.

The mountain is cantankerous, full of divots and loose rocks, holes and hidden danger. Each breath of air I take is thick with heat, and the August sun is having a good old time with the back of my neck. Less than an hour ago we walked into a fortress of slanted trees and rocks that don't appear to have an end. We've been marching an uneven path to perdition ever since.

Avery appears beside me, her jaw set. The sun catches strands of her hair, causing it to shine like gold. "*I'll* lead."

"You don't know where we're going."

"Up." She gestures in the direction we're heading. "We're going up, just like the Extreme Retreat employee said to do. It's not hard to figure out." Everything is a competition with her. I misstep on a twig, and losing my balance, bump into her. It's completely by accident that my elbow happens to shoot out at the exact moment it connects with her biceps.

"Ow!" Scowling at me, she rubs her arm. "You did that on purpose."

"Whoops," I say evenly, eyes trained forward.

Avery hurries past, her perfectly rounded ass emphasized by her microscopic white shorts with each upward lunge of her legs. Who wears white shorts to go hiking through a national forest? Really, I want to know. Turning from the view I wish I didn't enjoy, I look at another one. Blue skies and green trees have taken over the world. I drop my gaze to the unseen valley below, wondering how far our coworkers have gotten. I'm sure none of them are enjoying their time with their partner quite as much as I am.

"I hate this," Avery mutters once we crest a small hill. She sets her palms to her knees and draws air into her lungs. Her pale face is flushed, and dewy with perspiration. Avery's hair, normally smooth and straight, is forming waves I didn't realize it had.

"Hate what?"

"This. Walking. The heat. Bugs. Outside."

"Outside?" I give her a sidelong look. "You hate outside?"

"That's what I said."

"That's a pretty general statement."

We lock eyes, hers like smoldering fire. "Meaning?"

"Meaning it covers a lot of areas. There's nothing you like about outside?"

"No. Wait. Air. I like air. Air is outside."

"Yes. It is," I agree, and wait.

Avery sighs. "You're getting to a point, aren't you? What is it?"

"I find it interesting that you hate everything—besides air—that has to do with outside, since you were gushing to Duke about how excited you were to go on this wilderness team-building quest."

Avery's golden eyes land on mine and skirt past.

I gesture to her spotless pink Pumas. "I bet you bought those tennis shoes just for this, didn't you?"

The corners of her mouth tighten. "So?"

"I find it interesting, that's all." I tell myself I will not be the first to look away, but I still blink in surprise when she does.

Avery scowls. "Hiking in the mountains is not my idea of fun, but I always do what is necessary."

"With a lying smile in place," I murmur.

"Can smiles really lie?" she returns with an arched eyebrow.

"Yours do."

Her jaw shifts, but Avery doesn't reply.

After a couple minutes of walking, I ask, "Aren't you from Montana?"

"What's your point?"

"Do I have to say it?"

She gives me a look.

I guess I do. "How can you be from somewhere that is known for its mountains and have not a clue as to how to navigate through them?"

"Illinois is known for its high crime rate. Does that make you a criminal?"

Touché.

Avery straightens, running a hand through her hair. "I might have overstated my level of enthusiasm over this."

"You mean you lied."

She scowls. "Overstated."

"Lied."

She's been sweetness and goodness to everyone since she walked through the red door of Sanders and Sisters. She even has Duke Renner, the owner of Sanders and Sisters and a man who cannot be manipulated, captivated. She's a fraud, and I plan on exposing her. It could be said that, so far, my attempts have backfired. Case in point: where we presently are.

"Okay. Fine. I lied," Avery says.

"Was that so hard to admit?"

Avery rolls her eyes and faces the rocky walkway. "How much farther do you think we have to go?"

"Duke said it should take around five hours to find the flag and get back to the lodge, so, for us, it'll probably take twenty lifetimes. Here's to many, many years of torture," I tell her cheerfully.

"He said this is mandatory continuing education, whatever that means." She complements her next statement with a pout. "What is the purpose of this, really? Other than to make us miserable."

"True. The same outcome could easily have been accomplished by sticking us in a room together for two minutes."

"You're hilarious," Avery replies mockingly, swatting at something that dares to try to touch her. Probably a speck of dirt.

Twigs snap under the weight of my hiking boots. I squint at the landscape before me. In the distance, brown and gray rocks climb a path to the clouds. We both know why we're here, and it isn't because of any continuing education bullshit. "I wasn't kidding."

A prolonged pause follows that.

"I can't believe he did this to me," she finally says.

"Well, he did. And what's worse is that he did it to me." I've been Duke Renner's star employee for years; Avery's been around less than seven months. It chafes. It chafes a lot.

"At least you have something nice to look at. I just have...you," Avery says.

I turn around, studying the woman. "Careful, Avery. You're starting to show your true colors."

Avery crosses her arms and turns her head to the side. "I don't know what you're talking about."

"What's wrong with the way I look?" I don't know why I ask it, or why I care what she thinks. I know I'm not the best-looking guy around, but I've never had a problem getting dates.

"You're, you know..." She gestures vaguely to me.

I stand up straighter, hands on hips, and lift an eyebrow. "What am I? Please, do tell."

Avery makes a face. "You're not that tall."

"I'm five-ten."

"Exactly."

I decide not to point out that five-nine is the average height for a guy. Plus, she's barely five-four herself, if she's even that.

"What else?" I know there's more. That can't be the only thing about me she sees as a negative.

"You wear glasses."

I snort. "Yeah. A lot of people do, so they can, you know, *see*."

Sighing, she shakes her head and attempts to move around me. "Never mind. It doesn't matter."

I step into her path. She has to tilt back her head to meet my gaze. I don't point that out either. "Oh, no, let's hear it. I'd like to know all the ways I am visually unappealing."

"Okay, well, your hair is, I don't know, boring."

"Boring?" I narrow my eyes. "How can hair be boring?"

"I don't know. It just can. It lacks character."

"Are you serious?" I ask in a low voice.

Ignoring my glower, she adds, "And you're not nice."

My voice is unusually high as I sputter, "What the—"

"It makes you less attractive."

I stare at her hard, long enough that my vision blurs beneath the lenses of my glasses that apparently make me unattractive.

"You're not my type," Avery says, as if she thinks I want her to want me. The world goes unnaturally silent as my blood pressure skyrockets. I take a slow breath, keeping my eyes trained on Avery. She watches me with that fake innocent look she uses around the office. Whatever the scenario, I will not let her win. I will remain calm. I will one-up her, again and again. Because I'm too short, and wear glasses, and not her type.

I may not be a lot of things, but I am something.

I move closer. "Avery."

Avery lifts her eyebrows.

My gaze trails from her eyes to her mouth. I watch her lips part and sweep my eyes back to hers. "I think we both know *you're* not *my* type."

She gasps, her face going pink, and I turn before she catches my smirk. Satisfaction, warm and pure, flows through my limbs.

AVERY

I must have died sometime during the night and been sent directly here. Nothing else makes sense. I'm fairly certain, when Duke Renner set up this team-building mumbo-jumbo, he specified that it should be located in Avery Scottam's—that's me—least favorite kind of place: outside. Outside is gross. It's dirty, and there are bugs, and my hair does not respond well to heat.

To add more salt to the wound, Ben Stitzer is the last person I want to see me at anything less than completely composed, so of course Duke paired us together. It has nothing to do with the fact that I did something awful to Ben and he's hated me ever since. Things have been tense around the office, and wherever I turn, there's Ben, plotting his revenge. But that's not why we're here. Right. Nope. Not at all.

Our boss's words repeat in my head, bringing inner calamity and outer perspiration with them.

Wilderness retreat.

Improve team-building skills.

Rely on one another.

And the most upsetting words of all…

Ben and Avery, you're partners.

I shoot a look in Ben's direction. More likely, he chose the setting. As if sensing my eyes on him, his head turns, his eyes slicing me in two. The look lasts all of one second but has enough vexation in it to steadily burn through many, many lifetimes. There was one single night that could have been the start of something amazing, but I ruined it.

I think we both know you're not my type.

The words echo through me, bringing an uncomfortable twinge with them.

"I have no idea what you're talking about," I reply with a sniff. "I'm sure you made up some fantasy scenario in your—"

A bitter laugh comes from my side, cutting off my words. "Trust me, you're not in any part of my fantasies."

I stop walking, my eyes shooting to my coworker's. Ben gazes stonily back, his bespectacled brown eyes scalding me with their animosity. I sigh and face forward, absently scratching at the most recent of countless bug bites. Mountains, rocks, and trees greet me, splashing the immediate vicinity in shades of brown and gray, speckled with green. They remind me of Ben's eyes, actually, except without the perpetual loathing in them.

"What's the hold up?" he demands, hands on his hips.

"You."

One dark eyebrow quirks.

I know men fantasize about me. I'm not being vain. I'd rather only one man want me over all the rest, and it's the one next to me, looking at me as if I'm diseased and contagious. That's irony for you.

"If I simply stand here all day, will I wake up and realize this has all been a really bad dream?" I ask without looking at Ben.

"The better question is: will I?"

I swallow a snort and take the rubber band from my wrist, twisting my hair into a sloppy bun. I don't understand how Duke Renner could drop us off in the middle of nowhere with a gleeful wave and shouted well wishes. But then, since I started at Sanders and Sisters over six months ago, I've realized that the only constant with my boss is that he is unpredictable.

Things were much simpler in Montana.

Ignoring the sharp pain that accompanies thoughts of my life before I relocated to Illinois, I set my shoulders back and once again take on the dusty trail to an unknown destination.

"Where do you think the others were taken?" I ask.

Our six coworkers are somewhere within the miles-wide expanse of Shawnee National Forest, paired with the person they get along with the least, working on their own quests. I wonder how Juan Narvaez and Nate Schroeder are faring. Nate went out with Juan's ex-girlfriend a while back and came home that night to find all the beer in his fridge reduced to empty cans strewn about the kitchen.

To most people, that wouldn't be a big deal, but to Nate, who loves beer, it was catastrophic. Juan showed up to work the next day with the scent of alcohol seeping from his pores and a smug expression on his face, silently naming him as the culprit. Nate was not happy.

The wind picks up, bringing authentic country dust with it. Even though my mouth is closed, I still taste its gritty, chalky flavor on my tongue. I haven't navigated through much of Illinois yet. I have to say, I can think of better reasons to explore the state.

Ben's jaw is tight as he walks beside me. "We may be partners, and yes, we are obligated to work together to get through today but talking is not a requirement. In fact, let's not."

It's supposed to be four days of this. Four days of hell spent trekking over countryside with a man who loathes me. Wonderful. Exactly how I want to spend my time, following a map and compass with checkpoints through uncivilized terrain. I kick at the ground, hurting my big toe in the process.

I stop and pull the map from my back pocket, pretending Ben didn't say that. Pretending he isn't justified in his aversion to me. One day, he'll forgive me. I am going to make sure of that. But for now, we need to focus on what's required of us to pass our mandatory continuing education class.

"Let's see what we need to do first," I offer just to irritate Ben, and come to a stop.

Ben turns toward me and shoves his glasses up his long nose, the ever-changing shade of his eyes striking against the backdrop of his olive skin and dark hair. I envy the golden sheen of his skin. He's probably one of the lucky people who never burn, their skin only darkening with sun exposure.

Fair-skinned and fair-haired, I am prone to burn instead of tan. Regrettably, I freckle too. My skin is already feeling the effects of the early morning sun.

"I'm going to look at the map now," I announce loudly in an attempt to get a reaction from Ben.

There isn't one.

As the seconds tick by and I simply watch Ben, he gives me an exasperated look and gestures for me to continue. I lift an eyebrow, the map remaining closed.

His teeth are bared as he says, "Will you please check the map, Avery?"

"Yes, I will, Ben, thanks for asking," I reply pleasantly, hiding a smile when Ben rolls his eyes.

I unfold the map and study the colorful landscape paired with specific directives. Although I know it isn't, the marked-off area we are to navigate seems endless. It's pocketed with lakes, caves, trails, and other vague, ominous wildlife pictures. I chew on my lower lip, wondering about the sanity of this whole thing.

It seems an archaic form of employee bonding to me. But then Extreme Retreat, the company Duke hired to orchestrate this obstacle course of madness, is known for their wild, sometimes dangerous, means of bringing coworkers together. No electronic devices, including cell phones, are allowed. They didn't even let us have first-aid kits or flares. I think whoever runs the organization is partially crazy.

Their motto is actually "There is no don't, only do." Being nontraditional himself, I can see why this organization appealed to Duke.

Anne Dobson, one of our coworkers, got into a tug-of-war match with an Extreme Retreat employee when they attempted to take her cell phone from her. Besides the map I hold, all we were given is the backpack presently resting on Ben's shoulders and were told it has everything we're allowed to have, or will need for the day. Unless there is a room inside it with air conditioning, running water, and takeout cuisine on hand, I tend to disagree.

I read the first objective on the list. *Goal number one: Hike Crow Hill. Retrieve red flag.*

"The first checkpoint is at the end of a two-mile hike." I look up, frowning. Working at keeping my voice unconcerned, I say, "It's called 'Crow Hill.' Why do you think it's called that?"

Ben resumes walking, not answering.

I lengthen my stride, catching up to him.

He scowls and moves faster.

I do the same, minus the scowl.

We continue this way until we're jogging side by side up a narrow rocky incline with towering stones surrounding us. A worn green sign, along with an arrow, announces we're on Crow Hill. I'm not a runner and it soon shows. Panting, my legs and lungs scream at me to stop, but I don't slow down. I'm not slowing down until Ben does. I glance at him, taking in the determined set of his face.

I don't think he ever plans on slowing down.

I push myself harder when I begin to fall behind, full-on running now. Ben moves ahead of me, his legs long and leanly muscled. He doesn't appear to be sweating, whereas I already feel the salty wetness trickling down my spine and the sides of my face. A wheezing sound has replaced my normal breathing. I tell myself to pick up the pace, but my legs don't want to cooperate, and that is unacceptable. I force my legs to go. Anything Ben can do, I can do—sometimes, even better.

We briefly exchange looks crackling with intensity. As we near the end of the trail, it takes me far too long to realize what we're doing, and that it is exactly what put us where we are. Working against each other instead of together. There's friendly competition and then there's rivalry.

Duke was right to send us here. Ben and I have competed since the day I started working for the advertising company. It's instinctive, part of our natures. Why would I think now would be any different?

And it needs to be.

"We're supposed to be a team," I remind him around gasps of air.

"*Now* you want to want to be a team?" Ben scoffs, his form and breathing steady. "Forget it."

"We'll be in trouble if we don't."

He pulls up abruptly, jerking around to face me. I skid to a stop, gravel rolling beneath my tennis shoes. I fight to breathe, partially from the run, mostly from the man before me. Ben's eyes are alive with simmering emotion, sparking green and electrocuting with thunderous gray. His chest lifts and lowers as I watch, finally seeing a hint of exertion. Ben's hair is damp, the ends curling around his ears.

The air turns stifling as we stare at each other, the heat combustible. Ben looms over me, dark and furious. Desire streams through my veins, and I see it reflected in his eyes. I've wanted Ben since the moment I met him. I saw the same lightning bolt response in Ben. He tries to hide it beneath a shield of resentment, but sometimes, like now, it finds its way through the cracks.

"I won't be in trouble," Ben says confidently. He's probably right.

"Do you want to take the chance?" My voice is scratchy.

Ben studies me, his gaze dropping before slowly returning to my face. I feel that look as strongly as if he'd physically touched me. It steals my air; it turns my body to warm mush. Something unmistakable and equally unnamable glints in his eyes. "With you?"

He's toying with me. I know it, and I can't seem to care. Because he's looking at me in a way that makes me forget everything, even why I sought a job for Sanders and Sisters in the first place. Too often, Ben makes it hard to remember what I promised myself, what I vowed to my mom.

Unconsciously, as if I can't control myself, I step forward.

Ben steps back.

"Maybe," is all I allow myself to admit.

"You've never been very good at being direct, have you?"

I watch the fire die out, feeling the loss of it as if it's real and not only in his eyes. I bite my lower lip, not answering. If I ever decide to be brave enough, I'll be so direct with Ben he'll wish he could mute me like the volume on a television with a remote control. 'If' being the key word.

I cross my arms and reply with a scowl, "I know how to be direct."

He steps closer, bringing his heat and earthy scent. Ben stares into my eyes, his face devoid of expression, and lifts a hand toward my face. "Oh, yeah? How so?"

I hold my breath and go still, wanting to feel his fingers across my skin. I can't remember ever wanting anything more.

Toying with me or otherwise, I don't want this to end.

"Show me," Ben encourages silkily. "Come on, be direct. Tell me what you're really doing at Sanders and Sisters."

My heart lurches and I study his face. He can't know anything. Realizing that doesn't make me feel any relief. I open my mouth, but no sound comes forth. If we're playing games right now, Ben's winning.

Ben pauses, darkness billowing around his lean frame like a shadowy cloak. "You can't, can you?"

"Ben, I…"

Holding my gaze, he trails his fingers across my shoulder. I unconsciously shiver. Then he snatches his hand back, a red flag dangling from his fingers. Hardness claims Ben's features, wiping any hint of seduction from his bearing as he growls, "Don't forget who I am."

"I have no idea what you mean."

His eyes narrow. "I think you do."

I swallow hard, knowing what he's going to say before he says it.

Ben turns from me. "Remember, Avery, I know you. I know you better than anyone at Sanders and Sisters." He looks over his shoulder with a single glance that blazes and chars. "How could I not? I'm the person you royally screwed over."

I blow out a noisy breath, wrinkling up my nose. Yes, he is that indeed.

2
BEN

Duke Renner has never been much of a rule follower. Since he was in his mid-twenties, he's run Sanders and Sisters, a small, but prestigious company that centers on marketing words to the right buyer. The company, run by two aging sisters and their brother, wasn't much when Duke took it over, but he had the right amount of humor, bullheadedness, and charismatic personality to get his words noticed by the right people.

Inspirational quotes, greeting cards, business logos, makeup, clothing, and athletic apparel slogans—Sanders and Sisters handles that and more. Words are everything. They can be the difference between crying and laughter, a smile and a frown. Hope and giving up.

The Avery Scottam that Sanders and Sisters is familiar with doesn't complain. She doesn't have to, because everything is easy for her. Everyone wants to help her; I've even seen Duke fetch her tea as if it was his idea when she was the one who mentioned it. She writes some average saying a duck could think up, and her words are instantly sold. I wish Duke could see this Avery, and finally realize what I've known all along.

I tried to tell Duke, but he just thought I wanted to get her in bed and my sexual frustration was making me cantankerous. That was his word. Cantankerous. That wasn't it at all. Avery says I'm not her type, but she's not mine either. She is relentless in her pursuit of any and every client in sight. She outshines me, again and again. It isn't coincidental. It's personal, and I don't know why.

My stomach growls, or maybe that's just me. It does it again, confirming that it's my stomach and it wants food.

The last time I ate was at six this morning, and it's now early afternoon. Too long ago. Except for some sips of water and a piece of jerky each, Avery and I haven't had any real sustenance. We were told to ration what we were given, and I guess they thought bribing us with a gourmet meal tonight at the lodge would make it okay. I guess they were right, because here we are. This survivalist bullshit is a joke, and we're the ones being laughed at. I glance over my shoulder to Avery. She's unusually quiet—not that I'm not enjoying it. I'm generally a nice guy, but once someone deceives me, I'm done with them. Avery is the queen of deception. Sweat glistens on her sun-pink skin and a layer of grime covers the outfit I'm sure she bought specifically for today. She lifts an eyebrow when I don't immediately look away and shifts her eyes forward. I turn my head back around and focus on the path.

I've known Duke Renner for years. I consider him a mentor. Duke's always been eccentric, but have I ever considered his choices to be dangerous or illogical? Not until now. I told him this was a bad idea, and not only because I knew he'd pair me with Avery, but because none of us city folk have any right trekking through a mountainous countryside. He laughed and told me to grow a pair. Nice guy, that Duke Renner.

"Where are you going?" Avery demands when I veer off the path toward a tree.

"I'm taking a piss. That okay?"

"Yes, actually, it is, and by the way, I hope you piss all over yourself," is called from behind.

Half of my mouth lifts in a fleeting smile. Plain and simple, no matter that I can't stand her, Avery routinely amuses me.

I unzip my shorts and relieve myself, hearing what sounds like a squeaking sound as I finish up. Sure it's a rodent scurrying about, I'm not overly concerned until I turn around and find the area Avery-less. Which would be good under regular circumstances, but out here in the wild? Not so much.

"Avery?"

When there continues to be no response, I ask, "Did you find a mirror and get lost in your reflection?"

Silence greets me.

I turn, annoyance flaring through my veins that she's reciprocating my bad behavior toward her. Only one of us is allowed to be immature, and right now, I own that right. I take in my surroundings, looking for an inimitable shade of golden hair with matching eyes I've only seen on one particular woman.

Nothing but nature faces me.

A wisp of alarm threads itself around my chest, tightening enough to let me know something isn't right.

I turn in a slow circle, pausing to glance over the cliff's edge. I quickly step back. My stomach dips at the thought of how far up we are, and how far someone would fall if they went over the edge. I swallow. "We're a bit old to play hide and seek, don't you think?"

Not able to let fear become even a thought, anger takes over.

I storm back in the direction from which we came, eerie quiet my only companion. Even the birds and bugs are silent. It makes my skin crawl. With her white shorts and pink shirt and shoes, Avery should stick out like a peppy cheerleader-type target among the neutral-toned land. I spent the hour-long drive to our drop-off point wondering who in their right mind would wear white shorts to hike through a mountainside. Now, all I want is to catch a glimpse of her white shorts—and not only because they're microscopic.

"Avery."

Why is she not answering me? I run a hand through my hair, jaw jutted forward as I make my way around a rock ledge that partly covers the trail. I look for clues on the ground, but I'm not a detective of any sort, or all that good of a tracker. I see nothing in the dirt to let me know where my coworker went.

"Avery? Can you hear me?"

Another sound, much closer and definitely human, catches my attention. I turn to the left, looking at a small valley where trees reside, and come up short. I stare for a minute, trying not to smile as I meander toward one particular tree. My heartbeats slow with the knowledge that Avery's safe.

"How's it hanging?" I greet.

Avery smiles thinly, not replying.

"Let me guess—you're imitating a tree, right?" I tilt my head sideways to better meet her eyes. I probably shouldn't be enjoying this as much as I am, but it's Avery.

She stands at an odd angle, her hair held hostage by a tree limb. Her arms are crossed as she stares death at me. "I just thought I'd like to see the world from a different perspective."

I rub my jaw. "I see. How's that going for you?"

Avery's expression turns lethal.

I pat her shoulder, feel the muscles spasm beneath my touch, and turn. "Well, have fun with that."

"If you leave me like this, you're fired."

A patch of green-and-yellow shrubbery holds my interest as I weigh her quiet words. She's right, but I'm still considering it. I face Avery, watching her skin turn pinker the longer I gaze at her. Shifting my jaw back and forth, I remove a switchblade from my pocket, flick it open, and advance.

"What are you doing?"

I grin evilly.

"You're cutting the branch, not my hair, right?" Her eyes dart from the gleaming silver blade to me.

"Yes."

"Yes? Yes, *what*?"

Glancing down, I hide a smile before moving behind her. I allow myself one second to study the elegant slope of her neck before taking the limb in hand to saw it in two. It frays, then snaps, and Avery screams like I slit her throat instead of the tree branch holding her hair hostage. She hops around as she disentangles the limb from her hair and manages to trip over the same branch as it hits the ground. She falls, landing on her back in the dirt. A grunt leaves her upon impact.

I watch the rise and fall of her chest as she pants, her gaze deadly and aimed straight at me.

Her creamy skin is pocked with dirt and her shoulder-length hair is a golden poof around her head with twigs and leaves caught in it. The rubber band she used to pull back her hair is now but a memory. Avery's shorts and T-shirt are brownish gray with debris, and her grapefruit scent has all but dissolved. This is sweet justice, it really is.

Avery's eyebrows slant down, and she scowls up at me. "Why are you smiling? You're stuck with me for the next four days."

The smile drops from my face. I close the knife and shove it back in my pocket before I decide to use it on her. "You're welcome."

Avery huffs behind me, but luckily for me, she remains quiet.

I make my way down the rocky incline at a brisk pace, thinking the faster we find our flags and checkpoints, the faster we'll get out of this hellish place. I misstep on a pile of rocks and roll forward on my boots until I gain control of myself. A branch scrapes my cheek as I pass by a tree too closely. I breathe in the scent of crisp leaves and fresh air. If not for Avery, this might not be all that bad. I'm not much of a nature guy, but this feels peaceful.

"Ben! Wait up!"

I wince. And there goes the peacefulness.

The sun peeks through endless branches, heating my already hot skin. I almost cheer when I hear the sound of moving water. I slow my pace to allow Avery to catch up.

The end of earth comes upon me quickly, and for a moment, I feel weightless. I jerk back from the edge of a rocky cliff. Where the hell did that come from? Without warning, the world ended. My heartbeat takes a drastic leap directly into calamity, and I carefully step away from a ride I'd rather not take, putting a couple feet between me and the drop-off. I set a hand to the rough bark of a tree and look down hundreds of feet to the rushing water below. It looks unapologetically wicked.

"What is it? Why are you stopping?" she asks.

There is one instant—one immoral, spiteful second—where I consider letting her find out on her own. Chances are, Avery would stop walking before she fell to her death. Probably.

I partially turn and look over my shoulder. "Don't come any closer. It's a drop-off."

Avery skids to a stop, her eyes wide in her dirt-smudged face. A chunk of golden hair falls forward to obliterate one eye, giving her appeal she doesn't need, and that is wasted on me. Pretty face twisting, she throws her hands up. "What is the point of this? We're just supposed to wander around in the wild for days? This is asinine! There's no reason we couldn't learn how to work together as a team at a nice resort, not out in the wilderness. I don't understand why Duke would do this to us. It's like he's punishing us."

My lips press together. Oh, I am definitely being punished.

"I feel like we're in *The Hunger Games*," Avery mutters from my left. "Who does this anyway?"

"Duke Renner," I growl, for once in agreement with her.

"I thought we weren't allowed to bring anything," Avery remarks.

I look at her.

"Your pocketknife." She gestures to my shorts. "We were told to not bring anything but ourselves. Isn't that considered illegal?"

"Illegal?"

"You know what I mean. Against the rules."

I study Avery's features. "I would think you'd be glad I had it. Otherwise, you might still be trapped by a deadly tree."

Her jaw goes taut. "I think the idea was to get me untangled without using a weapon."

I shrug. "I've been wondering…how did you manage to get your hair caught?"

"You know what an even better question is?" She glares at me.

"Why has Duke forsaken me?"

Avery continues to glower at me.

I sigh and briefly explain about the pocketknife, "I don't go anywhere without it."

"Why?"

I climb over a boulder almost as big as me, calling over my shoulder, "If I tell you, you'll just make it into a slogan and sell it on me. You're good at that."

AVERY

We all have parts of ourselves we dislike. Some we can help, and others, we cannot. I've always hated my freckles and wavy hair. I can't permanently do anything about either of those.

I carefully heave my frame over the monstrous rock that decided to make its home in the middle of a trail. I scratch my palms and knees in the process. Once I get over it, and by that, I mean, I basically let myself fall over the side and ungracefully land on my feet, I lean over with my palms on my knees and take a moment to catch my breath. Sweat trickles down the sides of my face, stinging my eyes when some drips into them.

"We're wasting daylight," Ben says snippily.

"Coming," I say hoarsely.

I want people to like me, and because of that, I sometimes don't stay true to myself. The need for approval is strong, and knowing from where it stems, doesn't negate it. There are times I've done things I regret, or acted in a way that isn't really me, all to impress someone. I study Ben's profile as he takes in the scenery up ahead. I had control over whether or not I hurt Ben, and I did it anyway. Because I thought the bigger picture outweighed Ben's feelings. Because I made a mistake I can't fix.

My chest spasms, tight with pain, and I straighten. I slowly make my way toward my coworker and teammate, my muscles overtaxed and noodle-like. I'm not used to this much physical activity. Exercising is not my friend.

I stop beside Ben, my heart pounding with gusto. He takes one look at me and wordlessly offers a bottle of water.

"Thanks," I rasp, chugging the water so fast it dribbles down my chin.

"Easy, we need to make that last," Ben warns, moving to take the bottle from me.

I almost growl at him, but grudgingly relinquish the water.

He hands me a piece of jerky and I chomp down on it, tearing off a small piece and chewing it into oblivion until I can swallow it without the fear of choking on it. I do this until it's gone, my stomach longing for more. I don't even bother asking, the look Ben gives me saying not to waste my breath. I grimace and turn from him.

A wind forms, strong and cool. I close my eyes and tip my head back, letting it wave over me. This, right here, this is nice. The rest of it? No. But the breeze is like heaven to my burning skin and downtrodden disposition. It's enough to put a little pep back into me.

When it passes, I lower my head and open my eyes, surprised to find Ben watching me. Noting the intensity with which he views me, my mouth pulls down. What is he thinking? He quickly looks away, his throat bobbing as he swallows. I decide I probably don't want to know. I'm sure it's something hellish, like he wishes I'd break out in scabies or something. I'm not even entirely sure what that is, but it sounds horrible.

"It's beautiful out here," Ben says softly.

I turn a critical eye on the world below and beyond us. The landscape blurs the farther out it goes; its rolling hills blanketed with dense greenery and brown soil, and higher still, mountains are tipped in gray and white. Endless, and vast, it stretches out for miles and miles. Land layering land layering land. My opinion shifts from adverse to appreciative.

"It looks like it goes on forever," I remark, watching as clouds shift and part. It's dizzying to see from this height, and to know with a few steps forward, I'd be rolling down the side of a mountain. I put more space between me and the ledge.

A bird caws in the distance and I hum to block out the sound, refusing to look at anything but what is directly before me, which is a sloping incline. If I don't see them or hear them, they aren't really here. As another bird joins the first, my stomach lurches.

Over the undesirable sound of nasty flying creatures, I shout, "Can we get moving already?"

Ben gives me an odd look. "Why are you yelling?"

"I just like to yell," I yell.

His eyes narrow. "Since when?"

"Since now," I get out around clenched teeth, lunging forward when Ben doesn't move fast enough for me. He can stay here if he wants, but I am most definitely not.

"You want to tell me what's going on?" Ben easily catches up to me, keeping pace with my light jog.

"Not really." I huff along, feeling as if my chest is going to collapse on me. I have exercised more today than I have in the past decade. It's horrible and I hope to never have a repeat of it.

Something flies in front of my face and I swat at the air as I go motionless, closing my eyes so I don't have to know what it is. Of course, I ask anyway. "What was that?"

Ben answers carefully, "A bug."

"It felt really big and seemed to have wings, like a bat...or a bird."

"It was a fly."

"No way." I crack open one eye to find Ben staring at me. I snap, "What?"

"Bats aren't out during the day. You do know that, right?"

My skin suddenly itches, imaging phantom bugs crawling on me. Or real. They could be real. Tiny, microscopic, disgusting bugs. I scratch at my arms and legs. "There are exceptions to everything."

"Sure, but it wasn't a bat."

"Are there bugs on me?" Panic escalates, taking my sanity with it.

"No," Ben replies slowly.

"Are you sure? Because it feels like there are."

He continues to watch me, finally asking, "Are you having a mental breakdown?"

I scratch harder. "You'd like that, wouldn't you?"

"Well, I wouldn't exactly be sad about it."

I make a sound from deep in my chest.

"Was that a growl?"

I stop scratching long enough to glare at him. "I hate bugs."

"Got that."

I navigate the land, pretty sure we're descending directly into hell. The tight feeling in my chest is getting worse, as is my scratching. "There are no bugs on you," I tell myself, right before one lands on my shoulder.

I shriek as I jump up and down, swatting at my shirt. The bug is attached to the fabric, clinging to me for all it's worth. I hit myself harder in desperation. The bug is large, and black, and ugly. So ugly. As I spin around, I run into something hard and unmovable.

Ben stares down at me, gripping my un-bugged shoulder with enough force to keep me still. He holds my gaze as he calmly removes the bug from my shoulder and flicks it away. I look at the ground, my face flooding with heat now that that ordeal is over. That was a little embarrassing.

I straighten my spine and go about my walk as if nothing happened. My eyes briefly meet Ben's. He lifts his eyebrows.

I give him a dirty look and walk faster, my back stiffening at the faint sound of chuckling behind me.

3
BEN

Avery looks around, her expression less than cheerful. The sun is slowly lowering in the sky, mocking us with each hour that passes without us making any progress. Her tone is biting when she says, "Shouldn't we have found the next checkpoint by now? Or, I don't know, possibly the lodge?"

Or people. Other people would have been nice to see at this point. I'm really surprised we haven't run into anyone by now. I'm almost concerned. Are we so far spread out that it would be impossible to stumble upon our coworkers? Or have they all already gotten to the lodge? Not the most heartening thought.

"This is where the next flag should be." Woods stand before us, not a hint of a red flag in sight. I scratch the side of my head, my eyes searching again and again for something that isn't there.

Avery's tone is particularly peevish as she demands, "Then why haven't we found it?"

"I don't know." I turn in a circle, taking in the vastness around us. "Why don't you ask the trees?"

With sweetness coating her tone, Avery says, "Why don't you kiss my ass?"

I shoot her an irritated look, mostly because I'd probably enjoy it. "Check the map again."

"You check the map." A trifold pamphlet flies my way.

I snatch it out of the air, meeting Avery's grumpy look with a deadly one of my own. It doesn't seem to faze her. She drops to the ground, crossing her arms and legs before turning her face to the side. This is another side of Avery I haven't seen. She keeps them all well-hidden. I guess seeing her in such a sour mood wouldn't look good for her office image. I'd love for Duke to witness Avery right now and know what she's really like.

Although, being stuck in the mountains even has me in a bad mood, so maybe this is not the best example.

"We aren't in the right place," I announce.

"How do you know?" Avery looks at me suspiciously.

"This is near where we started, I'm sure of it." I study the landscape that looks the same in every direction I turn. "We're going in circles."

"How can we go up two hills and end up where we started?"

"I don't know, but we did," I retort angrily.

"But how do you *know* that?"

"I don't!" I lower my voice and add, "Not for sure."

Avery jumps to her feet, her eyes like live flames of golden wrath. "Then don't say you do."

"Something isn't right," I insist.

I swing the backpack off my shoulders and dig through it, pulling out a compass. I study the map, looking from it to the compass, and then I drop my hands and look at nothing, my vision going fuzzy. I don't know where we are, and looking at the map or compass for guidance is meaningless.

Before the trip, I read a bunch of articles about surviving in the wilderness, but it didn't prepare me enough for what's before us. According to where we should be, we need to head north. Only, I don't know if we are where we're supposed to be.

"This is such bullshit," I swipe an arm across my sweaty forehead and take my glasses with it. I lean down and shove them back on my face, the lenses smudged with fingerprints now.

"Give me the map." Avery motions for me to hand it over.

I think about whipping it at her like she did to me, but somehow show restraint.

"Maybe there are landmarks that will help us figure out where we are."

I snort, but keep my comments to myself.

A frustrated sigh leaving her, Avery lowers her hand and lifts her golden head. "We should have been tying things to trees."

"That's a good idea." I look at Avery. "Got any rope handy? Ribbon? No?"

"I'll use my damn shirt," she announces scathingly, already tearing at the hem of her shirt.

A couple minutes go by with me enthralled by Avery's antics. She grunts and tugs and jumps around as if she's practicing some space-themed dance move. When it finally happens, the ripping sound is unusually loud.

Avery lets out a cry of triumph as an uneven tail of pink fabric dangles from her hand. She lifts it with a raised eyebrow, part of her midriff taunting me as she does. I swallow around a dry throat. I tell myself to look away, but I don't. Avery went from hating everything to do with outside to survivalist instincts. She is one surprise after another.

Eyes riveted to the small expanse of lower back shown as she goes on her toes to tie a dirty pink knot around a low-hanging tree limb, it takes me a moment to realize something. "I have a red flag in the backpack. You could have used that instead of your shirt."

Avery blinks. "Well, I guess it's too late for that now."

Her unfazed expression pulls a short bark of laughter from me. "It is indeed."

Eyes sparkling, Avery nods toward a clearing to our left and away from the wooded area. "Come on, let's keep walking in that direction."

"Sure. Why not? It isn't like either of us know where we're going. Let's make it interesting."

Avery narrows her eyes. "Was that sarcasm?"

"Maybe."

BEN

Fifteen minutes later and another hill ascended, the silence is broken. By me. And lamely.

"Are you going to keep tearing parts of your shirt off?" I ask, the question on repeat in my head until it comes out of my mouth before I can stop it.

"Why?" Avery gives me a sidelong look.

Because I want you to, is the unbidden thought that pierces my mind. I shrug, aiming for nonchalance. "You'll get cold."

She goes still abruptly, and I almost run into her. Avery glances at me. "Did you see that?"

"See what?"

Avery turns in a slow circle, her head tilted back. "There are birds."

I frown. "Yeah. There usually are outside. It's where they—now, don't be too stunned by this—live."

Wide eyes lock on me. "I don't like birds."

"You don't like birds?"

Avery tugs at a string on the hem of her torn shirt, her next words a low mumble. "Scared of them, really. Terrified. I have nightmares about them."

It's my turn to go motionless. From badass to coward to bat shit crazy, I'm getting whiplash from all Avery's different personalities, and that's just today. "Are you serious?"

"I had a bad experience with one once, all right?" Her voice is high.

"Did it happen to flip you...the bird?"

Her eyes trained on something overhead, Avery flinches. "I'm not joking, Ben."

"I have to ask one thing: did you seriously not realize there were birds out here before now?"

"I tried not to notice."

I stare at her.

"I hummed. It helped."

"What's a little bird going to do to you? If anything, the worst you have to worry about is it pooping on you. You are washable."

The words come out through lips that don't move. "It isn't little—and there's more than one."

I frown.

Carefully raising an arm, Avery points up.

I follow the direction of her finger. A massive tree slants down the hill not far from Avery, the limbs crooked and thick. It looks as if millions of black leaves cover the branches, and it isn't until one caws and takes off that I realize why the branches droop so far down. The tree is filled with crows, not leaves. I readjust my glasses and turn to Avery.

She hasn't moved; she doesn't appear to be breathing.

I watch the birds for a moment. They seem to watch me back, one in particular keeping its gaze trained on me. . The sight of Avery's pale face and shaking form chips away at my resentment until it all but disappears. I sigh, hoping this isn't all an act. One never knows with Avery.

In a low voice, I meet her gaze and say, "Tell me what to do."

"Make them disappear?" Her tone is hopeful; her expression says she knows better.

"Sure. I'll wave my magic wand I keep right here in my back pocket"—I pat the backside of my gray shorts— "and that'll be the end of the crows."

"Yes." Avery nods her head rigorously. "Do that."

A crow separates itself from the others, twisting its neck to peer from me to Avery. I think it's the same one that stared at me. I watch it, literally jumping when it turns its head and I'm hit with its eyeless wonder. A jagged scar resides where an eye should.

Awe coats my voice when I say, "Do you see that? That crow is missing an eye."

"Is that supposed to make me feel better?" Avery screeches

I readjust my glasses, but the crow remains the same size. It's proportionate to a small cat, and with its one eye missing and a jagged white scar in its place, badass for a bird. It caws, and a strange choking sound leaves Avery. I face her, watching as what little color her skin holds drains away. She isn't joking. She's afraid. Or she's playing one of her games again. It's too bad that I can't be one hundred percent positive either way.

Releasing a sigh, I take a step closer. In a low voice, I tell her, "It won't hurt you, I promise. Let's just keep walking. It will go away."

She focuses on me. A crease forms between her eyebrows, splitting the smooth skin. Her eyelashes are impossibly long. Damn, she's got beautiful eyes. "Are you sure?"

Even with knowing I'll most likely live to regret it, I soften at the fear in her voice. "Positive. We're probably in their territory. We'll leave, and everything will be fine. Trust me."

"Okay," Avery says softly, nodding. "Okay."

We take slow, small footsteps, Avery's eyes finding the crows again and again. She continually knocks into me, bringing her scent and warmth each time. It's maddening to the baser part of me I try to tramp down in regards to the woman beside me. If only my brain was the lone high-functioning part of my anatomy.

The one-eyed bird squawks and takes off, the high branches shaking upon its departure from the tree. Leaves fall, spiraling to the ground.

I turn to Avery. "See? It's already leaving. I'm sure the others will follow." She grabs my biceps and squeezes until I stop walking. "What?"

"It isn't leaving."

Sure enough, the crow lands in a tree ahead of us, its profile in view and a single beady eye trained on us. I wonder how it lost the other one. It verbally announces its dislike for us once more. If I had to guess, I'd say its animosity is strictly toward Avery. Birds know. They can't be fooled by pretty exteriors and sugary words like humans. When the crow moves to a closer tree, I study it. It cocks its head, still and silent as we watch each other.

Okay, this is a little strange.

"Why won't it go away, Ben?"

I put large doses of confidence in my voice as I say, "It wants to make sure we don't hang around, that's all. It can probably sense your fear."

"What, are you suddenly a bird expert?"

"You asked."

"We're going to die," Avery whispers.

"Oh, come on," I scoff. "How is a crow going to kill us?"

"It's going to attack us, and peck out our eyes, and then we won't be able to see, and we'll fall off a cliff, and we…will…die."

I slowly look her way, waiting a moment to reply. "Do you think maybe you're overreacting a bit?"

Avery glares at me.

"Let's keep moving." I take a step and she takes one with me.

As soon as we move, Avery reaches for my arm, clutching it between her hands. We've intentionally touched a total of one time in the months of our acquaintance. But then, it only took once for everything to blow up around us.

I pause, glancing at Avery. She stares ahead, her expression resolute.

It is one thing to help her; it's another to get sucked into her warped reality. I'm not letting that happen. No touching is a good idea. I try to pull away and Avery only digs her nails more firmly into me. I grind my teeth around the sting and resign myself to the situation.

As we make our slow trek through uncivilized terrain, the bird flies from tree to tree, always keeping us within its sight. Its cry is freakishly loud, ominous. I get paranoid the longer it hovers.

It seems to be tracking us.

"It isn't going away!"

I open my mouth to respond but am unable to produce a sound as all the crows, seemingly offended by Avery's voice, spiral into the air, blackening the sky in a death cloud. Their shrill cries pierce my eardrums. I gape at the sight, never before seeing so many crows together at once. Even louder, and shriller, is Avery's scream as she dashes off. Her hair flies behind her like a waving flag of surrender.

I shout at Avery to stop, but she keeps moving, not even looking where she's going. Eyes trained up instead of ahead, her face is set in a caricature of horror. I grab her arm and swing her around when she almost sprints past me. She about ran right off the side of the mountain. "Avery! Avery, stop!"

Avery blinks and finally focuses on me. I squeeze her shoulders reassuringly, staring into her eyes. She looks terrified. I frown in response. The fight slowly goes out of her. She slackens against me, breathing heavy, smelling of fear. Avery trembles, but doesn't make any attempt to flee.

"What are you doing?" I ask quietly, gentling my grip on her arms.

"I hate birds," she whispers.

"I am aware."

Avery stiffens. "It's coming back!"

When the crow swoops toward us with evil intent, a curse falls from my lips at the same time Avery screeches directly into my ear. I shake my head to dislodge the ringing sound as a force rams into me and sends me off balance.

And then I'm falling.

4

AVERY

I am losing it. No, that's not right—I have officially lost it.

My one thought as a horrific scream is torn from me is this: *I am in hell.*

When the crazy bird dives toward my head, I react without thought. I screech and push past Ben, unintentionally bumping into him, and I sprint. I refuse to be bird bait. No beaks are touching these eyes. Heart pounding, I run without direction. I just have to keep moving, and then it won't get me. When Ben shouts from somewhere behind me, I know the crow has him. A small cry leaves me, picturing his intense brown eyes pecked away. I hesitate. He has glasses, so maybe he'll be okay. I mean, at least his eyes will be okay, and that's something.

Even as my stride shortens, my brain roars at me to keep going, to let him be the sacrifice to ensure my safety. I almost do it too, but my stupid legs, as if controlled by my heart, stop working. Panting, covered in sweat, I spin around. Eyes shifting back and forth, I search for my coworker and the bird. I find neither.

"Ben?" I say through a burning throat.

A single word reaches my ears, strangled and quiet. "Help."

Heart trying to jump from my chest, I rush toward the nearest drop-off. It's a downward ride of trees, rocks, and most assuredly, death. A body of water is far below, looking like a sliver of blue from this point. I try to swallow, but my throat is closed. The sweat on my body has been replaced by clammy fear.

Where is Ben? I heard him cry out. Didn't I? This whole excursion is to learn how to better get along with each other. If I killed Ben, I'll be fired for sure, maybe sent to prison. I can't spend the rest of my life wearing a single color for every day of the week.

"Avery."

My gaze drops and I freeze. Ten feet directly beneath me is Ben, and the only thing keeping him from plummeting down the ridge is a misshapen tree flush with the ground. "I thought you were dead."

I don't know how he manages to glare so thoroughly at me, especially in his present condition, but I feel the wrath of his eyes all the way to my soul. "Don't sound so disappointed," he gets out around gritted teeth.

I don't respond.

Ben's voice is surprisingly calm as he asks, "Did you push me?"

"Well…" I rub my forehead. "I mean…not intentionally."

"How do you unintentionally push someone?"

A change of subject is needed. "You lost your glasses."

"Yes, and my legs are tangled around a dead tree. It's a glorious day all around."

"Are you hurt?"

"I've felt better," he says darkly.

"How blind are you right now?"

"I don't know, things are pretty blurry. Why?"

I lift my middle finger and wave it back and forth. "How many fingers am I holding up?"

"I'm not *that* blind."

"Just checking." I set my hands to my hips and stare at my teammate. There is dirt smeared across his forehead and his red shirt is torn near the hem. "How are you going to get back up here?"

Ben lowers his head, his shoulders lifting as he inhales. His dark eyes are intent when he looks up at me. "I'm pretty sure I sprained my ankle. I don't think I can get out of this while holding on to the backpack. I'll have to throw it to you, and then I'll get myself up. Do you think you can catch it?"

I look from Ben to the ledge. If he underthrows, and I dive for it, I'll be in the same position as him, or worse. That's a chance I'd rather not take. I unconsciously take a step back, as if my body is readying for something my brain hasn't yet accepted.

"Avery."

I focus on Ben, going still under the intensity of his daze.

"Everything we need is in this backpack. The compass, the map, food and water…" Ben speaks after a brief pause. "Tell me you can do this, Avery."

Something about the way he says the words straightens my spine and returns my gaze to his. Ben's counting on me. He needs me. I won't let him down, not in this. I nod briefly.

He releases a long breath. "Okay. Great." Ben's expression turns serious. "Widen your stance, brace your legs, and no matter what, catch the damn thing, all right?"

"All right." I do as he says, arms outstretched and ready.

"Here we go. You can do this." Face twisting with determination and pain, Ben hefts the backpack over his shoulder and straightens his arm like a whip, the backpack soaring from his hand. It flies through the air, rocketing toward me as it gets larger and larger.

Just before it smacks me in the face, I catch it. I stumble under the force of it, and fall to my butt. I land on a small rock, but even the sharp sting that stabs my backside can't dampen my elation. My face splits in a wide grin as I hug the bag, smelling fresh air and Ben.

"Avery? Everything okay?"

"I got it! I got it!" I laugh and clamber to my feet, holding the bag as I jump up and down. I stop and point to the backpack. "See? I got it!"

For the first time in a long time, a genuine smile that is meant for me crosses Ben's features. Not the tight, fake ones he produces under the watchful eyes of Duke Renner, but a real one that makes Ben's eyes sparkle and his face light up. I falter under the power of it.

As if realizing what he's doing, Ben's smile disintegrates.

I swallow thickly, turning at the loss of it. "Can you get loose or not?"

His response is stiff and takes a moment to come. "Yeah."

"Maybe you can speed it up a bit?" I snap to hide hurt I pretend is nonexistent. "We have a lodge to find before nightfall."

"Anything for Queen Avery," he mocks.

I wait with my back to him as he hauls himself up the side of the mountain, silently fuming. I'm hot, and sweaty, and tired. I want to go home, where it's clean, and cool, and I can watch reality television as I eat takeout. My mouth salivates at the thought of pasta from my favorite Italian restaurant.

Rosa's Italian Cuisine is a little shop ten blocks from me, mostly undiscovered by the masses. It's been one of the best surprises since relocating from Montana to Illinois. All the meals are homemade by Rosa Rossetti and have phenomenal flavor. I'd give about anything right now for a big bowl of noodles slathered in sauce. I'd probably even forsake Ben, although I'm sure after I was done stuffing myself full of noodles, I'd feel a little bad. Okay, a lot.

I shudder as I think of the near attack of the crows, wondering where all the black beasts went, and when they'll make another appearance. Clamminess covers me with cold dread, and I instinctively take a step back, bumping into Ben as I fight terror no amount of counseling has been able to control.

"Watch it. I don't want a repeat trip down the side of a mountain," he snaps.

My eyes lock on Ben, remembering the way he carefully handled me during the crow situation. Ben's missing his glasses, there's a cut along his cheek oozing blood, and he's favoring his left leg, but he's in one piece, and that's what matters.

"You helped me. You didn't have to, but you did. Thank you." Warmth swims through me as I hold his gaze. It gives me hope that maybe, eventually, we'll be okay.

Ben's eyes flicker, and just as quickly, his face hardens. "Don't thank me. I did have to help you. You're my partner in this hellhole, and I need you in order to pass this. That's it. Don't make it out to be more than it was."

My cheeks burn. Apparently, we won't be okay any time soon. "Any kindness you show is a ruse, is that it?"

He steps closer, his voice low and husky when he answers with, "That's exactly it." Ben stares at my mouth before moving back, taking all the air in the vicinity with him. He smirks dangerously. "Everything I do has an ulterior motive, and a selfish one at that. You would know exactly how that works, wouldn't you?"

I stamp my hands to my hips as I show him my profile, frustration and guilt slamming into me. "I explained—"

"You didn't explain, Avery." Ben firmly takes my arm and turns me until I can only look at him. His scent is sweet and spicy, wrapping around me like a warm, angry blanket of sinful temptation. "You made excuses. Only thing is, there is no excuse for what you did."

Swallowing back the urge to try to, once again, make him understand my betrayal, I begin to walk. He's right. What I did was shitty and uncalled for, and I have no good reason for my actions. I have *my* reasons, but they don't justify my behavior, not toward Ben.

I have not been myself since I moved from my home state of Montana to Illinois. I felt it was necessary to change my public demeanor, and I've been lost for a while now. Until I can be completely upfront with Ben, things are at a standstill. Possibly irreparable at this point.

* * * *

The sound of Ben's voice directly behind me causes me to jump. "Have you seen the map?"

I turn to face my coworker. He's kneeling on the ground, digging through the backpack with a black expression on his face. One leg is straightened to keep his weight off it. The leg is toned and covered in fine hairs and cuts. He looks haggard and beat up by nature. I'm sure I don't look any better.

"I saw you put it in the backpack when we started up the last trail." I think.

The look on his face gets deadlier. "It's not here."

Ben turns the look on me. Without his glasses, the fierceness of his eyes is harder to ignore. My breath catches. I'm glad the glasses are gone; they were hiding such loveliness. I didn't mean any of what I said. I find Ben terribly attractive, even when he's scowling at me, as he is now, and I guess, pretty much always. He makes me so mad with his rude behavior and then I have to retaliate.

"We need that map," he all but growls.

"Maybe it somehow fell out of the backpack when you took a tumble down the mountain."

"Right. Only I didn't *take a tumble down the mountain.*"

The sharply spoken words echo through me, bringing an uncomfortable twinge with them.

"I have no idea what you're talking about," I reply with a sniff. "I mean, it's possible it seemed like I pushed you, but—"

"Where's the compass?" Ben cuts in, his voice rough and unpleasant.

"Compass?" I frown.

"Yeah. Compass." He turns to me. "The contraption that is going to tell us which direction to go and help us find the others, since we apparently have no map."

"I don't know anything about a compass. Didn't you have the compass?"

Ben turns to stone. "I handed you a compass before we walked up the last hill."

I scrunch up my nose. "No. I don't think so."

"I know I gave it to you."

"If you did, I'm sure I gave it back to you, or put it in the backpack. I don't remember." I truly don't, and who can blame me? This whole filthy, uncivilized scenario has me traumatized.

"Are you—are you *kidding me?*" Ben slams his hands on the top of his head and keeps them there. His shirt rides up, showing a hint of lean muscle.

My heartrate trips and I redirect my gaze from him. "If I didn't give it to you or put it in the bag, which I'm sure I did, it must have somehow been lost when I was attacked by that rabid bird. When I next see the employees of Extreme Retreat, I will demand to know why they allow birds out here. That's completely uncalled for."

He sputters, his face turning red. "You lost it? You lost it?"

Heat burns my cheeks. "Maybe? I don't know. It isn't like I planned on being chased by a crow. I could have gotten seriously hurt, and you're worried about a stupid compass. You know, you could have at least tried to help me out, instead of falling down the side of the mountain."

Ben mutters something.

"What? What was that?"

"Son of a bitch." Ben gets to his feet, heaves up the backpack, and flings it in the air. A bird squawks as the bag soars by, within inches of hitting it. He stalks toward me with a faint limp, danger dancing in the depths of his dark eyes. He looks like a beast. A virile, unstoppable machine of vengeance.

"That was unnecessary." I step back, and Ben follows.

His voice is low and controlled when he tells me, "We are now out of a compass. Because you took it from me, along with the map, right before we climbed up the mountain you shoved me off."

"Shoved? That's a little harsh."

I take another step back, and again, he closes the distance between us.

"Okay. Then we'll backtrack until we find it. It has to be around here somewhere." My face burns under the force of Ben's focus. "Why are you looking at me like that? What is it?"

Time pauses as I watch a vein bulge in his forehead, and then he explodes.

"How are we supposed to find anything without the map, or the compass?" Ben roars, kicking at a nearby bush. He swears, reaching for his bad leg he used to abuse the foliage. He spins away, and then turns back to add, "Have you also somehow missed the fact that we are surrounded by trees? How are we supposed to have any idea which way to go?"

"We'll find another checkpoint. They have to be all over the place."

Ben's jaw hardens.

"I guess..." My mouth is terribly dry. "I guess we need a compass or map to find those too?"

"We're—"

"Don't say it," I plead.

"Lost."

I close my eyes as my stomach drops. Guilt races through me. This is at least partially my fault. We are surrounded by treacherous earth and unknown danger, pretty much the worst scenario ever to find yourself in when lost. I hate when things are my fault. It makes my stomach queasy. Anger is better than guilt. I can handle anger.

I snap open my eyes, glare at Ben, and lie. "This isn't my fault."

He laughs at me. He actually laughs.

"I shouldn't even be surprised," Ben says conversationally. "Ever since you stepped through the red door of Sanders and Sisters, my life has been completely ass-backwards."

Ben's words evoke a flutter of disquiet in my chest. Because it's true. It's been one miscommunication after another with us since the moment we met. I turn from his view and look at what faces me on all sides. Tall, long-limbed trees, and whatever lives among them. They look ominous; I swear they're mocking me.

My voice is weak when I tell him, "That's a rotten thing to say."

"Am I wrong?" Ben counters.

Not having a comeback, I mutter, "Whatever."

"Did you or did you not make sure you had Duke's favorite breakfast delivered every morning?"

"So?" I shift uncomfortably when he turns to glower at me.

He steps closer. "First of all, that's *Anne's* job, and second of all, you were being an ass kisser."

"I was—"

He moves another step closer, until we're less than a couple feet from each other. "Because every morning when you took his food to him, you made sure you mentioned some great idea you had for one of the companies interested in using our advertising agency. There you sat, chirping away in his ear, making yourself indispensable to him."

He raises his voice to a high falsetto. "*Oh, Duke, what do you think of this? And I had the most wonderful thought last night. I think if we move the wording around, it will sound better.*"

My face flames. I jab him in the chest. "You purposely set up an appointment with Callie's Trinkets because you knew I already had one that day."

Ben blinks. "So?"

"Your time overlapped my time already scheduled. You did that on purpose to cut into my time with them."

He shrugs, but guilt lines his face.

"Last month you told me the wrong time for an important meeting," I add.

"That was an accident."

"Sure it was. You're no better," I finish.

Fire flares to life in his irises. "I wasn't trying to steal Callie's Trinkets's business from anyone, Avery. You were. I'd already done two campaigns for them."

"Well, maybe it was time for a change." I don't mean the words, and when I see how they hit Ben, I wish I'd never spoken them.

He steps back falteringly and turns his back on me. "Yeah. Maybe."

I clench my fingers to keep from reaching out to him and turn away. There are more important things to think about than whether or not I inadvertently wounded Ben's pride—okay, and hurt his feelings. I cringe. And maybe, in a way, somehow, sort of, betrayed him. Being lost is not an option. That is not acceptable.

With or without Ben's help, I'll find the compass and map, and I'll get to the rest of the group. Except, the whole point of this is to work together as a team. If I show up without Ben, or he shows up without me, we're done. My shoulders slump. We're stuck together, which is exactly what Duke wanted.

I scowl.

The lodge can't be that far away. I straighten my spine. Duke said this is a simple quest, and if we don't show up by the time everyone else does, they'll look for us. We won't be lost for long. I can do this. I will do this. *We* will do this. Nothing is impossible, unless you tell yourself it is. My mom told me that once. I haven't forgotten.

I tip my chin and head in the direction I think we came from.

"Where are you going?" Ben calls.

"I'm going to find the compass and map. I refuse to be lost!"

"Great idea. You do that."

"I am doing that," I reply.

"Have fun."

"I will have fun."

I glance back. Ben faces me, his arms crossed. The sun blazes behind him in a fiery backdrop. I can't see his expression, but I'm sure it's unfriendly. I face forward with a sigh, focusing on my feet as the ground steepens. The air cools as I head farther into the trees.

5
BEN

I rub the back of my neck as I take in the monstrous-sized mountains. Damn, it's an overwhelming view. Mountains high into the clouds, vast and out of focus. Like a painting—an image I'd rather be looking at on a wall instead of witnessing firsthand.

I cannot even begin to gauge where we are in relation to the path on which we started, but like Avery, I can't sit and wait. I'll look for some trace of other humans while Avery goes and gets herself even more lost. Yeah, that's what I'll do. I ignore the feeling of wrongness that creeps over me as the minutes of our separation grow. It's her own fault if she vanishes and no one ever sees her again. I tried to tell her.

Walking a dozen footsteps, I keep my eyes trained on the rocky hill before me, seeing nothing but insects, and a rodent or two. Lots of land, and lots of nothing. My shirt is damp with sweat, the sun unapologetic in its burn. I need food, and a drink or two, preferably of hard liquor. The terrain gets rockier the higher up I climb, and when I reach the halfway point, I know I'm not anywhere I want to be. There's no trail above me. I skid down the wall and jump back, picking another area of the vast, wooded fortress to check.

Time seems to drag to the point where I wonder if it's altogether stopped. We're supposed to be near Panther Den Wilderness, one of the seven parts of the national forest, but I haven't seen anything that tells me we are.

Try as I might, I can't concentrate, my thoughts spiraling back to Avery again and again. What if something happens to her? When I can't take it anymore, I look over my shoulder, spotting Avery's figure as it gets smaller and farther away with each step. Another few feet and I won't even be able to see her.

Panic sets in without any warning, and I vault from the rock ledge, tearing through the woods as if I'm afraid I'll never see her again. I'm not, I just—I don't want her to be alone if she gets hurt, that's all.

"Avery!" I land on a tree limb wrong and it shoots up to smack me in the forehead, adding a sting to the side of my face. I curse and keep going. At this rate, I'll be horrendously disfigured before nightfall.

She whirls around, a speck of golden light in the distance. Her voice reaches me before I can make out her features. "Ben? Ben, what is it? Did you find the map?"

When I'm close enough to see her expression, a fist slams into my chest at the way her eyes are lit up at the sight of me. It makes me feel like an ass, and then I feel like an ass for feeling like an ass.

"I didn't." I slow to a jog, stopping once I'm within a few feet of Avery.

"Oh." Avery bites her lower lip, the act sending life to parts I want to remain lifeless. "Why did you come after me then?"

"I didn't come after you," I quickly deny.

"Right." She eyes me. "Why are you here then?"

I look at the world around us, full of creatures and wildlife we can't even guess at. I shift my gaze to her expectant one. And I tell her why I really raced after her. "We're supposed to be a team."

"So you did come after me." She lifts an eyebrow and waits.

"All right, fine, I came after you," I admit reluctantly.

Avery turns her face, but not before I catch her smile.

* * * *

We've walked for what seems like hours—or in my case, hobbled. Not having a phone or a watch, I can't tell for sure. You would think, at some point, we would meet up with other people. Not necessarily our coworkers, but someone. Unless we're so completely off the grid, we're in a place people know better than to go. Which, yeah, sure, why not? That would fit right in with how our day is going.

If it was any other situation, I might feel a spark of satisfaction at the forlorn expression on Avery's face. As it is, I wish we were in any other situation. But we're not. We're here, together, lost in Illinois country inside of a national forest.

I look at Avery. Her legs are covered in scratches, her hair looking more brown than blonde from the dirt that's seeped into her scalp and around the locks. Her makeup is smeared, and faint enough that I see a smattering of freckles coating her nose and cheeks. I didn't even know she had freckles. She's an absolute mess—and she's prettier than I've ever seen her, a fact that puts an ache in my temples and in my groin.

Her face brightens. "Wait! I just remembered! The map! I remember I have the..." She reaches in her pocket, and then the other three. Her shoulders slump. The light fades from her eyes.

"You have the?" I prompt, already knowing what she doesn't have. That map is long gone by now.

"I have nothing. No, wait. I have dirt." Avery opens her hand, palm down, and brown dust falls to coat the ground.

"Now what, partner?" I don't mean to sound sarcastic, but I hear it drip from my words all the same.

Avery shakes her head, her face about to crumple. She whirls around, holding that pose until I hear a long exhale. When she faces me, her spine is straight, and her expression is fierce. "We keep going until we find a trail, or people. We find something."

I have to admire her drive, whatever my misgivings where Avery Scottam's concerned.

"Good plan." I nod, pausing a moment before I drop the information bomb. "Only we are in a national forest—a national forest that's over three hundred thousand acres in size. There are seven wilderness retreats inside it, and those make up only ten percent of the forest. The rest is unknown territory. And I don't know where one ends and the other begins."

"Then what do you suggest?" she says through her teeth.

I rub my face, already weary from this ordeal, and I get the feeling it's only just begun. "I don't know. Sit and wait? Moving around is going to get us more lost."

"No." Avery jabs a finger at me, grazing my nose.

"No?"

"No. I'm not sitting and I'm not waiting." She shakes her head. "Life doesn't come to you; you have to go to it."

I make an incredulous sound. My exasperation knows no bounds when it comes to this woman. "Avery, this isn't work. You aren't pitching some inspirational slogan or greeting card speech. There is no makeup account, no athletic apparel company. It's just you and me."

"I would win if there was," she retorts waspishly.

"Win? Did you listen to any part of Duke's speech last month? It isn't about winning. Any sale the company gets is good for all of us." I sound like a hypocrite as I spew forth Duke's words. I feel like one too. "We're not supposed to try to outdo each other. We're supposed to support one another at Sanders and Sisters. We're supposed to be family."

She just looks at me, steely-eyed and motionless.

I sigh. "All right, I didn't listen to the speech either. If I had—if we *all* had—maybe we wouldn't be here right now."

"Do you think he meant it?"

"Who meant what?" I ask, annoyed by the vague question.

"Duke. When he called us family, do you think he meant it?"

I find the question odd, as well as the way she waits expectantly, never once shifting her gaze from me. "I have not one clue, and frankly, I don't care right now."

"I wonder why we haven't seen any of the others," she says absently, her eyes skimming the vicinity as if she's hoping one of our coworkers will pop up from behind a tree and rescue us.

"Because they're where they should be, and we are not."

Avery looks at me, frowning. "You blame me for us being lost, don't you?"

"No," I bite out.

I don't blame Avery for us being lost. I do blame her for a lot of other things though, like us being sent here in the first place. Things were fine until she came along and upended Sanders and Sisters, along with my reality. She stole commissions from me one by one with an innocent smile and feigned ignorance. It was as ifshe specifically had it out for me, outpitching me any chance she got.

I was Duke Renner's number one, and then, I wasn't.

Avery turns to me, a hint of the sweet, citrus scent somehow remaining. "Do you have any idea at all where we are?" she asks. The determined set of her jaw wavered at some point over the last few hours; the fierce light in her eyes dimmed.

I rub my jaw. "I'm guessing we're on a direct route to hell."

"But really, do you?"

All I have to do is look at her.

Avery's shoulders slump.

Even though neither of us say the words out loud, she knows it as well as I do.

We are so fricking lost.

And I don't mean a little lost. I mean, we have not a single clue as to where we are, where we started, or where we need to go. I can feel us getting sucked into the wilderness; it's an unseen hand that guides us into nowhere. Clearly, the employees of Extreme Retreat overestimated our ability to stay on course, because we have nothing in the backpack to alert anyone as to our location.

Avery studies the land. "We have to run into someone else eventually, right? We can't be the only ones out here."

I don't even bother answering that. I'm a city guy from Illinois who's never set foot on anything remotely resembling a mountain. And Avery? Avery doesn't like to be outside. We're doomed.

Avery's quiet for a moment. "Is the national forest really that big?"

"Bigger than you realize," I answer honestly.

She quickly looks away, but not before I see the resignation in her eyes. Something about seeing Avery beaten down makes me uncomfortable, which is exactly the opposite of how I thought it would make me feel.

"I want to keep moving," Avery announces. "I can't stand not moving."

"I read that if you ever get lost you should stay in one spot."

Avery shakes her head. "I want to walk, Ben. I'll go without you if I have to."

"That's not smart."

She stares woodenly back.

I sigh and run a hand through my hair.

Avery doesn't move.

Maybe I'm as gullible as everyone else, I think as I contemplate giving in to her in order to not see Avery sad. I shake my head. No way that's it. But then I vow something I have no right doing. "We can walk for a while. We'll find the lodge, don't worry."

A faint shine returns to her eyes, some straightness to her spine, and I realize something. I am as susceptible to her charm as everyone else. I inwardly shake my head at myself. I'm a fool, plain and simple. The glimpses of a softer Avery Scottam are lies. They don't really exist. I have to remember that. Still, if any part of her is genuine, I hope it's the part she's showing me now.

I let out a noisy breath of air and lift an eyebrow at my teammate. "Ready for some more walking?"

Avery nods, and we continue on our path to an undesignated destination.

6

AVERY

The words that instantly come to mind are "Oh" and "God" when the sky splits open without warning. Rain pummels the earth, and us along with it. It only takes seconds to be completely sopping wet. Standing close to the ledge of a hill that feels more like a mountain, I look at Ben, who is equally drowned. I guess, at least, we're a little cleaner than we were moments ago. And the rain isn't cold, so that's another plus. Ben's clothes are vacuum-sealed to his body, emphasizing ridges and valleys I'd rather explore than anything presently around us.

"This is nice, right? Very relaxing," I say conversationally. It's amazing how clearly I can see his glower around the sheet of rain hindering my eyesight.

Ben skims a hand over his wet hair, a chunk of it rebelling and falling over his forehead. "This is ridiculous."

"But in a nice way," I remind him.

I'm sure I imagine the judgmental look on Ben's face, the expression stating that I am insane. The rain, you know...so distorting.

"No. Not in a nice way," he retorts, swiping an arm across his face. "As in, this is the last thing we need right now."

I watch Ben become taller and wonder how I'm shrinking. Then I realize I'm not shrinking, but sinking into the ground. I look down, amazed to find my shoes lodged in mud. How did that happen without my knowledge? The gap grows between Ben and me, and I catch his frown as I begin to slip down the slope. I look up just as the ground crumbles beneath me. I reach for something to hang on to, but there isn't anything. Unable to keep my balance, I fall.

A hand lassoes my wrist, stalling my ride. "Is that you, Ben?"

"No, it's the Jolly Green Giant. Yes, it's me."

"Don't be such a stick in the mud." I look at the rain as it splatters my face, laughing at the terrible joke.

"No one told me you were hilarious." His grip tightens on my arm when I start to move again.

"Well, I am. Now you know."

"Are you going to help me at all?" Ben demands, sounding slightly breathless.

"I don't know, this is kind of fun."

"For you maybe."

His attitude rubs me the wrong way and I attempt to fling off his hold, but he only reaches higher, his hand almost erotic in its touch as it skims the side of my breast and wraps around my elbow. Ben tugs me toward him until I'm looking into stormy features. He hovers over me, locking me in place with his lower body strategically placed crosswise over mine. We slide down the muddy slope an inch before settling once more in the mush.

"What?" I snap when Ben continues to study me, feeling overwhelmed and out of my element with our current positions.

Ben glares at me, his expression fiercer than any words that might leave his mouth. "You can't slide down the hill."

"Why not? What else do we have to do?"

"I don't know, maybe try to find a way out of here?" he returns.

When it comes to nature and everything it beholds, I'm pretty much a disaster. My mom tried to teach me that I can't live life afraid of the things around me, but my fears overrode her efforts. It didn't help that whenever I went outside, some kind of catastrophe followed. Part of the reason I agreed to this torturous outdoor adventure was to overcome my childhood phobias that followed me into adulthood—the other part was because I wanted to keep my job. I've since discovered jobs are overrated.

"What do you think we've been doing this whole time?" I ask tartly.

I find his words puzzling, along with the tingling sensation flooding my body. I buck my hips to dislodge him and only better fit our bodies together. We scoot down another inch or so. Ben's nostrils flare and he sucks in a sharp breath. Oh. I can feel him. And he feels glorious. I involuntarily part my lips as I look at him. Ben curses, shooting upright and away, and I shudder, wanting him back, wanting lots of other things I can't have.

"It isn't like I planned on falling." I sit up, pretending I am not a horny hussy where Ben is concerned. My hands are quickly covered in muck.

It's slimy and cool to the touch. I take a handful of sludge and pat my arm with it. I might as well take a mud bath at this point. "It just happened." Ben looks at me, mud smeared across his face and hair. "Right, like you didn't push me earlier."

Scowling, I look from him to the scene below, and then I shove off with my arms and career downward, laughing wildly as I shoot down the mud slide. Head back, I whoop as I fly along the ridges and dips of the hill, jostled and jerked side to side, which makes me laugh more.

"Avery! What the hell?" Ben hollers after me.

"Come on, it's fun!"

I land on a bump, the air knocked from my lungs, and skid off course, rolling the rest of the way. Peals of ragged merriment leave me as I go. I don't remember having this much fun ever. Maybe that one time when I was thirteen and my friend and I went on a carnival ride that made us spin upside down. I puked. I hope I don't puke this time. I land on my back, arms and legs sprawled, eyes closed, laughing so hard I hiccup.

A few short breaths later, Ben lands near me, his arm whacking my leg as he abruptly stops.

I lift my head and grin at him. "Was that fun or what?"

"I suppose sliding the rest of the way down the hill just happened too," he gets out, panting.

"You rolled all the way down, did you not?"

"Yes," he admits grudgingly.

"Did you have fun?"

"No."

I lift my eyebrows.

"Maybe a little." Ben winces and sits up. "I can't believe you did that." I eye his muddy exterior. "I could say the same about you."

The rain continues to come down, streaking our faces with tiny, dirty rivers.

"You don't fit with who you were at the office." He glares at me as if this knowledge is one more thing to hold against me.

"Yeah, well, neither do you."

"I am exactly as I've always been." Ben gingerly stands, mud plopping from his clothes to the ground.

Stuffy, by the books, anal. Yeah, he's probably right.

I sniff the air. It smells like worms, the realization jolting me to my feet in a flash. Worms can stay in the earth, where they belong. When the rain stops as suddenly as it started, and the sun appears, I blink in consternation.

We are covered in mud that will soon dry to dirt. Wonderful. But then I notice something to the left of us and I don't even care about the dirt.

"Ben, look." I grab his arm without thinking, squeezing as I point to the rainbow above the mountains, spanning forever and ending somewhere in the clouds we can't see. It's beautiful, and the sight of it brings me hope. I stand still, drinking it in. This is something I like about outside, along with air.

Ben turns, standing beside me, his arm brushing mine. "I see it."

"Isn't it breathtaking?"

He doesn't answer, but I don't care.

"*In life, remember that rainbows always come after rain*," I murmur as I take in the colorful beam, thinking of my mom.

"You pitched that for an inspirational greeting-card company."

"I did."

"After I pitched my own quote."

I bite my lip, turning away as I wince.

Resentment coats his next words. "The company picked yours."

"Mine was better," I retort. It was too; I'm not being conceited. "'*Only after the rain comes the rainbows*' isn't as catchy."

"It is almost identical." Ben sounds petulant.

"Well, Duke thought mine was better."

"You basically worded yours the same as mine but acted like it was way different because you rearranged the sentence and added 'in life'. So different."

I begin to walk, picking up my pace. "What's your point?"

"You stole my words and tweaked them. You're a thief."

My back stiffens. I might be a thief, but it isn't for stealing Ben's words.

"But then, I guess I already knew that," he finishes.

"Keep the barbs coming." I clench my jaw. "I know they make you feel better."

"Not especially."

"All right, Ben," I shout, throwing my hands in the air as I whirl around, startling him. "Let's have it!"

He blinks. "What?"

"Tell me all the ways you hate me," I urge. "Get it all out. Come on, it's obvious you have a lot of reasons."

A glower takes over his features. "You act like I shouldn't be mad about it."

"Mad? Yes. Yes, you should have been mad. But being mad forever does you more harm than it does me. It's over. It's done. I did a shitty thing and

I can't take it back. Either move on or—or get out of my life," I stammer, not really meaning the words.

His eyes harden. "Hard to do when we're stuck together."

"Well, as soon as we aren't, you can do it."

Ben nods. "I will do that. Because you know what, Avery? I quit."

Alarm puts a tight pressure in my chest. "What do you mean, you quit? Quit at what?"

"Sanders and Sisters." Ben looks as surprised as I am by his words, but then stubborn resolution takes over his features.

"You can't quit."

"I can do whatever the hell I want!" He steps closer, an edge to his voice, a glint of danger in his eyes. Ben looks like a swamp demon with the mud covering him and the maniacal glaze over his eyes. "You purposely made yourself indispensable to each Sanders and Sisters employee, but what pisses me off the most, is that for even one second, I actually thought you were genuine. You smiled pretty, and you laughed at the right times, and you acted like you cared."

I hide my eyes from Ben, my throat working but no sound coming forth.

"Then, you went around and stole contracts right out from under me, looking all innocent and sweet while you did. But that's not even the worst thing you did."

Still and silent, I listen to Ben's wrath.

Ben puts his face directly before mine, close enough that a lump of mud falls off his chin and onto my shoulder. "The worst thing you did, Avery, was make me think you were special."

My eyes shoot to his. That isn't what I expected him to say. This goes beyond that last inexcusable act I did before we came here. This is personal, and that means, I did more damage than I realized. Did he really care for me then? I assumed he didn't. If he cared for me even a little, it makes what I did a thousand times more reprehensible.

"Just tell me why." Ben stares into my eyes, into my very being. "Why did you do it?"

I want to answer him, but I don't know how. What words can make this better? I think only actions can really show Ben that I'm sorry.

Ben shakes his head, weariness replacing the anger. "Fine. Whatever. I don't care anymore. As soon as we're out of here, I'm gone."

"G-gone?"

"Yes." He glares at me. "Gone. You won, all right? You get the job, you get everything I had. I'm done fighting something I can't win."

"But...I...Ben." Sadness stitches itself into my frame. "That isn't what I want."

"Don't fucking care. You got it." He throws his arms out wide. "Congratulations. You won."

"Ben—"

He jerks away when I lift a hand, turning his back on me. "We aren't going to find the lodge by standing around yakking."

BEN

Of course, we don't find the lodge.

What we find is more rain, along with thunder and lightning.

Within seconds, the sun that briefly gifted us with its presence blinks out of existence, the sky turns the color of obsidian, and thunder rolls above our heads. It's surreal how quickly it happens. I look up just as fingers of lightning streak through the clouds. Rain falls on my face, cool and wet. It starts light, but quickly turns powerful. The wind picks up, slanting the rain. As if we haven't had enough rain for the day. Another crack of lightning shoots across the sky.

I turn to Avery. "We need to find shelter."

She darts for cover under a nearby tree before I finish talking.

"Not under there!" I snag her arm and haul her back, glaring at her. "Don't you know anything about lightning? You'll get electrocuted."

Avery turns wide eyes on me. Her face shimmers under the fallen water. "How would I know that?"

"School?" I guess. "Common sense?"

Her mouth pulls down. "I don't usually go outside when it's storming."

"Right." Or any other time unless necessary, apparently. How can anyone be as clueless as her? I shake my head, water dripping from my hair and into my eyes. "Outside bad. Avery no go outside."

Avery yanks her arm from my grasp, leans down, gathers a glob of mud in her hand, and then flings it at my head.

It grazes my ear. I stare at her, stunned.

She lifts her eyebrows and crosses her arms.

I fight the urge to smile, instead frowning at her. "You're lucky you missed."

"Pfft. I think *you're* the one who's lucky I missed."

"Fine. I'm lucky." I wipe the mud from my ear. "We need to find shelter, and fast."

"What do you suggest we do?" Avery asks stiffly.

My eyes shift over the dark terrain. The rain doesn't help my already weakened vision as I search for some kind of natural barricade from the elements. As I watch, the sky comes alive as lightning highlights what looks like a small pit or cave partially hidden by bushes and trees. I point. "Over there."

Mud has replaced the ground, making each footstep a struggle to keep the boots on my feet. My sprained ankle protests each movement. I grit my teeth and keep moving. I am aware of the exact moment Avery clasps my hand. I pretend it doesn't happen, even as my body tingles. Her hand is soft and small in mine. I want to yank my hand away, and I also want to squeeze it tight. Instead, I loosely hold her hand.

Fuck if I know what I'm doing. If she'd just tell me why she betrayed me, maybe I could get over this. Then again, I made a decision. In anger, yes, but as soon as I said I was leaving Sanders and Sisters, I knew it was true.

I'm at a dead end there. I can't go any higher up, not with my present mindset, and if I'm being honest, even before Avery showed up, I was restless. Maybe I didn't want it enough, and maybe she did. Could be that's what pisses me off more than anything. She's shown me what I've been trying to deny.

She betrayed you. Don't forget about that.

Avery stumbles and I twist around, grabbing at her to keep her upright. Instead, she takes me down with her, landing directly on top of me. The ground makes a strange sucking sound as my body is implanted in it, muck oozing up to outline my form. I slowly sink farther into the sludge as wide golden eyes stare into mine. It feels as if this has happened before. Strange.

"I'm...um..." she stutters, for the first that I can remember, at a loss for words.

I don't try to talk.

Even with the cold rain all around us, her body heat scalds me through our drenched clothes. Her breasts are pushed against my chest, her hips flush with mine. There aren't enough layers of clothing in the world to be enough of a barrier to thwart my body's reaction to hers. It comes alive immediately and hardens painfully.

I shift, cursing and immediately going still as a soft moan leaves Avery. I don't want to move, and I want to move like I can't believe. "You need to get me off—"

Her eyes pop.

"I mean...*fuck*..."

A squeak leaves Avery.

"You need to get off me—without moving," I say through gritted teeth. If she moves, I might do something I'll regret.

"How?" she croaks, sounding as flustered as me.

"Just…stay still. I'll figure it out." I close my eyes, the muscles in my neck taut. I lift my hands and clamp them to her waist, but that only pushes her hips down. I groan, in pain, in pleasure.

"Ben?"

I look at her face, see the heady desire pulsing in her eyes, and catapult her from me. A squeak of surprise leaves her as she lands on her ass in a puddle. Brown, thick water splashes up to coat her.

"What the hell, Ben?" Avery cries, spitting out dirty water.

"Sorry." I'm not sorry at all. It was either that or end up naked, and that is not happening.

With dizziness swimming in my head and my ankle screaming as I shift my weight, I carefully sit up. The position puts our faces inches apart. The salty scent of sweat and woman mixed with rain meets my nostrils, wrapping around me like a drug. Avery's plump lower lip is captured by her teeth. Fire licks my skin as she slowly releases it.

"Stop it," comes out hoarse.

Avery frowns. "Stop what?"

As if she doesn't know the power she has.

I go to my knees, hunch over, and tighten my hands into fists to steady them. Tremors run through my frame and they have nothing to do with being cold. I don't get how I can want someone so bad while at the same time be unable to stand them. It's madness.

"You didn't need to throw me off you like I'm a sack of potatoes," she grumbles.

I laugh as I get to my feet, looking at her through the rain. "Trust me when I say that no one could ever compare your body to a sack of potatoes."

"That almost sounded like a compliment." Avery carefully stands, showing me her backside.

I choke back more laughter at the sight of her brown shorts. They will never be white again.

From over her shoulder, Avery gives me an irritated look. "What's so funny?"

I simply point.

She cranes her neck and looks down with dismay. And she sighs. That's it. Just sighs. That anticlimactic response softens me a bit toward her. I expected her to whine, or complain, maybe even cry. Avery is contradictory in every sense of the word.

"Come on," I say in a voice roughened by need I'll deny having until my last day on this earth. "The storm isn't going to stop for us."

With quick, awkward steps, we navigate toward temporary salvation. Avery finds my hand again. I blink and keep moving, carefully holding it. She pulls back at the entrance to the cave, forcing me to stop. "Wait. Maybe we should find somewhere else to wait out the storm. We don't know what's in there."

I eye the shallow cave, catching flashes of rock each time lightning pierces the sky. It looks empty to me. "I'm going in. You can stay out here if you want."

Ducking under the low lip of the cave, I enter a small, dark space that is downright cold compared to the stormy weather happening around it. It only goes back about four feet, and other than dirt, leaves, and other debris, there is nothing inside it. The ceiling is low enough that I have to be hunched over to fit under it. Tight quarters, but mostly dry.

"Did anything eat you, or are you still alive?"

"Yeah, I got eaten by a one-eyed crow. It's just ghost Ben in here now."

"Ha ha." Her golden hair is like a flashlight as she enters the cave. "Maybe ghost Ben can see if there's any food in the backpack."

Avery sits across from me, her muddy shoes near my legs. They are no longer pink, that's for sure. She looks as if she decided to roll around in a mud puddle, jump in a lake, and then roll around in the mud puddle some more. It's interesting to see her this unkempt. It's sexy, and I'm not even sure why. I look longer than I should at her sleek legs, only turning my attention to my own mud-splattered legs when she notices.

"I think there is a big bag of trail mix in the bag." I grab the backpack and unzip it. For some reason, it seems lighter than it should.

Her nose crinkles. "I'm not *that* hungry."

I snort and zip the bag back up. Food doesn't sound especially good to me right now either. "It's nice to see you haven't lost your discriminatory outlook on things you consider beneath you. What's wrong with trail mix?"

"I eat food that tastes good. I care little about nutritional value."

"Well, what about when you're hungry and that's all that's around?"

"I might consider it." Avery brings her knees to her chest. She rests her chin on the tops of her knees and closes her eyes. "Is there any jerky left?"

"No, we finished that earlier. There's water in the backpack. Do you want some?"

She shakes her head without opening her eyes.

Shifting to get more comfortable on a naturally uncomfortable surface, I watch the grassy scene beyond the opening of the cave, the trees and ground as bright as daylight each time lightning hits. Neither of us speak as the rain competes with the thunder. At least if we aren't eating or drinking what little supplies we have, they'll last for a while. I wonder how long it'll be before we're found.

I wonder if we *will* be found.

7

AVERY

My teeth chatter as chills take over my body. I am woman enough to admit that the flimsy T-shirt and shorts I picked out for my hiking outfit wasn't the most practical wardrobe choice. The wet clothes combined with the coolness of the cave is making me quite miserable. I snap my teeth together to keep from complaining, even though I really want to. Ben looks as dejected as I feel.

He removed his boot and sock not long after we got situated, massaging the swollen flesh of his sprained ankle. Ben's leg is now straightened, his toes near my hip. They're cute toes, long with clean, evenly trimmed nails. I inwardly shake my head at the direction of my thoughts. Since when do I have silent commentaries on feet?

"What time do you think it is?" I ask when I can no longer stand the silence.

Ben's eyes are closed, his head resting on the rock wall behind him. "I have no idea, maybe four, maybe later."

Since I've been in Illinois, I have only portrayed myself as sophisticated, strong, and yes, tenacious. As far as Ben knew, I didn't have any weaknesses, and I certainly never looked anything less than perfect. That all got blown away within minutes of being outdoors. It figures, as it is my least favorite place to be.

"How can Extreme Retreat not allow their participants to have some means of protecting themselves?" I voice thickly. "A radio, or flares, or…I don't know…*something*."

"We're supposed to rely on our teammates," is Ben's low response. "Extreme Retreat is known for their hardcore team-building excursions. We all read the manual."

"It's ridiculous," I huff.

Our eyes meet across the space of the small cave.

Water pings at the back of the cave, gathering in a small pool on the earthen floor. I think about how I fell on Ben. My pulse spins. I think about the feel of him pressed against me, the look on his face. The fire in his eyes. I think I need to think about something else. I switch my brain to my boss, someone I'm interested in learning more about.

"How long have you known Duke?" My pulse is at odds with the calmness of my voice.

"I've worked for Sanders and Sisters since I graduated from college, so about four years."

"Where did you go to college?"

"Illinois State University." Ben pauses. "You?"

"Just a community college in Montana."

Ben narrows his eyes. "You say that like it's a bad thing."

I shrug one shoulder. "It's not as impressive as a four-year college."

"Who cares?" he retorts.

I blink, and then I slowly nod. He's right. Who cares? Surprised and grateful by his nondiscrimination toward anything that has to do with me, I return the conversation to our boss. "Can you tell me more about Duke?"

Ben lowers his chin and levels his eyes on me. "You know what he's like."

"As a boss, yes, but…not as a person."

"Why do you ask?"

I shrug, dropping my gaze to my ruined clothes and dirty, scratched skin. My mouth wobbles at the thought of how horrible my hair must look and that Ben's seeing me this way. I guess I should be glad there isn't any kind of mirror nearby.

Ben goes still, a curiously blank look flashing across his face. Disgust, maybe anger, shoots through his eyes. His voice is dangerously soft when he speaks. "Tell me you aren't interested in Duke Renner."

My stomach spins at the thought, and not in a pleasantly giddy way. It's more of a going-to-be-sick sensation. "No! Definitely not. I mean… not the way you think. Just, you know, he's my boss, and I don't know a lot about him."

Ben's next words show me I might as well have not spoken, because he isn't listening. "He's old enough to be your father."

"I don't know what you're talking about," I snap, anger and frustration churning through my stomach.

He laughs scornfully. "I shouldn't even be surprised. You'd do anything to get ahead in your career. You've already proven that."

That stings as if he slapped me across the face. I briefly touch my cheek, expecting a welt. There's just the one on my heart, and it aches. I can't even respond to that; I look at Ben and wish things hadn't gotten so twisted between us.

Ben stares back, the fury melting away to guilt as we silently watch each other. "I didn't mean—"

"Don't lie, Ben. You did mean it." I launch myself to my feet and head toward the entryway.

Ben lunges for me, barricading the exit with an arm in front of me. "Where are you going?"

"Anywhere but here."

He turns his head to the side to meet my gaze. "You're not going out in the storm."

"You don't get to tell me what to do." I shove at his arm, but he only strengthens his grip. "Get out of my way."

"No."

"I mean it."

"It's dangerous out there," Ben says.

"Why do you care?" I retort.

He gets a strange look on his face before answering, "I don't."

I silently fume, not moving.

"Please, sit down," he tells me in a quiet voice, his expression beseeching.

I give him a withering look before complying.

Ben sighs and runs a dirty hand over his even dirtier face. He hobbles back to his spot and carefully sits. "Duke is a hard-ass, but he's fair. He's egotistical, but he also has a good heart. He made his fortune out of nothing and he did it all on his own. That takes guts, brains, and talent. I respect the hell out of him as a businessman. And personally, Duke's a pretty decent guy."

"How so?"

"My parents decided to cancel Thanksgiving last year to instead go on a trip out west. My sister wasn't coming home because she was going to her boyfriend's. Having nowhere to be, I was going to hang out at home, watch some movies, maybe eat a frozen pizza. Duke found out and insisted I go to his house. Most employers wouldn't do that, let alone ask their employees about their Thanksgiving plans."

"Does he…" I take a shaky breath and start over. "Is he married? Does he have kids?"

Ben's look turns inquiring, his keen gaze studying my expression.

"I didn't see anyone with him at his birthday party last month and I wondered," I quickly explain, heat creeping up my neck and into my face.

"He was married, but it only lasted a couple years, and it was long before I knew him. Duke's too much of a workaholic to make a relationship last. Sanders and Sisters is his life; it comes first. No kids."

I put a hand to my now flip-flopping stomach and close my eyes. It takes me a moment to get my breathing even enough to respond. "I see."

"Do you think you'll stay at Sanders and Sisters?" This time, Ben sounds curious instead of vindictive.

"Maybe," I answer honestly. "I enjoy working there. Everyone is really nice, and I like the work."

"Even Juan?"

I smile, thinking of the man who pretends he can't speak English to mess with people. He had me practically trying to mime for weeks as a form of communication with him before someone finally told me he understood everything I was saying. He and Nate are in charge of ad development and production. "Even Juan."

The Sanders and Sisters building itself is tiny and white with a red door, but like they say, it isn't about size. That red door accurately states the motto behind Sanders and Sisters. It's a power color, and Sanders and Sisters is dynamite when it comes to advertising pitches and transforming a thought into a product stamp. To me, it's impressive to be small but fierce in an always-changing business world. You have to change along with the trend or be the one who starts it. Otherwise, you get left behind. Duke knows what he's doing. For barely knowing him, I feel oddly proud of the man.

"Are you really going?" I ask, eyes down.

Without looking, I know he shrugs. "What did you do before you came to Illinois?"

The question startles me. Ben having any interest in me is rare. "I worked in the marketing department for a clothing store."

"And you left there because?"

I shrug, avoiding the question the same way Ben avoided mine.

"Aside from the job, I also like the area where I live," I tell Ben.

"You're in Lake View, right? That's a pretty part of the city."

I nod. "At the Marymount on Elaine Place."

Ben lets out a low whistle. "Fancy."

"It's beautiful," I admit. "The brick and rock walls add amazing character to the place."

He doesn't reply.

"At first, it seemed so lonely." I'm not sure why I tell him that. At Ben's blank look, I explain. "This is the first time I've lived on my own. It took a while to adapt to it, but now I like it. I'm used to small-town living too. Chicago is like another country compared to where I grew up."

"Who did you used to live with?"

Pain pools in my chest, in my heart. "My mom. We...we're really close. She's my best friend."

Ben's eyes reflect the dark skies. There are questions there I cannot answer.

"And, most importantly," I say to change the subject. "There's this amazing Italian restaurant not far from my apartment."

"Oh, yeah? What's the name of the place?"

"Rosa's Italian Cuisine." My mouth salivates at the mention of it. Although, trail mix is beginning to sound just as good.

Ben sits up, animation returning to his drawn features. "I love that place."

My eyebrows shoot up. "Seriously?"

"Their breadsticks and pasta?" He rolls his eyes and sets a hand to his chest. "Delicious."

I laugh, liking the sight of the sparkle in his dark eyes. I want this to last, and I also know it won't. I decide to enjoy the easy conversation until he remembers he hates me.

"Definitely. Maybe we can go there sometime."

The light dies, and he settles back against the wall, shadows settling over his features. There it is: the moment he remembers.

Ben's voice is deadly as he tells me, "The people at Sanders and Sisters? They're nice because they've only been shown one side of you."

I pull air into my lungs, turning my focus to the storm. The thunder and lightning have lessened, but the rain is heavier now. I twist my fingers around the hem of my damp shirt, only now realizing I am no longer cold. I am, in fact, hot from Ben's words. I wish I could explain my actions, but I don't think it would matter.

"You don't have to hate me," I say quietly.

"That's where you're wrong."

The funny thing is, when Ben says the words, I don't hear resentment. I hear regret.

BEN

Out here, it feels as if we're the only people in the world. This is a perfect setting for murder and mayhem, maybe some mutilation by wolves or bears. Even while knowing there are animals around us, I have yet to see any of significant size. They'll probably make an appearance in the dead of night while we sleep and gnaw off an arm or two. God, I hope we're still not here tonight. With any luck, they'll decide Avery tastes better than me.

I don't mean that.

Mostly.

My conscience says it's possible I am being unfair to her. My pride doesn't give a damn.

"I don't think we're going to make it to the lodge before everyone else," Avery states as the rain stops and wind takes its place.

I snort. "I'm pretty sure everyone but us has made it there."

I am mentally kicking myself in the ass for not having more interest in Cub and Boy Scouts as a child. I vaguely recall my dad encouraging me to sign up and me flatly refusing, speeding off on my tricycle. I was four or five. Still, he asked every year and every year I said no. I didn't like that kind of stuff. I liked operating fast things and sports. My parents knew that, and they didn't push it. How I wish they would have pushed it.

I take a drink of water, offering the bottle to Avery. "Drink some, but pace yourself."

Avery takes a careful sip, longing in her eyes as she hands it back. It makes me want to give her all the water and go without, just to not see that look on her face. I shake my head. How does she do that, make me forget what she's done, again and again? I would blame it on magic, if I believed in such things.

"We should set out again as soon as the storm stops so we are visible to the search team." Her stomach growls, stating its needs for food. When I don't say anything, she adds, "They'll find us. I'm sure a rescue team is already looking. It won't be long now."

Avery's voice is determined. I know we'll be found; I just hope it's before anything really bad happens to us. I draw lines in a dirt patch with a stick, eyes down.

"You don't think they'll find us today, do you?" she asks.

I look up. Somehow, in the dimness, her eyes glow. Like they captured the sun and that's why it can't be seen. "I don't know about today, but I think they will," I answer slowly.

"I don't want to be lost out here forever, Ben." Avery takes a shaky breath, her eyes shining with unshed tears. She averts her face when she realizes I can see them.

"You won't." When she looks doubtful, I add, "If anything, we'll die before we can be lost forever, so there's that."

Her next words are firm. "If they don't find us, then we'll just have to find them. We'll figure out the way back, I know we will."

We did a top-notch job of that this afternoon.

I sigh and drop the stick, moving to a small pool of rainwater to wash dirt from my face and hands. The dampness of my clothes has seeped into my skin, turning me into a human cooler. It's to the point where I don't feel the cold much anymore. I move to take off my glasses before remembering they're most likely a chew toy for some wild beast. Lucky for me, my eyesight isn't terrible. Face and hands feeling a smidge cleaner, I return to my spot.

Avery holds herself tighter as the wind picks up and is sucked into our inadequate shelter. I watch her shiver, and before I can talk myself out of it, move closer to add my warmth to her. Avery tenses before relaxing against my side with a small sigh. I loosen my stiffly held arm and put it around her shoulders, ignoring the pinpricks of awareness that flood my body as she melts into me.

She still smells good, somehow. I smell like sweat and mud.

I close my eyes, listening to the strong beats of my heart. If we only have each other, we have to take care of one another. That's all it is. I'm looking out for my partner. Animosity has no place out here. I mean, not much anyway.

An animal howls in the distance and Avery presses tighter to me.

"What was that?" she whispers.

"It was just a dog," I whisper back.

Her soft laughter floats over me and I find myself smiling in return. It drops from my mouth as soon as I feel the bend of it.

We should both rest, but any time I think about it, I see an image of us lying next to one another on the ground, spooning for warmth. I'd like to avoid that for as long as I am able. So I talk.

"What happened with you and a bird to make you scared of them?" I ask.

Avery clasps her hands, showing off dirt and chipped fingernails painted pale blue. Her mouth turns down. "I was eight. My mom took me to the park to play. While there, I noticed a nest on the ground and I went over to look at it. There were eggs in it. I wasn't going to touch them; I just wanted to look. I guess I got too close because this bird came diving at me from the sky and then proceeded to chase me around the park. Its feet even got caught in my hair at one point."

She shudders, and then her mouth quirks. Avery laughs softly. "My mom was simultaneously trying to catch me and swat at the bird, along with screaming at it to get away from me and at me to hold still. People were staring at us. I imagine it looked pretty funny. The bird finally gave up on me after we put enough distance between us and its nest. I didn't want to go outside for the rest of the summer."

A smile hitches to one side of my mouth.

"It's still my least favorite place to be, and not just because of that. I swear nature has it out for me."

"What else happened?" I surprise myself by actually wanting to know. This isn't just about passing the time; it's about getting inside the head of the enigma sitting next to me. I want to know Avery, and then I want to know why she set out to sabotage me. I guess being stuck together could have a couple advantages. Namely, she can't run when I decide to grill her about her duplicity.

She shakes her head, her hair barely moving with the motion. Not surprising with the fifty pounds of mud imbedded in the locks. "Tell me something about you," she says.

"There's no point in talking about me. I'm an all-around boring guy. It isn't only my hairstyle."

Avery frowns, but she doesn't say anything.

Sighing, I give a minor detail. "I had braces. See? Bor-ing."

Avery's eyes drop to my mouth. "I guess I wouldn't know whether or not your teeth are straight, since you rarely smile."

I decide to let that one go. "How did you find Duke?"

Avery stiffens and pulls back. "What do you mean?"

I turn my head toward her, bringing our faces close. She truly is one of the most visually attractive women I've seen in my twenty-six years. Her nose is straight, and her eyes make me think of liquid gold. The normal shine of her hair is openly envied by the other women in the office. With her lips full and glossy, and perpetually posed for a kiss, it's not surprising that they've become the subject of too many conversations among my male coworkers. And her body—my mouth goes dry and I shift my eyes from her.

Even covered in grime as she is, there is no way to not see how well-made she is. Avery's beautiful—and she's also a spoiled, power hungry snob who may or may not be on a quest to seduce our boss. The thought makes me sick, and furious, and I'm not completely sure why. It's personal though;my guts are twisted up inside and there is no way to unknot them.

"I mean, how did you find Sanders and Sisters? What made you apply for a job there?"

"Oh. Some…things happened and I thought it was best to make a change. I was looking online for jobs in states other than Montana when I saw the ad for Sanders and Sisters. I've always loved to write." Avery lifts and lowers a shoulder.

"What do you like to write?"

"I've been writing poetry since I was a kid. Before this, I did freelance articles for a couple magazines, but it wasn't on a regular basis. When I saw the ad online, I sent in a bunch of my poems and other work. I figured, the worst that could happen was that I wouldn't get an interview, but I did. Then I told myself I probably wouldn't get the job, but I did. And here I am."

"I have a hard time picturing you writing poetry." It doesn't mesh with her narcissistic image. Poetry is for ones who speak from their soul. I was positive she didn't have one.

Avery's voice is soft when she answers. "That's because you don't really know me. Everyone has endless sides to them, Ben, and a lot of the time, we only get to know a few. You said our coworkers are nice to me because they've only been shown one side of me. I guess you're right. I didn't want to show them more."

I look at her, finding Avery's gaze fixated to me. My breaths cuts off before I can exhale, and I quickly turn from the silent words shouting from her eyes. I don't want to know whatever it is she's trying to tell me. Avery can either say what she means, or not bother telling me anything. I'm done playing her games.

"Try to get some rest," I tell her roughly as I settle in the opening to the cave. "I'll be on lookout."

8
AVERY

Something wet slides along my face.

I mumble and swipe at it. "Stop licking me, Ben."

The cold wetness comes again, and I swat it away, rolling to my other side, away from the tongue. "Ben. *Stop.*"

I'm huddled in a ball. There is a crick in my neck, and consciousness brings coldness and body aches. Sleep sounds way better than wakefulness. I'm about to settle back into the darkness, but then I hear Ben's voice.

"That isn't me, Avery."

My eyes snap open and I vault upright, screaming at the sight of the four-legged creature. It makes its own cry and staggers back, unease widening its eyes. I scramble back as far as I can, the back of my head knocking against the rock wall and forcing me to stop. The animal hops and trots around before going still. I rub the throbbing spot on my scalp as we stare at each other, woman and beast.

"How did that thing get in here?"

"I'm assuming it walked in on its legs."

"Why did you let it?" I demand.

"Because I needed to take a piss and had my back to the cave, is that all right?" Ben snaps.

The animal tilts its head and lets out a sound that sends a shudder down my spine. "Did I mention I also hate animals?"

"Why is that?"

"They're smelly and they drool, and they have no manners."

Ben chuckles. "You know, for hating everything that has to do with outside, nature doesn't appear to reciprocate the feeling. Maybe that crow really just wanted to be close to you, give you a big kiss like our friend here." My eyes cut to Ben. He stands in the doorway of the cave, arms crossed, leaning against the rock. For someone caked in dirt, sporting a sprained ankle, partially blind, not to mention lost in the wilderness with his nemesis, he appears especially chipper. I narrow my eyes. Sunrays silhouette his frame, letting me know the storm has passed.

"How long was I out for?"

"Not long enough," Ben mutters.

My eyes go into slits. "What was that?"

"I said, a couple hours."

"What is it?" I demand as I turn my gaze back to the white creature.

"That, my dear Avery, is a goat. A rare animal, indeed. Found only in all fifty states. It's no wonder you have no idea what it is."

I scowl at the mocking quality of his voice. "I thought they had horns."

He cocks his head, saying with disbelief, "It's a baby. Can't you tell by how small it is?"

"What's that have to do with it not having horns?"

"Well, they aren't born with them, you know. Unlike you."

"Are you insinuating that I'm the devil?"

Ben's all innocent-looking when he replies, "Would I do that?"

The goat, white and skinny and not especially cute in appearance, takes a step toward me.

I try to take a step back and hit a rock wall. "Make it go away."

"It won't hurt you."

I shoot a glare toward Ben. "I don't care. Make it go away."

Ben straightens from the wall, annoyance taking over his features. "Sure, I'll just get out my leash I keep here in my back pocket for situations such as this, you know, along with my wand, and snap it around its collar and walk it back to its home. How's that sound?"

"Maybe if I leave the cave, it will stay." I eye the goat and it blinks.

"Go for it." I pretend his words don't ooze amusement.

When it opens its mouth, showing off nubby yellow teeth, I shudder. Thinking fast, I reach down and grab a small rock, tossing it toward the back of the cave. The sound of it making contact distracts the goat, and I sprint toward Ben. He jumps to the side before I reach him. I wasn't going to run into him again. Probably.

Instantly blinded by the sun, I squint my eyes and whirl around, hoping to see nothing behind me. Instead, there is the goat, mere feet from me.

A squeak leaves me at its proximity. It snuffs or sneezes and looks at me expectantly.

I back up another step, careful to keep my footing balanced as the incline deepens.

It waits a beat and follows.

"I can smell you from here," I tell it, wrinkling my nose. It has a musky, wet fur and dried manure scent. Flies appear around it as I watch.

"Sure that's not you?"

"Shut up, Ben."

The goat makes that terrible bleating sound again, and inches nearer. I tense. "Why won't it leave? What does it want from me?"

Ben stands off to the side, watching us like this is the best entertainment he's seen in a while. "Why don't you ask it?"

I sweep at the air with my hands. "Shoo. Shoo. Go on now. Go home."

It lowers its head and paws at the ground, its nostrils flaring as it exhales.

"Why is it doing that?" I ask curiously.

It does that sneezing, snuffing sound, only louder this time.

"Avery."

Ben's tone sends alarms through my head and my eyes snap to his. "What?"

"Run."

I frown. "Why—"

Head bent, evil dancing in its eyes, the goat charges me. With a shriek, I spin forward and race down the mountainside, shouting unintelligibly. I trip over my own feet, almost pitching forward to land on my face, but somehow manage to straighten and keep going. By sheer will, I'm thinking.

I run until I find a body of water, and I run right into that, hoping the goat won't follow. The iciness freezes my lungs as the water swallows me. I kick my feet and shoot up, coughing from water that went down my throat and nose. I try not to think about how deep the water is, or how dirty, or what's in it with me.

The goat stands near the edge of the water, bleating at me.

"Get out of here!" I splash water at it and it scoots back when it gets hit by the cold droplets.

The goat growls, or makes some other equally unpleasant sound.

"You are not allowed to eat me," I shout at it, jabbing a finger in the direction of its angular face.

Its eyes are yellow and bulgy. Ominous and evil. I shudder when it stares at me head-on. It looks like an alien. Maybe that's what goats really are.

"It might just eat your hair."

I whip my head toward Ben's voice. He stands with a foot propped on a fallen tree, elbow resting nonchalantly on his thigh, a satisfied smirk curving his mouth.

"That alien-goat-thing is not coming near this hair."

"Alien-goat-thing?"

"Never mind. The point is, I've spent way too much money on my hair to let an animal feast on it."

Ben eyes me with a dubious expression. "I can tell. It's very stylish. I especially like the part up front that's sticking out sideways from your head."

"You're enjoying this, aren't you?" I unsuccessfully attempt to tame my tangled hair, but it's no use.

The water ripples around me and I go still. *Don't think about what you're standing in. You're fine. Nothing is around you.*

Ben straightens, not even trying to mask his amusement. "Of course I am."

I glare at Ben before shifting the look to the mangy animal watching me. We stare into each other's eyes, me seeing nothing but dark, soulless, black. I narrow my eyes and give it a death stare. The goat sneezes, trots backward, and spins and sprints away.

I look at Ben, mirroring the satisfied smirk he recently wore.

He snaps his mouth shut, blinks, and scowls. "How the hell did you do that?"

"Voodoo."

"I don't doubt that."

"Careful, or I'll think you're scared of me," I taunt.

Ben looks directly into my eyes. "Terrified."

With a shake of my head, I turn from him. He sounded serious. Like anything about me is threatening. If Ben knew me before I came to Illinois, he'd know how plain I truly am. I never thought I'd want him to know that person, but I do.

Spine straight and lethalness in my eyes, I march farther into the water with the intent to wash myself up. There's no reason to be unclean, along with everything else going on. My heartrate escalates as I imagine invisible creepy-crawly things finding homes in my skin, but I take deep breaths, telling myself I'm safe.

I grudgingly concede that we're lost, but we won't be for long. They will find us, and soon. We'll be back at the lodge, clean and sated, by tonight. That's what I choose to believe, and that is what is going to happen. And nothing in—or out of—the water is going to eat me.

I nod to myself, just before I step on a drop-off and directly into a bottomless pool of icy water. I'm completely covered before I have a chance to do anything. A gurgling sound fills my ears as I inhale water. Panicking, I propel myself up, breaking the surface with a gasp. My lungs are on fire. Something from behind grabs at me. Alarm sets in, quick and overwhelming. The goat fear is too fresh, and I instinctively fight back, elbowing whatever has me with all my might.

"Damn it, Avery! Quit that!"

I spin around, treading water as I focus on Ben.

Ben's eyes are like dark lasers on my face. "What was the point of attacking me?"

Teeth chattering, I say, "You scared me."

"I'm beginning to think everything scares you."

I blink as the urge to cry comes forth. It's not true. I'm out of my element here. Normal things don't scare me, like when I'm inside. At Sanders and Sisters, I seamlessly go about my day with minor worries.

"There's a drop-off there," Ben informs me dryly when I remain quiet.

"Thanks for the warning," I reply stiffly.

His hair is plastered to his forehead, water dripping down his face. The cuts and planes of his features are sharp at this proximity; his firm lips are within kissing distance. My pulse quickens; my lips tingle. Somehow, we're closer than we were a second ago. Somehow, the water is warmer, or maybe that's me. Ben stares at me, his gaze dropping to my mouth. Heat dances in the depths of his brown eyes. His eyes meet mine.

"Don't forget we are not friends, Avery," Ben says warningly.

The water turns cold again.

The distance from him to me expands.

I sniff as I turn, doggy paddling toward land.

Not wanting to be in the unknown watery depths any longer than I have to be, I vault from the water and throw myself to the grass. I don't know why, but the moment I catch my bearings, hunger strikes, vicious and undeniable. It twists up my guts and makes me feel faint. I go to my elbows and gulp air into my lungs, the sun fierce against my back.

"You know," Ben says conversationally. "I kind of feel like you have a thing for catastrophe."

I flip hair from my face and look up at Ben. Or rather, I glare. "A thing?"

"Yeah." His expression turns heated, his mouth supple as his eyes trail over my features. Ben lowers his voice and says, "Do you get turned on by danger, Avery?"

Maybe if "danger" is synonymous for Ben. Too bad I know his loathing for me is greater than his attraction to me. I shift my eyes from his, not wanting him to see the clash of longing and sorrow I am presently feeling.

"Somehow, you look worse than you did before you went in the water." He unlaces his boots, tugging them off, along with his socks.

"What are you doing?" I ask suspiciously when he reaches for his shirt.

"Gettin' naked." He wiggles his eyebrows at me.

"Don't you dare take off your clothes."

"Funny, I remember a night when you wanted them off."

My face burns. I twist onto my back, my eyes trained skyward to keep from traveling toward Ben as he undresses down to his boxers. "Are you always going to bring that up?"

"Strange, isn't it? That you wanted someone like me, someone you apparently don't even find attractive—"

I don't know why I do it. I guess because I'm so sick of hearing Ben tell me about all the stupid things I say. Believe me, I already know. I jump to my feet, grab his face, and pull his head forward until my lips touch his, and then I kiss him. His mouth is unresponsive, so I press my lips more fully to his.

Ben's hands clamp to my waist, his fingers dig into my sides, and he kisses me for one blazing hot instant where the world tilts. It makes my hunger for anything but him vanish. He tastes like everything I could ever need to survive the elements. Ben's lips are luscious, and commanding, and oh my, I want it to never end.

But then it does end.

* * * *

Tearing his mouth from mine, Ben lifts me and firmly sets me aside. I watch the rise and fall of his chest before lifting my gaze. His eyes snap with passion and recrimination. He points a shaking finger at me, and in a voice I don't recognize, says, "Don't do that again."

"Or what? What's big bad Ben going to do?" I taunt, hands on my hips. My pulse thrums with anticipation. If we're going to be stuck in this hellhole of nature, I might as well make it interesting.

His eyes lower to my thrust-out chest; my skin hums under his gaze. "Don't push me, Avery, or you'll find out, and you won't like it."

"Promises, promises."

I don't know what we're doing, but we both keep doing it. It is a dance of control and willpower, a chaotic storm of want and need, loathing and lust, and we spin and dip and fall into each other, over and over. It's maddening, and exhilarating. Ben makes me feel alive in a way I haven't for a long time.

Ben steps closer and I forget to breathe. I tremble when his brown eyes light into me. They have so much energy to them. Instead of kissing me, like I want, he hauls me over his shoulder and marches into the water. I open my mouth to scream just as my face meets water.

Accidentally inhaling, I get a mouthful of water. I come up screaming, punching, and gagging, all at once. "Get me out of here!" comes out sounding like Chewbacca overtook my vocal chords.

Vices have my wrists hostage. "No way."

"I mean it!" I wrestle Ben, ineffectively trying to get away from him and out of the water.

Brown eyes drill into mine. "You started this, Avery."

"And now I'm ending it!" I fight harder. I can't breathe the longer I stand where I don't want to be.

"Hey!" Ben grapples with me, grabbing my wrists and squeezing to halt my attack. "It's just water. It's not going to hurt you."

"How do you know that?" I shriek, wrenching my hands from his to shove him.

Ben falls back before steadying himself. He blinks at me, confusion filtering over his face. "I was just trying to get some of the mud off you, okay?"

"You made me drink parasites!"

Ben laughs. "What?"

I hit his shoulder and his laughter cuts off. "You heard me! There are probably microscopic worms crawling around inside me right now."

"You went in the water on your own a second ago, but since I put you in the water this time, it's not okay?"

I nod vehemently. "Yes. Correct."

"You're overreacting."

I stare steel at Ben. My blood boils and a red film descends over my vision. "Stop...saying...that."

Ben frowns. "Avery, come on, you're fine."

"I do not want to be in this water," I screech in a voice I don't recognize. The longer I think about it, the more I cannot stand not knowing what is around me, behind me, beneath me. Even now, I wonder what mutated beings are swarming me, ready to attack.

Ben looks quite calm considering my outburst. "Why?"

"I don't know how deep it is, and I don't know what's around me, and I want…to…get…out…of…it—and I want to stay out of it," I state around a taut jaw.

He pauses, and then slowly nods. Not saying another word, he takes my hand and turns, tugging me along to dry ground. Once there, I stand with crossed arms, shivering as cool air collides with my wet skin and clothes. I don't look at Ben, ashamed and angry at myself and him. I can't control my freak-outs or what's going to set them off. I can't control anything. My throat tightens, and I swallow hard.

"Are you all right?" Ben asks after a moment. He actually sounds as if he means it.

"No. I'm not all right. I want to go home. I hate this place. I hate not knowing where we are, or when we'll be found. I hate it all." I turn my face from his searing eyes.

"It's not exactly your idea of a vacation, is it?"

I wordlessly shake my head. The distant caw of a crow causes me to flinch. I don't know how much longer I can handle this. I want to be where I feel secure, where I have some form of control, even if it's an illusion.

Turning from Ben, I drop to the prickly grass, lift my knees to my chin, and close my eyes. I feel exposed. He's finally seeing the real me, the part I try to hide, and she isn't too impressive.

The air shifts as Ben sits beside me, his body heat warming my side. His arm touches mine, and his closeness lessens the ache in my chest, just a tad, just enough. I'm surprised when he doesn't immediately move to put distance between us, and I'm grateful that he doesn't. I don't think I could take that right now. It helps to know I am not completely alone, even though I know I'm the last person Ben wants to be around.

"I figured out your problem."

I finally look at him, noting how the sun hits his face just right, turning it into a wonderland of planes, dips, and angles. Ben has sharply honed looks that could be considered too severe by some. I find him magnetically attractive; he pulls me to him each time he's near. I wish I could tell him that, but I know he'd only mock me if I did. I wish I could tell him a hundred things I'll never be able.

"So now I only have one?" Where did that raspy voice come from and how is it mine?

He studies me for a moment, water droplets coating his long eyelashes. "You have phobias."

I scoff, even though I know I do. But who doesn't? Anyone would have a bad reaction to being thrust into a world they don't understand. "I do not."

"Yes. You do. How do you function on a daily basis?" I would get mad if he was being cruel, but he sounds legitimately confused.

"I exist perfectly well when I am where I want to be." My jaw aches with how tight it is.

Ben faces forward, crinkles lining his eyes when he looks toward the sun. "How's that working out for you right about now?"

9
BEN

Avery jumps to her feet and stomps toward a copse of trees, her shoes squishing with each step. Her white shorts became see-through from her encounter with the lake. I catch glimpses of rainbow-printed panties as she moves. It makes me want to sink my teeth into her soft flesh and—I pull air into my lungs. *Down, boy. Remember: Even if you like certain things about her—a lot—you don't like* her. That cancels out everything else.

I slowly stand and swipe fingers through my wet hair. "Where are you going?"

She whirls around, her eyes snapping as she announces, "I'm getting out of here!"

That look in her eyes, remembering the feel of her mouth, her body emphasized by her wet clothes—it's too much. I grind my teeth together and jerk around as if I'm not in control of my body. And let's be honest: I'm not. The last thing we need is for Avery to see the imprint of my erection through my shorts. A fricking furnace was flipped on inside my boxers.

"You don't—" My voice cracks. I clear my throat and start over. "You don't know what direction to go."

"I don't care. These circumstances will not beat me. I will not let them. I am done feeling sorry for myself," Avery rants. "I'm walking, Ben, even if it's to nowhere, and if it is to nowhere, well, as long as I'm not sitting here feeling sorry for myself, that's fine. I'll just keep walking and—what are you doing?"

I try to think of something that sounds legitimate, but before I can produce the words, Avery has a hand around my biceps and pulls me around.

Her gaze drops, her face pales, and she backpedals as if she's scared or horrified. I cross my arms and roll my eyes at her reaction.

"What is that?" she whispers, her focus riveted to my lower half.

Feeling oddly embarrassed, I snap, "It's a dick, Avery. Don't act like you haven't seen one before."

"Oh my God, it's moving!"

What the hell is her problem? In a bored tone, I comment, "Yeah, it likes to dance when it gets excited too."

"Ben."

"What?"

Avery's wide eyes finally lift to mine, her lips still even as quiet words leave her mouth. "I think it's a leech."

I freeze, a hum beginning in my ears. I can barely hear my own voice when I ask, "What?"

She points, a grimace on her face. "On your thigh. It looks like a leech."

"Get it off."

"Ben."

I jerk my head back and forth, not wanting to hear whatever she's going to say. "Get it off."

"Ben!"

"Get it off," I roar, squeezing my eyes shut. I can feel the blood as it drains from my face and probably goes directly into the little bloodsucker's mouth. *Don't pass out*, I tell myself.

I'm not generally scared of anything smaller than me, but leeches? Hell yes, I'm scared of leeches. Do they even have eyes . . .? And those serrated suctioning needle teeth? Anything involving blood makes me feel sick, and when it's my blood going places it shouldn't, as in outside my body and into a monster worm's mouth, it's a million times worse.

"How?" Avery asks.

I fight to stay on my feet. I can barely hear the words even as I say them. "I don't know. Just do it."

"Okay. I can do this. Okay. Okay." Avery moans, a whimpering sound leaving her. "I don't want to touch it."

"I don't want it sucking my blood either!"

"What if latches on to me next?"

I sway forward, feeling grayness creep over me. "Avery...please."

"How, Ben? How do I get it off?"

"Just..." I stab a finger into the air. "Just let me think for a moment."

Sweat breaks out on my skin as I try to remember what I know about leeches. I read all the articles I could find on them after watching *Stand by Me* when I was fourteen, but that was a long time ago. I clap my palms to my eyes and press. I remember that the reason I can't feel the leech draining my blood is because once they attach to a host, they release an analgesic substance that numbs the skin. They drink until they're full and then they fall off. I know that they can't be removed easily.

Think, Ben, think.

I drop my hands and look at Avery.

She looks expectantly back.

"You have to hook your thumb under the sucker from the side and pop it off."

She gulps, her face turning white. Avery shakes her head. "Oh, no. I can't. I can't do that."

I take her face in my hands, refusing to look down, refusing to look at anything but Avery. "Yes, you can. You survived crows and a goat; this is easy in comparison. You can do this."

Avery blinks, her hands forming to the backs of mine. Within instants, resolution hardens her expression. She nods once. "You bet your ass I can."

I barely have enough time to allow a small smile to form on my lips before Avery leans down. I close my eyes as a tiny tugging sensation forms on the front of my upper thigh. With a small cry, Avery stomps her foot down just as I open my eyes. Looking repulsed, she runs the sole of her tennis shoe along the ground and announces, "It's gone."

I force air in and out of my lungs and still can't seem to get enough.

"Do I have to siphon the wound?" she wonders, eyes on my thigh.

I contemplate telling her yesto mess with her, but instead, I shake my head. "It'll be fine."

"You're bleeding."

"A lot?"

She shifts her eyes to mine. "Why don't you look?"

"Blood makes me queasy."

Avery snorts and crosses her arms. "And you say I have issues."

I narrow my eyes at her. Tearing off the end of my shirt, I wrap it around my thigh and knot it. I must look pretty ridiculous sporting nothing but boxers and a makeshift bandage for clothing. The thought raises the level of my irritation. "At least I'm not scared of water."

"Seeing as how you got a leech on you from being in it, maybe you should be."

"Take off your clothes," I croak.

She blinks. "What?"

"Take off your clothes. We need to check each other over for more leeches."

"I am not getting naked in front of you," Avery declares with a sniff.

"You don't have to get naked," I say irritably. "You can leave on your bra and underwear."

With lifted eyebrows, I wait for Avery to unclothe.

She hesitates. "Let me check you first."

With a shrug, I turn and show Avery my back. Time seems to pause as a featherlight touch slides down my spine. I stiffen but don't move. I like it too much. Her voice wobbly, Avery tells me I'm clear.

I take a shallow breath and turn. Avery's heavy-lidded eyes hit me, and my body responds as if lightning strikes it hard, everything going taut, everything tingling. The way she looks at me undoes some tightly locked part of me.

I reach for the hem of her shirt and pull her toward me. Anything telling me to stay away is now silent; even my conscience is waiting to see what happens next. The need to touch her is fierce, my hands palming her waist before I can talk myself out of it. My fingers reflexively tighten, not wanting to let her go. She's shaped like a goddess, softly curved, kissed with peaches and pinks. Avery doesn't fight, doesn't make a sound. Hooking my fingers around the thin material, I slide my hands up her sides and tug the shirt over her head. My mouth goes dry at the sight of her lacy pink bra

Time ticks by, bursting of unfulfilled desires brought on by undeniable chemistry.

Her socks and shoes come off next. Then Avery tugs off her shorts, baring shapely legs and the rainbow panties that are way more seductive than they should be. I realize it's her—she makes everything sensual. I drink in her curves and hollows, knowing I'll never witness a more perfect female form.

"You're beautiful," I rasp, speaking truthfully.

She looks back, swallowing once. Passion dances in her eyes. That, and something else. Something that makes her seem more human, almost vulnerable. Something I don't want to think about right now.

"The tattoo on your back," she murmurs. "What does it mean?"

It's the kind of tattoo a college kid gets when their baseball team is undefeated and they're feeling invincible—a baseball with their jersey number on it underneath the head of the school's mascot, Reggie Redbird. "Just something I got in college."

I turn her around, freezing at the sight of two black, slimy blobs between her shoulder blades. The desire instantly cools, clamminess taking its place. I close my eyes and take a deep breath. "Avery." "What is it?" she whispers. When I don't answer, panic enters her tone. "What is it, Ben?" "Don't freak out, okay?" She turns to stone. "Don't say another word," Avery warns. "Just... take care of it."

Closing my eyes was a bad idea. I envision the mutant worms with their gaping mouths and teeth sucking the blood from Avery's body. The sick sensation in my stomach grows, until I am positive I am about to vomit or pass out, possibly both.

"Get them off me, Ben. I did it for you."

That should make me feel like a wimp, but machoism left me at the knowledge of a leech making a meal out of me. I tell myself to be a man and take air into my lungs. Trying not to think about how disgusting the worm feels to my fingers, I work at navigating my thumb under the sucker. I swallow back a gag at the feel of it on my skin.

"Is it gone? Is it gone, Ben? Ben!" Avery shrills, on the cusp of losing it. And then, when my fingers won't cooperate with my brain and remain motionless, she does.

"Oh, my God, of my God. Get it off me! Get it off me!" Avery screams and commences to hop around in a circle. She feels herself up, which would be erotic, if not for the screaming.

"Stop it! Avery." I grab for her, but she dances away, her own cries overpowering mine. "Hold still!"

She sobs and moans, getting close to the water and out of reach.

I lunge for her before she tumbles back into the water, pulling her around to face me. She's stronger than I realized, her elbow connecting with my chin at one point. I shake her until she stops fighting me. "Hold still and let me do this!"

Tears and dirt cover her cheeks; her eyes are bloodshot and swollen. When Avery's mouth trembles, my heart lurches. Forcing calmness I don't feel into my tone, I say, "Look at me, okay? Just look at me and nothing else. I'm going to be brave now, all right? But you have to be too."

Her forehead slowly smooths. Avery's shoulders relax, and she stares into my eyes.

"There. That's better." I give her a crooked smile. "I'm going to turn you around now, okay?"

Avery studies me for a moment, and nods.

"Good," I continue softly. "I need you to hold still so I can get them off you."

"Them?" she squeaks.

I wince at the blunder.

Avery demands in a high voice, "How many are there?"

"Two."

Suspicion enters her eyes.

"I'm not lying. There's just two. Now turn around and let me get them off you. I'll be fast."

With a look of resignation on her face, Avery turns her back to me.

I tightly grip her shoulder in one hand, tell myself I'm braver than I really am, and coming in from the side, hook my thumbnail under the sucker. My stomach heaves as it detaches, imagining I hear its high-pitched shriek of indignation at being removed from its food source. Worried it will somehow turn around and attach to me, I fling my arm wide, toward the lake.

"Are you done? Please tell me you're done."

"Shut up," I tell her without any real heat.

A welt is left from the leech; a small stream of blood leaks from the puncture wound. The wrongness of its mark on Avery's creamy skin is enough to make me dizzy—that, and the sight of her blood. Saliva enters my mouth, my throat working against the inclination to throw up.

With a grimace on my face, I remove the last one and pitch it in the same direction as the first one. I put pressure on her back, the small amount of blood sticky against my palm. The rust-and-salt scent makes my head swim and I breathe through my mouth. "There. They're gone."

Relief lightens Avery's eyes as she faces me.

Her gaze drops; her lips part. Avery's breath catches as she stares. I can't breathe. Need, powerful and unquestionable, shreds me, making me its slave My dick swells like a prideful peacock under her scrutiny. Running my eyes across Avery's frame, my attention lingers on her barely covered breasts before lowering to the apex of her thighs. No matter how many times I swallow, my mouth stays dry. An uneven tempo has overtaken my pulse. My hands shake—hell, my whole body shakes.

Avery jerks her gaze back to mine, the pink of her face darkening to red. She stumbles back a couple steps, her hands fisted at her sides. She breathes, and it comes out sounding like, "Ben."

I hold myself still so that I don't reach for her. I want to, badly. Desperately.

"T-thank you."

I nod brusquely and march for the water, quickly washing her blood from my hands. My stomach lurches in disapproval at the sight of it. I stand motionless until my body calms down, but then a vision of her near nakedness flourishes inside my head. Rounded hips, heavy breasts, skin like silk. Desire in her eyes.

I take a hitched breath, and another, fighting for control. Because if I know nothing else, I know I have to keep my hands from Avery Scottam.

I consider taking my chances with another bout of leeches by jumping in the lake to cool down. Instead, I tighten the strip of fabric around my leg.

10
AVERY

Ben wants me.

He may deny it until the day he dies, but he wants me. Still, I want more than lust from Ben. I want him to want me as a person more than his body wants mine. Knowing he never will, and that it's my fault, makes me crabby.

"I'm hungry," I announce waspishly as we trample around trees and more trees. As we've walked, the sun's lowered in the sky. How much more daylight do we have?

This is like the never-ending forest of doom, and if we ever make it out of here alive, I might write a book titled exactly that. Probably, though, I'll just be traumatized and never leave my home again. Most people look at the vastness of the world as amazing; I look at it as a cesspool of things I'd rather avoid.

Without speaking a word, Ben stops, pulls the backpack off his shoulders, and hands it to me. He hasn't said anything since the almost-naked-leech incident. I shudder as I remember the horror of it all. Seeing his nicely muscled body wasn't horrible. In fact, that was quite nice. The rest of it? Yes, definitely horrible.

I swing the backpack my way with a little too much exuberance and end up toppling backward. I swear there's an instant where Ben considers letting me fall on my face, but in the end, he grabs my arm. Only thing is, he pulls me forward hard, which in turn puts him off balance. The end result is both of us on the ground with me partially lying on Ben, the cut on Ben's cheek reopened and bleeding. He must have hit it on something sharp as we fell.

Ben is motionless as I lean into him, nothing but a whisper between us. My senses are heightened by his nearness, raw with need. His heart pounds wildly against my chest. My body feels submerged in liquid flames. I keep my eyes lowered. If I look up, I don't know what I'll do. Probably lustfully attack him. I take a shallow breath and focus on the line of blood cutting a trail across Ben's cheek.

I gingerly finger his marred flesh, careful to keep my touch light. He flinches, but holds himself still. "You're bleeding."

Ben's face whitens. "Thanks for pointing that out for me. Exactly what I wanted to hear."

My teeth capture my lower lip and work at it nervously. "Are you going to pass out?"

A muscle in his jaw flexes. "We can only hope."

"Right. Pass out. Great idea. Just leave me alone out here with wild beasts and flying horrors and biting insects."

"You got it," Ben says much too smoothly.

"It needs to be cleaned," I tell him, narrowing my eyes.

"It's fine."

"It's not."

"It is," Ben says through his teeth.

"It will scar."

"Maybe it'll make me more interesting."

I shrug. "Fine. Let it get infected then."

"I will. I like infections. The more puss, the better."

"You're disgusting," I tell him firmly.

Ben cocks his head and checks off his fingers. "Disgusting... unattractive...boring. Anything else you'd like to add to the list?"

My face flames. "Yes. Stubborn."

"Stubborn. Got it." Ben nods and turns his molten gaze on me. "Can you please move?"

He lets out an audible whoosh of air when I lean back. Ben's hands are fisted in his lap, and I wonder why. To halt the need to push me away, or pull me closer?

I meet his eyes, my nerve endings jumping in response. "There's more water in the backpack, right?"

"Yes." Ben doesn't make any effort to get up.

"Okay." I wait.

He stares.

"You want to get the backpack and look?" I ask, my mood presently set to snarky.

Lindy Zart

"Of course I want to do that for you, Avery. I live to serve you." Ben vaults to his feet and stomps toward the backpack.

"Glad you finally realize that," I call after him.

I get up with less exuberance, knowing I'll be covered in bruises by tomorrow, and look at one of countless mountains looming above. I have to tip back my head to see all of them, and there still are parts missing from view. Monstrous mounds of rock, dirt, and grass seamlessly meet with the sky and clouds. I can't believe Ben fell down something like that and came out with nothing more than a scratch and a sprained ankle. Well…and no glasses.

Ben tosses the backpack at me.

I catch it and kneel on the rough ground to dig around inside the bag. "There's hardly anything in here." I look at him accusingly. "Did you eat and drink everything we brought?"

His brows furrow. "I didn't touch anything."

I hold the backpack upside down and two bottles of water and the package of trail mix fall out. "Is that what there was to start?"

A black expression takes over his features. "No. It wasn't. Are you sure you didn't have anything? We need to make what we have last."

The accusatory tone makes my jaw clench. "I would remember eating disgusting nuts and even more disgusting dried fruit."

"That's not enough food and water to last us even until tomorrow."

What annoys me the most is that Ben says it in a tone that implies this is my fault.

Ben yanks the bag from my hands and inspects it, the look on his face obliterating any light the day may have. "There's a fucking hole in the bag."

He heaves the bag to the side and clasps his head in his hands, going to his hunches. I watch Ben's frozen form, not sure what's happening. His shoulders begin to shake, a choking sound leaving him. Ben sets his palms to the ground and leans forward, his forehead almost touching the grass. I stare at the man, stunned to see him reduced to tears.

"Um…Ben? Are you okay?" I awkwardly pat his shoulder. I didn't realize Ben was so sensitive. I guess anyone who gets squeamish at the sight of blood would tend to be. "It'll be okay. There, there, don't cry."

Ben drops to his back, his eyes closed, his face contorted in some kind of mad humor. He's *laughing*? How is this funny?

"There's a fucking hole in the bag," Ben chortles. "Everything—everything we had fell out. The compass, the map, most of the food… gone!" He laughs until he's gasping for air.

"Wait." I step closer, looking down at his sprawled form. "So when you accused me of losing the compass and map, they probably really were in the backpack?"

"Does it matter?" he cries. "It's gone. It's all gone."

"It does matter," I shout back, trying really hard not to kick him. "You blamed me for us getting lost when it was probably really the stupid bag's fault!"

Ben laughs harder. "You're right. Let's blame everything on the bag." His laughter sends my anger spiraling into a blazing inferno. "Maybe if you weren't blind, you would have noticed the hole in the bag!"

Ben jumps to his feet and puts his face directly in front of mine, his eyes as hot as my fury. "Maybe if you hadn't thrown me down a mountain, I wouldn't be blind!"

"I didn't throw you down a damn mountain! But if there was one handy, I might," I scream back at him.

The air crackles. We stare at each other, desire and rage at war within us. We're either going to kiss or kill one another. His eyes turn to slits, and just as suddenly, his forehead smooths and he steps back.

"Do it," he says evenly, quietly. "End my misery."

I look into despondent eyes, my ire snuffed out like a match. I swallow hard. "You don't mean that."

"You're right. I don't. I'd much rather walk around for days without food and water and hope to be impaled or eaten by some mountain cat, or, I don't know, lost forever with you." Stone-faced, Ben turns and continues walking, leaving me and our meager food behind.

"Where are you going?" I call after him.

"I'm going to find poisonous berries and then I'm going to eat them!"

I retrieve what's left of the food and water and hurry after him. "At least wait for me so I can watch!"

Ben halts, his back straight.

I eye him warily as I wait for a reaction.

He carefully turns to face me. Expressionless, Ben stares at the ground for half a dozen seconds before the oddest thing happens. Half of his mouth curves as he lifts his dark head.

As soon as our eyes meet, he bursts out laughing. It makes me laugh, and pretty soon, we're both laughing. It could be delirious-sounding, but that's okay.

* * * *

"What do you want, Avery?"

I jerk at the sound of Ben's voice, lost in the lull between wakefulness and slumber. We decided to rest when the thought of more walking had us both rooted to the ground. I am so tired of walking. "What?"

Like Ben doesn't have a care in the world, he lies on his back, hands behind his head, face upturned to the sky. I guess if you can't beat a situation, you might as well find a way to make it bearable.

He turns to his side, his chin resting on his hand, and studies me with careful eyes. Looking at me as if maybe he doesn't hate me. Probably all part of his vendetta against me. Be nice, confuse the subject, attack.

It's like, okay, I get it, you hate me. Let's move on. Even though I can't seem to move on from him—our inescapable close proximity might have something to do with that. Who am I kidding? Even if we weren't together, I'd be mooning over him somehow, probably while watching sappy love movies on the Hallmark Channel and drinking hot chocolate.

"If you could pick one thing to have, what would it be?" Ben says.

I want to be happy, I say inside my head. It isn't that I'm unhappy. I'm...misplaced.

"I want to be home." It's not a lie. I want that very much. But to me, home isn't a place. It's a feeling. And I think that's why I'm homesick, so lost and confused. I feel like an orphan. Where is my home? Where is my family? Where do I belong?

"Yeah, I want that too," he says with a nod. Ben returns to his back, face toward the sky. "But you know what I really want?"

"To get washed up?" I get to my feet and move toward the layered rock wall to the left of us with a tiny waterfall gliding down its face. It's to the point where dirt has become a part of me.

Ben kneels beside me, cupping water in his hands and smoothing it around his face. He shakes his head in answer to my question. "Nope."

Our elbows touch as he shifts. It's sad how much I savor that miniscule amount of contact. It makes me annoyed with myself, but not enough to move away. "To sleep in your own bed? Shower? Have whole pieces of clothing to wear?"

"Well, yeah, those are all a given, but I'd even take a steak over any of that. If someone appeared right now with a nice, fat, juicy steak and gave me the option of eating it, or being able to have all that other stuff, I'd pick the steak, no questions asked, and continue to take my chances in the wilderness."

"Steak is good," I agree, almost drooling at the thought.

The sun lazily dips behind clouds. My lips are chapped and my skin itches from the sun more than the bug bites I've accumulated. I imagine I look like a scaly lobster right about now—a bumpy, scaly lobster, to be exact. "But?" Ben turns his head to the side at the same time I do. His eyelashes curl up, pretty enough to be on a girl.

"But what really sounds good right now is Malt-O-Meal," I confess, looking to the side and back.

"Malt-O-Meal?" he repeats suspiciously.

I sit back on my heels, my ankles protesting until I shift to my butt. My throat feels thick as I explain, "My mom made me Malt-O-Meal just about every morning when I was a kid. Not because she didn't want to or couldn't make anything else, but because that's what I wanted, every day. I especially looked forward to finding lumps in it. The lumps were the best. I miss Malt-O-Meal."

It isn't the only thing I miss.

Ben frowns, his body held still. "You sound sad."

"I'm not sad," I deny immediately. "I'm...reflective."

He doesn't look as if he believes me. "Where is your mom now?"

"Why do you care?" I toss back, no longer enjoying the conversation. I know I brought it up, but now I want to forget I did.

His face goes blank and Ben stands, stiffly replying, "I don't."

"Good. Let's keep it that way." I clamber to my feet and brush off my backside. Why, I don't know. My clothes are ruined, a little more dirt isn't going to matter.

Ben retrieves the backpack and settles it over his shoulders. I watch the muscles in his arms flex as he moves. His face is scratched and he favors his hurt leg as he stands. Scruff lines his jaw. His dark hair is usually combed in an orderly fashion, but nature has had its way with it. Ben's always so put-together at the office. The image of unkempt masculinity he now portrays makes my heart beat faster.

I ask a question I've been wondering since the leech incident occurred. "How did you know how to get the leeches off?"

"*Stand by Me*," he mutters.

"Why?"

"What?"

"Why do I need to stand by you?"

Ben shoots me an exasperated look. "It's a movie."

"Oh. I'm going to find berries," I announce, randomly picking a direction to pursue. I need something to do, and for some reason, looking for berries seems like a great idea.

"There's trail mix left."

I shake my head, the thought of eating any food actually making me feel ill right now. "I don't want any."

Ben studies me. "You've barely eaten anything."

"I'm not hungry." When he just looks at me, thinking whatever it is he's thinking, I sigh and begin walking. Again.

"Do you know what kind of berries are edible?"

I jump at the unexpected nearness of his voice, shooting him a glance as I head into a heavily wooded area thick with shrubbery. "No. I figure I'll try one and if I don't die within the hour, I'll try some more."

"That sounds like a solid plan."

11
BEN

It is late afternoon when Avery collapses to her knees. I hear it before I see it, jerking around as she hits the ground. Her head is bowed, and she sways side to side, her hands flat to the grass, shoulders hunched.

Fuck.

I stride for her. She needs food, but more than that, she needs water. My tone is harsh when I speak, but only because seeing her like this sends worry crashing along my spine. "Get up."

Avery shakes her head, her golden hair swishing around her shoulders. She has yet to lift her head. "I can't. I'm thirsty, and hungry, and so, so tired. I just want to rest a minute."

"Not here, not now," I state firmly.

It's almost dusk. We need to decide what we're doing for the night, and we need to make sure we're safe. We're out in the open, completely unprotected from anything that may decide it wants to eat us. What concerns me even more than the thought of a feral animal attacking us is the thought of an unpredictable human wandering about looking for whoever is trespassing on their land, because I know, with absolute surety, that we are no longer in Shawnee National Forest. I have a sinking feeling in the pit of my stomach; it's telling me we're on someone's private land.

"Please." Avery finally raises her eyes to me and the look in them about does me in.

"Get up," I repeat, my voice like steel.

A sob is wrenched from her. It's full of despondency. My anger shoots to the surface at the pitiful sound. This isn't like Avery. She doesn't give up, and if she's ridiculous enough to think she has that option right now, I'll make sure she realizes she doesn't.

"Ben, I can't..." She wordlessly shakes her head.

I grab her under the armpits and haul her to her feet, holding her to me when she stumbles. We stand like this for seconds that seem to last lifetimes, her heartbeat thundering against my ribcage. Damn, she feels good in my arms. I absently smooth down her tangled locks, briefly pressing my cheek to her head before I harden my jaw, harden myself to Avery's forlornness, and do what needs to be done.

"You don't have a choice in this, Avery."

"Just leave me here. I'll be fine. Besides, I know you'll be glad to have some peace and quiet," Avery pants, the joke as weak as her shaking form.

Fury pulses in time with the twitch under my eye. She did not just say that.

"What are you doing?" she cries when I move us toward the nearest body of water.

"Making sure I am guaranteed not a single ounce of peace *or* quiet." I drag her to the water's edge and force her to the ground. The water is shallow and clear enough to see the pebbles littering the base, and to me, that means it's clean enough to drink. We emptied the last water bottle hours ago. This is all we've got.

"Ben, no! Stop!" Avery fights me, but her efforts are lacking.

"You need to drink something."

"I will not drink that water! I will not let parasites swim around inside my mouth again! I will not swallow them!"

Under less dire circumstances, I might smile at that declaration.

I grapple with Avery, eventually getting her to her back and locked between my legs. I squeeze, not enough to hurt her, but to keep her still, and to let her know she can't escape. Sweat covers her face and collarbone, and Avery gasps for air, staring up at the sky. I study her, intrinsically aware of her breasts and legs. She's beautiful, and sexy, and sweeter than I realized.

"You don't have a choice in this," I repeat, my tone hard. I look down, getting a little lost in the golden depths of her eyes when she finally brings them to mine. "You're drinking the water."

Tears fill her eyes, making them shimmer. "I don't want to be sick."

"You'll be sick if you don't drink something," I tell her gently. A muscle jumps in my jaw as I sweep my eyes over her sun-abused skin. There are shadows beneath her eyes. Her lips look dry and swollen. She's taken a beating from nature, that's for sure.

Even so, she's strong enough to get through this. I know that. She has to believe it too.

I hold her gaze and give it to her straight. "It's almost nighttime, Avery, and no one's come for us. We need to drink, and eat, and find shelter. You know the routine. We have to do what's necessary to survive. All right?"

Avery sniffles.

"You can do this."

A transformation takes place as my words sink in. Avery's eyes harden, and her spine straightens. Taking a rattling breath, she blinks away the tears and puts a hand to my legs, pushing until I release her. Avery goes to her hands and knees, looking down at the water. I watch her warily, posed to tackle her should she run. Motionless, quiet, Avery considers the drinking source.

"The water won't get any cleaner by staring at it," I let her know in my driest tone.

"I knew I wouldn't look good, but...I look horrible," she says in a shocked hush, staring at her reflection.

"That's not possible." The words come without thought, a simply stated fact.

Avery swings large eyes to me and I shift my attention to the water. I kneel beside Avery. "On the count of three, we both drink."

A faint smile flutters across her lips and disappears.

"Ready?"

"Sure." Avery's confirmation doesn't sound the least bit sure.

"One...two...three."

I cup my hands and bring them to the water, capturing the clear liquid between them. I quickly bring it to my mouth and swallow. It's cool and tastes like minerals. Avery shudders as she does the same.

"Not bad?" I ask after I've had my fill. The water doesn't help the gnawing hunger clawing at my guts, but it's refreshing.

She scrunches up her nose. "As long as I don't think of the fish poop I'm probably drinking along with the river water."

I laugh. "I'm sure there are worse things in there than fish poop."

Avery scowls. "Thanks. That's what I wanted to hear." She takes a couple more drinks. Shifting back, she gives me a curious look. "*Do* fish poop?"

Unable to hold back a smile, I tell her, "Yeah, I'm pretty sure they do. This is a lake, by the way, not a river."

She stands as I do, her attention on the water. "How can you tell?"

I gesture to the hills and mountains surrounding us. "Lakes generally have land on all sides, and they're still more than moving. Plus, they're cleaner."

"How do you know that?"

"I read a lot," I say with a shrug.

Avery eyes me doubtfully. "But we've seen multiple waterfalls. I didn't know lakes could have waterfalls."

"None of them were big ones."

Her daintily arched eyebrows lower. "They seemed big."

"It's all about perception."

Avery looks at me and quotes, "'*Everyone's perception is their reality; let yours be epic.'.*"

I am speechless for about a minute. I had no idea Avery even knew that saying. "I wrote that."

"I know. It's the slogan used for 'Epic Computers'. It was one of Sanders and Sisters' biggest deals."

Pride pulses through my chest. That was my biggest sale with the company. The feeling of accomplishment fades as soon as it appears, and my jaw hardens. It was the biggest deal Sanders and Sisters had in a long time, until Avery made an even bigger one with a makeup company last month. '*Beauty is more than skin deep. Show the world what you're made of.*' That was the pitch that caught Elliot Accessories' attention and made them ours.

Her smile fades as I say, "I see you did your research on me. Like to know your competition, huh?"

"You know, everyone at Sanders and Sisters has always been really nice to me—except for you." Avery says it thoughtfully, like it's a puzzle she's wants to solve, but so far, cannot.

"I was nice, at first."

Her expression says otherwise. "Even then you were aloof. Polite, but aloof."

There could be some truth to that, but although I had reservations about her character, I was willing to give her a chance. Until she began to usurp my work, and eventually, deceived me. The muscles in my neck tighten. What pisses me off the most is that she couldn't understand my reaction to her duplicity. Avery acted as if she did me a favor, when really all she did was advance her own worth in the company.

Now I know why too. She has a thing for Duke. Somehow, that makes it all twenty times worse. She didn't even do it for herself, but for him.

Duke Renner is an attractive guy. Even I can see that. True, he's overly tan and his teeth are cosmetically straight and white, but he works hard on being fit, and he's aged well, looking younger than his fifty years. Even so, he's still twice the age as Avery.

I grind my teeth together. I swear she exudes invisible magic that has the power to reorganize my memories to her benefit. Because when I'm around Avery, I start to forget what she did, and that makes me angry. I forget that she's the kind of person who would contemplate seducing her boss to get ahead in her career.

As if to mimic my mood, darkness descends quickly and unapologetically. Clouds take over the sky, blocking the sun as the wind picks up and dusk falls upon us. Night is coming, possibly bringing another storm with it.

"We need to find a place to sleep before it's dark." I stride past her, not waiting to see if she follows.

It is long moments before Avery speaks, her voice close but soft. "You're hard to figure out, Ben. Most of the time, I think you hate me…but other times, I think you might like me more than you want to."

"Trust me, Avery…" I swing around to confront her, to tell her that I despise her, completely and unconditionally, but I can't spit out the words.

She waits, already looking crestfallen.

"When I say that if we don't find shelter soon, we're going to regret it," I slowly answer.

Avery looks down, hiding a small smile. "Right. Let's find a hotel."

"A hotel?"

"I think I saw one over there." She points toward the highest mountain in the far distance, glancing at me as her smile grows. "Do you think they have any vacancies? Maybe we can get a drink at the bar."

"Are you delirious?"

Avery continues on as if I never spoke. "Oh! Do you think they'll have room service? I'd kill for a big, fat juicy cheeseburger and fries."

I glower at her because I really want to smile. "Stop being…cheeky."

Avery blinks up at me. "Why? Would you rather I collapsed to the ground again and refused to move?"

"No," I answer cautiously, not positive what is the right response to that.

"At least this way, it's harder for me to want to sink into a deep, dark depression where I'm positive my life is about to end. You should be glad about that. Right?"

"Right," I reply, again wondering if I should agree with her.

"Glad that's settled. Race you to the hotel." She sticks out her tongue and marches ahead of me, swinging her arms as she goes.

I tilt my head, staring after Avery for a moment, wondering if she's had some kind of mental breakdown. Maybe the lack of water, combined with the heat of the sun, has somehow dehydrated her brain, if such a thing can even happen.

12
AVERY

I look at Ben. "Now what?"

Ben gestures to an area to the left of us that is clear of bushes and trees. "Now we make a fire and settle in for the night."

"Do you know how? Because I don't."

"I haven't started a fire since I went camping with some buddies when I was eighteen." He reaches into his pocket and pulls out a lighter. He flicks his thumb across it and a small flame appears. Ben looks at me, the tiny fire casting wicked shadows across his lean features. "But I'm sure going to try."

"Also illegal." I'm jealous of the gadgets Ben seems to produce from nowhere. Does he have secret pockets in those shorts or what? Why didn't I think of sneaking things?

Annoyance flickers across his face. "What are you, the Extreme Retreat police?"

I don't respond. If I were the Extreme retreat police, I might handcuff him just because. Carnal images follow that thought and I clear my throat, turning my attention to anything but Ben.

We are bunked beneath a gang of trees, surrounding shrubs and high grass forming somewhat of a barrier from the elements, and whatever beasts are about. Of course, if the beasts are in the grass with us, it isn't really doing its job. I glance behind me, seeing nothing but plants. I guess this is as good as any place to sleep. Not that we have options. That cave we found is somewhere we will most likely never see again. I wish we would have stayed there. It's my fault; I wanted to move.

"Eat the rest of this." Ben shoves the sad-looking bag of trail mix at me.

I shake my head. I'm so hungry that the thought of eating food actually makes me nauseous.

"Take small amounts, chew slowly, make it last until morning," he instructs, not moving his hand away.

"What about you?"

"I'll be fine," Ben says shortly, turning back to the fire.

"No. I'm not eating the last of the food."

"You don't have a choice." He doesn't look up. "Eat it."

"Are there mountain cats out here?" I whisper, as if loud noises attract the animal in question. Which, they might, I don't know. I pop a nut in my mouth, sucking the salt from it. My stomach revolts and I take deep breaths until it steadies.

Ben mutters to himself as he tries, unsuccessfully, to start a fire with whatever earthly things he can find. Gathered in a pile are twigs, dead leaves, and other miscellaneous items. He's been working on it for what seems like forever, but I'm sure has really only been about five minutes. Fantasies about my king-size bed, with clean sheets and warm blankets, torment me as I watch.

"Ben?"

"What?" His focus shoots to me.

"I asked—never mind. Why hasn't anyone come for us?" The question pierces the silence, demanding an answer. Once I chew the nut for a minute, I move on to a raisin.

"You mean Duke?"

I glare at him, not responding. Let him think what he likes.

Ben partially turns my way before going back to his present task. "Do you really want to know the answer?"

"Yes, I want to know. Why are we still out here?" *And what is out here with us?*

I sit huddled against a large tree that scrapes my back with each violent jerk of my shivering body, eating the trail mix at the rate of a snail. My skin that burned earlier is now startlingly chilled. The night sky is dark gray streaked through with midnight blue. As soon as the sun started to go down, the temperature dropped.

I wonder how cold it will get when it's fully night. On the plus side, I have yet to see another crow—and it's cool enough out that the bugs are staying away. Although, I can hear them, and they seem closer than I like.

Ben sighs and drops a pile of twigs, frustration adding lines to his face. "Because we aren't where we are supposed to be anymore. No one knows where we are—I don't even know where we are—and the chances of them finding us at all are pretty slim. The longer we're out here, the less likely it is we'll be rescued."

I begin to hum over his voice near the end of his declaration, refusing to register Ben's dismal words. I can't accept the possibility of our demise in the wilderness. I won't. Okay, so we weren't found today. That's understandable. They probably just now realized we're missing. Someone is looking for us. Someone will find us.

"What are you doing?" Ben looks at me as if I've lost my mind as I continue to make magic with my vocal chords.

"Humming."

"Why?"

We'll probably wake up at exactly the moment they stumble upon us. Everything will be fine. I will not freeze out here, or starve, or become a pecking post to ferocious birds or a meal to mountain lions. I will not die, definitely not. No way. Panic squeezes my chest and I keep humming, louder and faster.

"Avery?"

I finally look at Ben, take in the quizzical look he's got set on me, and abruptly stop.

"*Now* are you having a meltdown?" he asks.

"No. I was humming because I don't like your attitude." I watch Ben work, the brush catching fire almost instantly. Smoke fills the air and my nostrils. It's a welcome smell.

As soon as it starts, the fire dies. Ben curses loudly and harshly.

I get up and move toward him. "Can I try?"

His expression is full of derision as he gestures for me to take over. "Have at it."

"It's weird."

"What's weird?" He hands me the lighter.

"You. You always seem so by the books, but you're not. You do things you aren't supposed to."

Ben snorts. "Because I brought a pocketknife and a lighter?"

"I didn't bring anything," I point out grumpily.

He begins to gather more broken twigs and dead leaves, adding them to a growing pile. After a brief pause, Ben adds, "I wanted to be as prepared as I could be, but it still wasn't enough."

I run my thumb across the wheel and a flame appears. I set it against the brush as a flame forms and watch it expand. "I like it."

Ben wipes his hands on what remains of his shirt and focuses on me. "Like what?"

"That you don't follow the rules all the time."

"Glad you approve." Ben haunches down and gets to work on helping me. He rearranges the sticks, making a teepee.

I ask curiously, "How do you know how to do that?"

"I don't. Most likely, it'll smoke out again."

"Way to be positive."

"I'm trying to be realistic."

"There's a difference between being pessimistic and being realistic," I mumble, watching as the fire crackles and pops and grows.

"I'll be whatever it takes to keep us safe while we're in this shit-pile of existence, for however long it takes," Ben retorts hotly.

"Are you saying there's a chance we're going to be stuck in the wilderness forever?" I purposely lighten my tone and concentrate on the snapping flames.

"God, I hope not."

I laugh at the revulsion I catch in his voice. "I'm not that bad, Ben, I promise."

When he doesn't say anything, I look up, going still at the unusual expression on his face. It isn't horrified. It's contemplative. And watchful. Maybe a twinge sad. Ben studies me, his eyes holding mine captive. I can't look away. He finally does, briefly lowering his head.

"Take this," he murmurs as he lifts his hand, offering the pocketknife. It looks ancient, possibly something handed down through the adolescent Stitzer line. It probably doesn't have a lot of monetary value, but to his family, is priceless. I have a couple things like that from my mom, nothing at all from my dad.

I take the knife warmed by his body heat and look at the fiery pile of tinder and brush. "What do I do with it? Stab the kindling a couple times and hope it stays lit?"

Ben's breath fans my hair as he quietly chuckles. "I'm not going to tell you no if that's really what you want to do. Or you could hold it for me while I show you some magic."

I twist my head, bringing my face close to his. My lips tingle with longing for a taste of his. Ben's eyelids become hooded, his face split by shadows.

Ben nods toward the ground, breaking the spell. "Do you want me to show you or not?"

"Um...yeah. Please." I swallow hard and turn my back to him, but that's worse, because now his front is flush with my spine, and his heat scorches me as he leans over me, his arms on either side of mine.

"My dad insisted I do Boy Scouts when I was a kid, said it would come in handy one day." Ben pauses. "I wish I'd listened to him."

I glance over my shoulder, daring to look directly into his eyes for a millisecond that alters my whole concept of him. Ben is ever-changing eyes under dark, swooping eyebrows with blades for cheekbones. He's gorgeous. "You're winging this, is that what you're saying?"

Ben offers a self-deprecating grin. "Yep. But don't worry, I did play baseball all through school and college. It's basically the same thing."

We share a smile, and I swear the sky lights up from the power of it. Or it's lightning. I wait, eyes to the sky, looking for another bolt. None come. I look back at Ben. It's just him, and how I feel when I'm around him.

Ignoring the thunderous beat of my heart, I turn my attention back to the task at hand. We need a better fire, and fast. My fingers and toes are slowly turning to ice. The only frozen feeling I like is the kind you get from ice in a cocktail.

"Okay, mountain man, show me what you got," I encourage.

"Abracadabra!" Ben wiggles his fingers at the fire.

I stare.

Ben looks at me and laughs. "Just kidding."

"Are you going to be serious now?" I deadpan.

He nods solemnly, looking adorably sweet. "As serious as a fire."

It takes way more concentration than I'm equipped to handle right now, to the point that my head starts to pound as we work the twigs and leaves and brush just so to stabilize the fire. Soon, my arms and hands are tired and don't cooperate like I want. But after countless attempts, all while being cocooned by Ben's arms, the fire holds.

I shriek and hop up without thought, knocking the back of my head against Ben's chin. He grunts and falls back. I swing around and hug him, overjoyed that we got the fire to hold steady. It will be a spectacular fire, of course, when it's at its full potential. It will keep the cold away, and hopefully, animals.

"We did it, Ben! We did it!" I grab his shoulders and shake him,and fling my arms around him once more. My voice is muffled when I say, "This hug would work way better if you participated."

"I might be more inclined to hug you if I could move my arms."

"Would you really?" I ask hesitantly, breathless with hope. I pull back to peer at his face, disappointed to find the answer in his expression. He wouldn't. It makes me angry. We have no idea what's going to happen to us out here and he's holding grudges. "Admit you hate me a little less than before we got here."

Ben's eyes darken. "Why? Would admitting that somehow benefit your career with Sanders and Sisters?"

"Not everything is about my career." It never was about my career.

"Could have fooled me. I'm sure you'll use this whole unwanted experience against me in some way too, right?"

"What do you mean?"

"You figure it out."

I settle back against the tree, eyes forward. I'd rather freeze to death at this point than be near Ben. I tuck my hands under my crossed arms and pray for sleep to come quickly. My breaths are visible poofs of air and the tip of my nose is cold. I'm done trying to figure things out for the day.

I think Ben realizes it. With a sigh, he shakes his head and situates himself before the fire. It's going to be a long night.

BEN

I wake up with a crick in my neck. The fire is dead with not even a trail of smoke left. I squint as I search the area not yet touched by the sun. It takes me another moment to realize my arms and legs are wrapped around Avery. I blink, vaguely remembering getting up in the middle of the night when I couldn't stand to watch her shiver another second.

Her face was softened by the glow of fire, her hair like golden silk around her shoulders and face. It was odd to watch her through the flames; she was part of them, possibly the bringer of them. She certainly produces sparks when she's near. But not enough to keep her from shivering in her sleep.

Avery's face is buried in my neck, her body contorted into a ball. My throat bobs as I try to swallow. Without a conscious thought to do so, I smooth hair from her face.

"Avery." My voice comes out thin and quiet.

A small sound leaves her.

My arms tighten around her a second before I disentangle our limbs roughly enough to jar her awake. She shoots upright, her eyes wild and wide. "Where are we? What's going on?"

I don't say anything, wishing I could tell her this is all a bad dream and that as soon as she wakes up for real, she'll be back home.

"Ben?"

I get to my feet, wincing as my muscles and joints protest. I glance at Avery, unease stabbing through me. I don't know how much longer Avery can do this. "Are you ready to get moving?"

Avery looks at me, disillusionment dulling her eyes.

"Come on," I tell her gently but firmly. "We should get some water to drink and try to find something edible to eat. Then we'll try to retrace our steps from yesterday."

We were lucky not to be visited by any animals during the night, but I feel them. I know they're nearby. At times, I feel as if we're being watched. By man or animal, I don't know. I haven't told Avery. God only knows how she'd react to that.

"Avery," I say in a harsher tone when she doesn't move. "Let's go. We aren't going to be found if we aren't in the open."

Avery finally stands, weariness casting shadows on her face.

Sheer willpower and the need to keep Avery moving are all I have to rely on. My muscles are overtaxed, my sprained ankle twinging with every other step. My stomach is painfully empty. *Keep going, just keep going.* I backtrack to the nearby creek we drank from yesterday.

As we finish up drinking, a scent hits me, sweet and welcome.

"Do you smell that?" I ask, scanning the foliage around us.

There.

I walk toward the plants with pointy leaves, elation quickening my pulse. It smells like mint and looks like mint. I pick a leaf and bring it to my nose, a clean, refreshing scent hitting me. Mint is better than nothing. Mint is great right now.

I pop the leaf in my mouth and chew the coarse herb until it is mush, swallowing quickly. Although there is a faint sour aftertaste, my mouth feels twenty times better. I gather some more, shoving it in my pockets.

"Eat this." I hold a mint leaf before Avery's face.

"What is it?" She warily takes it from me, eyeing the leaf.

"Mint."

"How do you know?"

"I don't know a lot about nature, but I did read up on it some before we came here. This is a step in the right direction. If we can find this, I'm confident we can find other edible plants." *Stay positive.*

Avery slowly chews the mint, taking more as I offer it. Self-reproach can be heard in her voice when she admits, "I wasn't prepared for any of this." She lifts her gaze to mine. "Thank you."

I give Avery a brief nod and turn from the sight of her trampled golden beauty. Her gratefulness sends a large dose of guilt my way. I could have been more prepared. I should have been. But I didn't know. How *could* I have known we would end up lost in my own state? I mentally shake off the thought and focus on the task at hand.

In a moment of clarity or delusion, I tell Avery, "I'm going to climb the nearest mountain as high up as I can, see what's below. Maybe we'll get lucky and find people or a campsite, something."

"What? No. Why are you going to do that?"

"It will be fine, Avery, trust me."

Finding the wild mint is a sign. Things are looking up. Today is the day we find our way back to civilization, I can feel it. I tilt my head back and examine the mountain I'm about to ascend. There are sporadic ledges, which can be used as lookout points and somewhere to rest. It looks promising, as in, I probably won't fall to my death. Up can't be worse than any other direction we've gone. It's a stretch, but I'm at the point where I'll try just about anything.

"Don't go." Avery latches her hand around my arm and squeezes.

I look at her hand, then meet her eyes. "I won't be long."

A crease forms between her eyebrows, and with reluctant fingers, Avery releases me.

With slow, careful steps, I make my way to the slanted wall of earth. A fly buzzes near my ear. I stare at the tumultuous terrain for a moment, take a breath of fortitude, and I begin to climb. Grabbing at trees and whatever else I can find, I carefully work my way up the incline.

"Ben. Ben, wait!"

I pause, shooting a look over my shoulder. "What is it?"

Avery looks at me, twisting her fingers together but not speaking.

My grip loosens, and I skid down an inch. Gritting my teeth, I reinforce my hold on the rock, the jagged edges digging into my skin. "Any time now, Avery."

"Remind me again why you're doing this?" Avery asks, worry lining her face.

"So I can see what's around us, maybe find someone or something that will help us get out of here. Remember? We need a plan, and right now, the plan is find out what's nearby." I pant around the pain in my ankle as it gives an especially sharp throb, pushing through it as I move higher.

"But...do you have to? What if you fall?"

"It isn't anything I haven't already done." When silence greets me, I press my forehead to the rough stone and tell her, "I didn't mean anything by that."

Even her mocking tone lacks sincerity when she calls, "Right. Well. Good luck. I'll just...wait here, I guess."

You do that.

I'm less than a third of the way toward my destination when I hear, "How long do you think you'll be?"

I pause at the nervousness I catch in her voice, again gazing over my shoulder and down. Avery stands with her arms wrapped around herself, her gaze divided between me and her surroundings. She jumps at the sound of a faraway bird call. Shaking my head, I face forward. She hasn't voiced many of her qualms lately, but I know they're there, eating away at her sanity. There's nothing I can do about that. Avery has to find a way to get over her irrational fears herself.

"I'll get there quicker if you stop interrupting me."

Something rumbles overhead, causing the earth beneath me to shake. Maybe it's a landslide, aimed right for me. Whatever it is, it can't be any worse than what I've already endured. Nothing is keeping me from reaching the top. The sooner I get up there, the sooner we can once more be on our way, the sooner we can reach civilization.

"Um...Ben?"

"I don't have time for this, Avery."

"But..."

I tune her out.

"Ben," she hisses.

I crane my neck and glare down at her. "What is it? If you haven't noticed, I'm trying to—"

The expression on her face mutes any forthcoming words. In fact, the air freezes inside my lungs. With a white face, wide eyes, and a thin slant for a mouth, she looks beyond me. Chills skim along my flesh. I really don't want to know what has her spooked. The earth vibrates again.

Avery shifts her gaze to me.

My eyes are held captive by hers as a snuffing sound comes from overhead. "What is it?" I ask.

She shakes her head when I begin to turn mine. The whisper of, "Don't look," reaches me as I do exactly that.

There is a good seven feet between us, but it might as well be inches. This particular animal is not supposed to be here. I specifically checked for that when I read about the forest. A face of matted black fur with long yellow teeth peers back at me. The beast sniffs the air, the muscles of its body rippling as it shifts. It's bent toward me; I don't even want to imagine how tall it would be standing upright. Its paws are as big as my head, sporting sharp claws. The eyes are small and fixated on me, and through them, I see my mortality. It leans closer, probably basking in the scent of my terror. Its mouth opens, hot breath wafting over me as I see the full effect of its teeth.

Fuck.

Me.

"Just...don't move," Avery says softly.

Really? Because I thought I'd do a little dance.

Hunching down, its face directly before mine, it lets out a spine-tingling roar.

"Bear," I croak.

13

AVERY

The bear is monstrous, and ugly, and when it lets out a sound that stiffens Ben's shoulders and gives me heart palpitations, I know fear in a way I've yet to experience. There isn't enough space between man and animal. One swipe of that daggered mitt and Ben is done for.

It makes me ill, where I literally am on the verge of vomiting. This can't be happening. The crow has nothing on this black brute. The bear paces back and forth, intermittently letting out that horrendous sound.

On the outside, I'm frozen in place. Inside, I'm pacing right along with that bear.

I decide something: I can't leave Ben to the fate of a bear. A crow, maybe, but a bear? No.

"You can't have him," I whisper, eyes on the black beast.

Shoulders back, jaw tight, I move forward. Even as I step toward danger, I wonder why now, when I should be running, as opposed to before, when I did run, I am resolved to stay and help. Even if I never let the thought fully produce, I know why.

Before I can force myself forward another step, the bear turns and moves out of sight.

I let out a choked exhalation and watch as Ben slides a few feet down the side of the mountain. Maybe it won't come back. Maybe something will go our way for once. Fingers clenched, I hop from foot to foot as I silently will him the rest of the way down the mountain before the bear decides to come back.

"Hurry."

"Trying," Ben rasps.

Panic shoots into my core as the bear returns, holding on to something that looks suspiciously like a scrap of my pink shirt I tied around some random tree branch in hopes of someone seeing it and finding us. Before too long, we'll both be shirtless. I mean, if we're still alive.

Arms outstretched, it almost looks as if the bear is offering it to Ben. Sadistic bear. It plops down on the ground, the strip of cloth looking diminutive within its massive paws. With unimaginable strength, it shreds it in an instant, roaring with displeasure when only pieces remain. Luckily, with its newfound toy, it isn't paying attention to Ben.

"Come on, come on." I gesture for Ben to move faster, even though his back is to me.

Ben hits the ground hard enough that his knees buckle, a grunt leaving him. With a wince, he straightens and hobbles toward me. He reinjured his ankle. There is a sympathetic lurch in my stomach knowing he's in pain.

I hurry to meet him, my hands ready to help him. His hair sticks up in front; there is a wild cast to his eyes. His hands and arms are pocked with dirt and blood. Ben is filthy and wounded, but most importantly, whole.

Our eyes collide, silently communicating the need to survive.

Side by side, we race down a jagged slope, away from the black bear. I only allow myself to look back once, and to my relief, the bear is still occupied by the pink material. That's one bear—how many more are there around? And what else is out here? I just want walls around me. Is that too much to ask? *Yes, it is,* a fierce part of me I didn't know existed replies. *So get your shit together and be brave.*

When Ben stumbles, I help steady his steps. When I almost land in a hole, he hauls me over it. Pulse sprinting along with us, my throat and chest burn with each breath of air I manage to inhale. I smack into tree limbs that sting upon contact and shrubs that feel like nettles against my skin. We run down and down, into a condensed forest of high trees. My leg muscles ache and there is a cramp in my right side. I'm sunburned, thirsty, dirty, lost, hungry, and on the run from a black bear. All things I never want to be. The urge to stop is strong, but even stronger is the need to persist.

We come to a clearing, our pace finally slowing to a stop. The far cry of a disgruntled bear reaches my ears and sends shivers dancing along my spine. *Please don't find us. Please don't let your friends and relatives find us either.*

My lungs burn all the way into my throat, to the point where even my teeth hurt. I look behind us, spinning in a circle until I'm dizzy and the sky is a blur of blue and white. I see trees and nothing else, so many trees they almost entirely block out the sky. We're safe, for now. I stagger to a stop, one hand braced against the bark of a tree.

Neither of us speak as we catch our breath. I feel as if I'm going to be sick. I bend over, my hair a curtain against the world. I close my eyes for a moment before straightening. "Do you think…" I suck in a lungful of air and attempt words once more. "Do you think there are more of them?"

"Definitely," Ben wheezes, bent at the waist with his hands on his knees.

Adrenaline spikes my pulse into overdrive and I immediately scan the trees for vicious, black creatures lurking about. "We should keep moving."

"I agree. Let's keep moving."

My heartbeat has navigated into my eardrums, giving our voices a surreal quality. I guess that muted sound could be reality leaving me, growing fainter and farther away as I sink into a nightmare of bears on the hunt for one Ben Stitzer and one Avery Scottam. "Sounds good. Let's do that. Where?"

"Not a clue, but if it means we're not eaten by wild animals, we can be lost the whole time we're here. We can walk in a never-ending circle for all I care," Ben tells me once he has his breathing under control.

I nod jerkily, agreeing without hesitation. "Want to know another reason I hate outside?"

"Besides birds and bugs being around?"

"Yes. Bears."

"It's like things that start with the letter 'B' are detrimental to you."

I stare into his eyes. "Not all things."

He doesn't answer me, just studies my face. Dirt streaks his face, sweat adding a sheen to his skin. This close, without his glasses, his eyes seem more expressive, deeper. They are greener than I thought. He searches my face as I admire his. "You didn't run."

My stomach dips. "We're teammates, remember?"

He opens his mouth.

"Don't bring up the bird."

Ben smiles faintly.

I want to hug him. The need is strong. To feel the surety of his heartbeat, to be touched by his warmth. Looking at him and seeing that Ben is okay isn't enough. I move forward with the intention of doing just that, damn the consequences, but before I can reach him, Ben walks off, a look of concentration on his face.

He scans the ground and then focuses on me with lowered eyebrows. "Where's the backpack?"

I shake my head. "I don't know. We must have dropped it when we were running."

Hands on his hips, Ben faces the direction from which we came. "I'm going back for it."

"Are you kidding?"

"No."

I take in Ben's taut jaw and know he is deadly serious. "Why? There's nothing left in the bag that we need. Leave it."

"No."

I fling my hands up in frustration. "The bear could already have it! It could be gone."

"I don't care!" That crazy glint is in his eyes again. "Even if I have to pry the backpack from the bear's mouth, that bear cannot have that bag. I forbid it."

"Ben."

He seethes.

"You're being insane."

Ben turns his head and focuses on me, his left eye twitching.

Or he's past that.

I realize it isn't about the bag, and really about all sense of control being taken from us. I get it. I struggle with that on a daily basis. Even though my pulse is racing with fear and this is probably one of the worst ideas to bring to fruition, I nod and tell Ben, "Okay. Let's go get it then."

He blows out a noisy breath and returns the nod, grim-faced. "Let's go get it."

* * * *

My stomach dips the moment we turn around and backtrack. Returning to an area we ran to get away from seems like a poor choice to me, but we do it. We stay to the trees, Ben leading. He keeps one hand behind him, fingers locked tightly around mine. My eyes dart around, seeing bursts of green and nothing worrisome, which, of course, worries me.

The trees abruptly end, and we stumble to a clearing that was taken directly from a postcard. Shrubs flourish with blossoms in pinks, oranges, and purples. Mountains, covered in green and white, hover in the expanse.

To the right of us is gently moving water colored blue-green, wider than I can see. A bird chirps, and it doesn't sound threatening. I shiver and set my eyes on the point where the distant mountains meet the skies.

Vibrant colors mix with pastels, curves contorted by jaggedness. With the white and gray clouds hovering above it all, I admit the view is beautiful. I've been terrified since we got here, but right now, looking at this, I feel free.

"What is this place?" I ask breathlessly, my voice full of awe.

"I'm not sure," Ben answers. "There are seven parts to the Shawnee Nations forest, but I have no idea where we are. I don't think we're even in the national forest anymore."

"Do you know the names?"

He shakes his head. "I remember Burden Falls Wilderness and Garden of the Gods Wilderness, but only because they're interesting names. The Panther Den Wilderness was where we started."

"Panther Den Wilderness?" Panthers? There are panthers here?

Noting the look on my face, Ben says, "Easy, there aren't any panthers."

"Right." I gulp. "And were there supposed to be bears here too?"

He winces, confirming what I thought. Wonderful.

I take a deep breath, refusing to think about it, and focus on the world directly around us.

"It's pretty here. Peaceful." I turn to him, finding his eyes already on me. A funny look crosses his features. I'm curious as to his thoughts, but not brave enough to ask what they are.

Ben sets his hands on his narrow hips and views our surroundings. I follow his gaze, taking in the faraway mountains. I hug myself, wishing I was anywhere but here. I am on display for all wildlife to see, and hunt. I could be being sized up right now by an unseen bear thinking I'll be its next meal. It isn't a pleasant feeling.

"Do you see it anywhere?" I ask Ben, wanting to be on the move again. Being out in the open doesn't make me feel safe. It's peaceful here, yes, but it's also an illusion. This place is full of predators.

"No." Ben sighs, going still in the next heartbeat. "Do you hear that?"

I cock my head and listen, catching the faint notes of something inhuman and sorrowful. "What is that?"

With stealthy steps, Ben moves forward. He pauses to look over his shoulder and gestures for me to follow.

I vehemently shake my head.

Ben lifts his eyebrows.

I shake my head some more, firmly staying rooted in placed.

With a shrug, he turns and disappears between two large bushes.

That jumpstarts me into action and I sprint after him, quickly catching up.

Ben looks straight ahead, his steps slow and silent. He stops without warning and I bump into him, sending him stumbling forward a couple steps. I mouth, "Sorry," when he gives me an annoyed look. I look at what holds his attention. My stomach drops to my feet, and then it drops some more.

I am looking at a furry black thing that isn't all that much smaller than me and appears to have its head stuck in the opening of the backpack. It paws at the bag, making those mournful sounds. Even though my eyes know what I'm looking at, it takes a couple minutes for my brain to process and accept it. It's a bear cub, and if there's a cub, its mama is nearby. And a distressed cub? That will most likely bring a pissed mama before too long.

"Ben," I whisper, wrapping my fingers around his biceps and squeezing the dickens out of it. "We have to go now."

"It's stuck."

"Yes, and that's probably the only reason it hasn't attacked us." I try to back up a step, but with Ben not cooperating, I either have to let go of him, or stop moving. I stop moving. "Ben, let's go."

He looks at me, resigned and apologetic. "I can't, Avery."

"What do you mean, you can't?" I tug at him.

Ben turns back to the cub, seemingly unaware of my struggle to navigate him away from danger. "I can't leave it like that."

"Yes, you can. Now get your ass moving!" I yank on him, growling when he shakes me off.

He finally turns to face me. "I know this seems irrational, Avery, but I have to do this."

"What's wrong with you?" I cry. Damn him for caring enough for the wellbeing of another creature to put his own wellbeing at risk.

Ben smiles faintly. "Absolutely nothing."

The cub whimpers, falling to its side with its head still trapped. Its breaths come fast and short, its movements slow and weak. I feel its fear like a lash to the heart. I know why Ben has to do it. Seeing another creature suffer is one of the worst things to witness, and if you can help, why wouldn't you? I look at Ben, becoming aware of another side of him I didn't know was there until now.

He steps forward and I am a step behind him. Ben frowns at me. "What are you doing?"

"I go where you go." My mind is set, my back is straight, and I am ready for whatever is about to happen.

Ben looks as if he's going to argue, but then he nods. "Stay back a little bit, all right?"

As if sensing our approach, the cub stills, and then doubles its efforts, its cries painful to hear. Ben talks soothingly, his voice low, as he gets nearer and nearer. The cub breathes hard, its body shaking. Ben leans down, palm outstretched. I watch, feeling as if my heart is going to blow up in my chest. I pray that the cub doesn't freak out on Ben, and I pray that its mother is not nearby.

"Easy there, little guy. I'm not going to hurt you," Ben murmurs, his hand inches from the quivering animal.

The bear cub can't be that old, probably just a few months. It looks to be between fifteen to twenty pounds and two to three feet tall. Even though it's small, it still has paws with claws. Its fur is thick and seems soft, browner than black in color on the underside. I stare so hard my eyeballs dry out, waiting as Ben gently runs his hand along the animal's back. Its stubby tail twitches back and forth. I jump when it lets out a pitiful wail, but Ben continues to pet and talk, and eventually, it settles down, relaxing onto the ground as if Ben is a bear cub whisperer.

With one hand stroking the bear, Ben reaches with his other one and carefully works at loosening the backpack from the cub's head. The cub growls at one point when Ben tugs too hard; another time it whimpers. Hands clasped, I watch with awe and apprehension as Ben finally gets the backpack from the cub's head. I start to clap and then stop myself, eyes shifting. We don't need any animals wondering what all the ruckus is about and coming over to investigate.

The cub falls to its butt, shaking its head as it lets out a plaintive sound. It's adorable, and possibly ferocious. I study its large eyes and ears and narrow, fluffy face, wondering what it will do next. My heart wants to melt, but my brain is stone cold with distrust. It gets to its feet on wobbly legs and looks at Ben, sniffing the air with its head forward.

"Ben." I back up a step, ready to run should the need arise. "I think it's time to leave now."

Ben slowly straightens, a smile on his face. "I've never been this close to a bear before."

"Well, now that you have." I motion toward the direction we came from. "Let's continue to live and be on our way."

The bear sneezes, almost toppling over, and Ben laughs. "I want one of these for a pet."

"Right. And then one day you'll wake up and your sweet little cub won't be a cub anymore, but a giant monster bear and it will tear out your throat and eat it for breakfast," I say all in one breath, drawing in a large lungful of air when done.

Ben quirks an eyebrow at me.

"What?" I snap. "You act like that isn't a possibility."

He swings the beat-up backpack over a shoulder, looking rugged and manly. "All right, fine, let's go."

I turn my back to the cub, glancing over my shoulder with each step I take. You never know, it could decide to attack us. It merely sits, watching us. When we've gone a dozen steps, it lets out a mournful cry that has us both stopping. Our eyes meet, and I know what Ben is going to say before he says it.

Ben partially turns, his eyes on the bear cub. The shadow of stubble along his jaw accentuates his cheekbones and jawline, causing my heart to pitter-patter. He gets more attractive the longer we're together.

"It's odd that it's alone, right?" He scratches at the thin cut on his face. "What if it doesn't have any family?"

The cub looks between the two of us, its head tilted.

"What if it does?" I counter.

"We can't just leave it."

I turn him back to face me and try to reason with Ben. "We can, and we will. We have ourselves to worry about; we can't worry about a bear cub too. Besides, we can't take it home with us. You already helped it enough."

Why am *I* the logical one right now? When did that happen?

Ben runs fingers through dirty, crazily styled hair and begins to walk. "You're right."

The final look he gives the cub, regretful and despondent, tears into me. I pretend I don't see it, but it stays with me as we trek over the uneven terrain. Time seems to freeze as we quietly walk, each of us lost in our thoughts. I wonder if we're actually getting anywhere, or simply walking in place. That's what it feels like. No matter how far or which way we go, the landscape always looks the same.

Ben finally lets out a sound of frustration and stops. "It's hard to know which way to go when we have no idea where we are."

"Or really simple," I add with a shrug. "If we pick a random direction and keep going, we're bound to find something."

Ben lifts his eyebrows. "Are you always this optimistic?"

"No, but when I'm not, I give myself a mental kick in the ass until I am. They'll find us," I tell him, needing to hear the words again, needing to believe them. I need Ben to believe them too. "And soon. We just have to hang in there a little longer."

He gives me a sidelong glance. His expression does not show a glimmer of conviction.

"They'll find us," I repeat sharply.

"Sure. Yeah. They'll find us." He doesn't say it, but I hear it all the same: What if they don't?

"Hey." I smack my hand to his shoulder, the sound sharp enough to make me cringe and Ben to flinch.

"Sorry," I apologize, my hand still resting on his hot skin. It burns my palm the longer I keep it there. I snatch it back, my face as blistering as my hand. I step closer, bringing my face close to his, and drill resolution into his eyes. "They will find us."

My hope was flagging; Ben wouldn't let it. I will not allow him to do the same. We can't give up.

"You don't let anything have a chance to get better if you give up," I state firmly.

Ben watches me as he mulls over my words.

"You wanted to go up before; let's go up. Like you said, maybe we can see what's around us." I point over my shoulder toward the tallest mountain peak I can see.

"Avery," Ben begins.

"I don't want to hear anything negative. We need direction, purpose. We need a plan. Your plan was to go up. I feel like that's what we should do."

He takes in my determined expression nods, even as a flash of apprehension hits his eyes. "You got it."

14
AVERY

It seems innocent enough. The faint sound of moving water is nothing to cause alarm. I'm envisioning a stream about three feet across and maybe two in depth. What I find at the top of an unassuming hill is a raging waterfall not ten feet from us, and we're standing inches from a drop-off that will send us directly into it. I stumble back into Ben. One fall on this hellish excursion was more than necessary.

We can't get to the mountain; the water separates us from it.

Ben palms my waist, his hands firm, his chest hard and hot on my back. When he lets out a breath, I feel it on the side of my neck. It's a balm to my overheated skin. This would be wonderful, if not for the screaming rapids beneath us, and the fear that Ben may decide to push me.

"You see that, right? The waterfall? And the large gap between us and the mountain?" I ask, to be sure I'm not hallucinating.

"It's hard to miss." Ben's voice is close to my ear. My skin breaks out in goose bumps at the sound and feel of it.

I spin around, which isn't such a good idea, with being so close to a watery descent I can't imagine I'll enjoy. Ben tightens his grip on me until I'm squished to him and walks us back until we're a safer distance from the ledge. I tip my head back and meet his lowered face, our eyes immediately locking. One move and we'd be kissing. One move and we'd probably be in the water too.

Ben gives himself a shake and drops his hands at the same time he steps back. He scowls and gives me a nice view of his broad shoulders. "This isn't the way we want to go, unless we want to try some freestyle whitewater rafting."

"Not especially." My stomach rumbles, announcing the fact that I'd like to eat something. Unless I have an appetite for tree twigs and leaves, I'm not sure what's available to me. I swear I've lost five pounds since the start of this.

Ben glances toward my midsection. "You need to eat."

"Are there restaurants nearby I don't know about?" I joke as we turn right, following the water.

"I'd kill for some ribs from Jones's BBQ Shack."

I stop and stare at his back in wonder before remembering I need to put one foot in front of the other to get anywhere. A feeling of pure joy and kinship bursts through me. "I love that place almost as much as Rosa's!"

"You do?" Ben glances over his shoulder, a faint smile lining his face.

"I do," I reply enthusiastically, a bounce to my step. "Their onion flowers are ah-ma-zing, and the homemade sour cream and chive chips? The best." My mouth salivates at the thought of the fried food.

"Right? Everything there is good."

"Well...except for the deep-fried shrimp." I wrinkle up my nose, sidestepping a prickly bush to my left.

Ben gives me a look from over his shoulder. "You don't like shrimp? What's wrong with you?"

I shrug. "I don't like crunchy fish things."

Ben laughs, the sound short and surprising. "Crunchy fish things?"

I smile and look toward the water. There's only been a few times where Ben and I have had an actual conversation. We generally spend our time together growling, glaring, and snapping at one another.

"Whenever my family comes to visit, that's where they want to go," Ben supplies, startling me with the offered information. I know next to nil about him, not for lack of trying.

"Your family doesn't live near you?"

"My parents live in a suburb about an hour from me. We don't see each other as much we'd like. My sister is in Wisconsin, so we meet up even less frequently."

I nod, trailing my fingers over a red flower as I walk. He has a whole family with one dad, one mom, and even a sibling. A stab of discomfort hits my heart and I talk around it, pretending it isn't there. "I eat there at least once a week. It's on my rotation of restaurants."

Ben gives me a sidelong glance. "Rotation of restaurants? Do you ever cook?"

"Not by choice." That's not completely true. When it was my mom and me, I enjoyed cooking. I guess because I had someone to cook for. There isn't much point in cooking elaborate meals for one person.

"Why is that?" he asks.

I wrinkle up my nose. "Cooking equals work. I'd rather have the food ready for me instead of wasting time cooking it first."

Ben snorts. "I don't get to Jones's too often. It's a twenty-minute drive one way for me."

"But it's worth it, isn't it?" I turn and give him a grin. We are now walking side by side, even though I have no recollection of when he shortened his steps for me to be beside him instead of behind. "The delivery drivers and I are on a first name basis—all five of them."

Ben laughs again.

I like the sight of the sparkle in his multi-faceted eyes. I like the sound of his laughter. I even like how stubborn he is. It's the times when he sheds his armor, however briefly, that Ben becomes irresistible to me. I should be glad I see his fun, caring side infrequently. Once was all it took though. Just one magical moment where he spoke to me and looked at me as if I was everything.

I trip at the memory of the night of Duke's birthday, righting myself before Ben notices.

"I guess the mountain idea is shot," I muse. "Got another one?"

Ben shrugs. "Backtracking is good, but also impossible when everything looks the same. We could follow the sun? At least that way, we're going in the same direction."

"All right." I nod. "Let's do that."

The incline deepens as we follow along what has to be a river. We're past the waterfall. The water is calmer now, and closer. The span from land to land is also wider, and I'm guessing the water is much deeper. I shudder at the thought of what unknown slimy things are in its depths, along with countless leeches. I don't like water dirty enough that I can't see what's swimming around me. I also used to be terrified that sharks were in the local swimming pool, even though I could see in that water. Ben's right: I have issues.

"There's got to be edible berries around here somewhere, right?"

"Sure." He shoots a glance my way. "We found mint; we can find berries."

A flash hits my eyes and I close them against the blinding light. I bump into Ben, who grunts upon impact, and then I fall to my knees. I shake my head and lean back on my heels, opening my eyes to Ben's nicely muscled legs before moving them up to his face. Ben watches me for a minute, not speaking. My skin heats under his scrutiny.

He finally asks, "What are you doing?"

"Oh, you know, just checking the stability of Earth." I pat the ground a couple times. "Yep, seems stable."

Ben crouches beside me, his eyes never straying from my face. He waits, patient and silent.

"Something blinded me," I confess.

"My amazing good looks?"

I smile faintly. "Did you actually just make a joke?"

One eyebrow lifts. "Are you saying I'm not good-looking?"

"I don't know." I purse my lips and examine his head. "Your hair's kind of boring. Remember?"

His forehead wrinkles. "Again I ask, how can hair be boring?"

"That's what I'm wondering." I set my chin on my hand and peruse the dark strands. "How *do* you manage that?"

"Whatever," is Ben's quick comeback.

I fight a grin as I stand. There's nothing boring about him. I even like his glasses. The nice thing about his lack of them at the moment is that I can see his eyes more clearly. Although, it does suck for him that he's sort of blind right now.

Ben scratches at the skin near the nasty cut on his cheek, never actually touching it.

"We should clean that," I tell him again.

"It's fine."

I shrug and nod toward an especially gnarly looking tree about six feet from us. It's lower down the slope, and off to the side, almost as if nature decided to hide it from the direct view of humans. "The sun caught something shiny near that tree, blinding me when I looked at it."

Ben moves in the direction I nodded. I catch up to him as he kneels. I step, unknowingly kicking something forward, and watch as a knife bounces across the grass. "That must be what I saw."

Frowning, Ben picks up the blade by the handle. The knife is big, and looks sharp. He peers around us, slowly straightening to his full height of around five-ten. Suspicion darkens his face as he turns to me. "Why would there be a knife out here?"

"Maybe someone dropped it?"

"I don't think someone would drop something like this, and if they did, they'd want it back," Ben muses, again searching the area as if he thinks someone, or something, is out there watching us.

"Stop that," I tell him, shivering as paranoia tries to clamp on to me. The image of thousands of glowing eyes studying us from unknown shadows runs through my brain. There's probably a gang of bears, or whatever a group of them is called, in wait to ambush us. I swallow, wishing I could retract that unwanted thought.

Ben turns his frown on me. "Stop what?"

"Let's just keep walking, okay?" I hurry past him, hoping with all hope that we are close to finding a search team. If they can't find us, we have to find them, right? There's no way us being missing for this long has gone unnoticed, nor unaddressed. It's only a matter of time before we're reconnected with civilization.

The knife is proof of that. Where there is a knife, there is bound to be a human—I really hope it's a nice person.

It feels as if hours go by as we tramp through brush and over fallen tree branches, but it's really only minutes. My legs are crisscrossed with cuts and my skin is sunburned, and I'm pretty sure my hair is a frizzy halo around my head. My muscles scream to rest, and I smell bad.

This is a nightmare, pure and simple, and we're trapped in it.

BEN

The land is level and flat, the waterfall a blurred spot on the horizon, when we stumble upon what we believe to be non-poisonous berries. They're round and reddish black in color. I tilt my head and study them, wondering if I'm about to poison myself.

"Do you know if these are okay to pick?" Avery asks.

"Not a clue. How about you?"

"Nope," she answers with feigned cheerfulness.

"I think the red ones are supposed to be okay."

"Supposed to be." Avery nods. "Wonderful."

We both take a couple, and look at each other.

"You go first," Avery urges, motioning to me with her free hand.

I laugh outright at that. "Are you going to wait to see if I keel over?"

"Yes." Avery smiles, and laughs too.

Her laughter is a happy sound, and I find I enjoy it, like I enjoy a lot of things about Avery I'd rather not. Her mouth…I really enjoyed her mouth on mine. In fact, the longer I'm around Avery in this surreal reality, the more I find her irresistible. I'm being drugged by her eyes, and her scent, and each paradox I unveil.

I turn from her, dropping my gaze to the berries in my hand. Things would be so much easier if she was unlikable. I consider telling her that to see if she'll accommodate me, but I doubt that will happen. If anything, she'd most likely lay on the charm a little heavier, make me fall irreversibly in love with her or something.

As if that would ever happen. I'm not that stupid.

"I've never seen *Stand by Me*," she announces, her eyes locked on a berry as she moves it between her fingers.

I give her a dubious look. "Really?"

"Really. What's it about?"

"It's a book written by Stephen King that was turned into a movie," I begin, pausing at the sidelong look she gives me. "What?"

"Isn't he, like, crazy weird and only writes about scary and gross stuff?"

I scowl. "He isn't only a horror writer, you know."

Avery doesn't comment.

"He wrote *The Shawshank Redemption*, *Dolores Claiborne*, and *The Green Mile*, which aren't horror novels," I state.

She shrugs. "I've never read a book by him nor watched a Stephen King movie."

"Never?" My tone is incredulous.

"Never."

I give her a distrustful look. "What *do* you like to read and watch?"

"Some romance, but mainly funny stuff."

"Funny stuff?" I repeat. The idea of her never reading a Stephen King book is plausible, but to not even have seen one of his movies? Unbelievable.

"Yes," she snaps, looking irritated. "Funny stuff—and since you brought it up, I don't understand why anyone would want to read books or watch movies about scary or sad things. There's enough of that in reality."

I let out a huff of air and continue. "Nothing scary happens in *Stand by Me*. It's set in the 1950s in Oregon. The scariest thing that happens is that there's an incident with leeches."

Avery narrows her eyes. "Is that really how you knew how to remove a leech?"

I nod. "After watching it, and being completely grossed out by the leech scene, I read a bunch of articles on leeches. I remembered some of what I read."

"That was helpful."

I shrug.

"What else was the movie about?"

I squint at the sun, the blue sky swirled white with clouds. "A group of friends learn the general location of a dead body and go in search of it. They meet up with older, dangerous kids during their adventure, and some other trouble."

"And you liked it?" Avery faces me, curiosity evident in the tilt of her head.

"The kids become better friends. They learn how to be brave. It's a great movie," I assure her.

Avery seems to be mulling over my words. She meets my gaze and says, "Maybe I'll watch it someday."

"You should. If you have no desire to watch any other Stephen King movie, at least watch that one, and possibly the other ones I mentioned." When she smiles faintly, almost absently, I swallow.

"You know how yesterday I said I felt like we were in *The Hunger Games*? I've never actually read or watched *The Hunger Games* series," Avery admits as if it's a deep, dark secret she's withheld for years.

"Oh?"

"I tried to read the books, but I got sad by the first chapter and had to stop." She shrugs. "Like I said, I'm all about the funny stuff."

"What do you like that's funny?"

"Pretty much anything with Bill Murray in it. *What About Bob?*, *Scrooged*, *Groundhog Day*, *Ghostbusters*, *Kingpin*, and *Zombieland*, *Caddyshack*," she rattles off. "There are more, but I can't think of them all right now."

I blink, surprised by her answer. The layers of Avery are being pulled back, one at a time. I wonder what I'll find when they're all off. I doubt I'll expect it.

"How's your back?" I ask a moment later. There are small blood stains on the back of her shirt that I continually try to avoid with my eyes and instead find each time I glance at her.

"I think it's okay. You?"

I work at relaxing my shoulders and shrug. "I don't feel anything dripping down my leg, so I'm guessing it's scabbed over."

She gives me a chastising look. "You still won't look?"

"Nope."

Avery's eyes fall to my leg. "I don't see any blood."

I hold her gaze when she looks up. "Thanks."

Her eyes soften, and she pauses as if she's about to say something, but instead Avery nods and remains quiet.

Funny, but I want to know what she was going to say.

"How did you get from Montana to Illinois?" I ask curiously.

Avery frowns. "What?"

"Did you fly on a plane, or drive? I ask because you're scared of... things. Are you scared of flying too?"

"I drove. But I'm not scared of flying."

"Why is that?"

"Planes aren't living," she says.

"I'm not sure I follow your logic."

"Animals and insects are alive; planes are not," Avery explains impatiently. "If I were to have anxiety over anything, and I'm not saying I do—"

I snort.

She glares at me. "It would be over something that can react with emotion, instinct, anger, whatever, not a machine."

"But pilots fly planes; they don't fly themselves," I point out.

"Just...don't worry about my phobias, all right?"

"Contradictory as they are," I murmur.

Avery shoots me a final wrathful look before lifting the hand holding berries. "Well, here goes nothing."

I grip her wrist as panic shoots through me. "I'll try them first."

"Maybe we should both wait." Avery swallows, a faint tremble to her hand.

I give her a look. "Wait for what?"

"I don't know." She shifts from one foot to the other. "Something. More mint plants?"

"What if we can't find more? I'll try the berries, Avery, it's no big deal."

"It could be a big deal!" She jerks her hand from my grasp. "Just let me try them."

I grab her hand once more. "No."

Her eyes scan my face. "Please, let me do it."

I am flummoxed by her present behavior. "You're willing to try them, but you don't want me to?"

"I don't want either of us to try them," Avery says. "But especially not you."

Interesting. I scrutinize her pinched features, looking for clues as to what thoughts are going through her mind. I lift my hand and Avery hits the berry from it. My voice is remarkably calm when I ask, "What was the point of that?"

Her eyes plead. "Just...wait. Don't eat it yet."

Impatience trickles into my tone. "One of us has to try them to see if they're edible. I'm doing it."

"Why does it have to be you?"

"Why do you want it to be you?" I counter. "Is it guilt or something that makes you think you have to do this? You don't."

"No. Yes. I just—" Avery's expression falters and then clears as she gives me a hesitant smile. "It's almost like you don't want me to die."

I pop a berry in my mouth and chomp down before Avery has a chance to react. Tart juice squirts into my mouth and I swallow the berry, wondering if I signed my own death sentence. "It is, isn't it? Strange."

"Why did you do that?" she moans, dropping the berries she holds to set her palms to her forehead.

I'm not entirely sure. I just know that if it comes down to one of us surviving, it's going to be her.

As the minutes grow, Avery holds her breath, her eyes wide and riveted to my face.

I make a choking sound and reach for my neck.

"Ben? Ben!"

Avery dashes for me, pulling up short when I drop my hands and grin.

"You ass!" Avery smacks my arm.

"I couldn't help it." I laugh.

"That was a crappy thing to do," she says with a scowl. As quickly as it appears, the scowl fades and worry pinches the skin between her eyebrows. "How long before we know?"

I shrug one shoulder and look around us. "An hour or two, I would guess." I meet her gaze. "Avery, if something happens to me—"

"Nothing's going to happen," she interrupts firmly.

"But if it does—"

Avery claps a hand to my mouth. "No."

I smile at the ferocity of her expression. I carefully remove her hand from my mouth and tell her, "First thing, take my clothes. I won't need them; you will. They'll help keep you warm at night. Try to find another unoccupied cave and stay near it during the daytime, so you remember where it is—something we should have done and didn't."

A guilty look sweeps across her features.

"I know; waiting is not what you do." My tone says I do not judge. "If at all possible, stick close to a water source. And don't go exploring anymore. We've done enough of that already. Someone will find you. You'll be okay, Avery."

"Shut up, Ben. I don't need to hear any of this." Her tone is harsh, but her eyes shimmer with tears. "You're going to be fine."

"But if I'm not, you have to be prepared."

Avery shakes her head. "I am not removing clothes from your dead body, so you just better stay alive."

"So you can remove them from my living body, is that it?" I joke.

"Yes, and with pleasure," she states plainly.

Blood surges through my extremities, assuring me I am one hundred percent okay. I have no response to that. I think of her slowly peeling away my clothing, one article at a time, and lust floods my system. I smile thinly and turn my back to her until I can get myself under control. It isn't easy, and I wonder how much longer I can fight the pull to have Avery in my arms, under me, and around me.

"How do you feel?" Avery asks a couple minutes later.

"Meh."

Avery touches my arm, her fingers like electrical currents on my pulse. "You feel *meh*? Is that an emotion? What's wrong?"

I look at where her skin meets mine and raise my eyes to hers. "I want you to know—"

Avery's mouth wobbles and she launches herself at me, her arms encircling my neck to the point where I can't breathe. A cut off exhalation is all I can manage before I'm smothered by woman. I suppose it isn't the worst way to go.

"Please don't die. I didn't mean any of what I said. Your hair isn't boring, and you're not short, and I think you're handsome and I lied when I said what I said and I'm sorry. I always say and do the wrong things with you and I will never get over it if you die," she babbles, choking me in the process.

"Avery," I gasp, trying to untangle her arms from around my neck. I basically drop to the ground with Avery still hooked to me.

She covers my face in kisses, speaking nonsense the whole time, her lips finding mine. It's a head rush sent directly to my core. I tell myself to pull away, and instead, I go still, our lips pressed together and nothing more. I carefully move my mouth over hers in a sweeping motion once, twice. I pause as her body relaxes into mine, our forms fitting together entirely too well.

I watch her face with her eyes closed, something sharp and sweet piercing my heart. I feel myself caving already. I realize I don't stand a chance, not when there is no way to distance myself from Avery.

She opens her eyes.

It's the look in them that is my undoing. There is fear in them, and sadness, and regret. I know it's all for me, and I almost wish we could go back in time and do things differently. I wish we had that choice.

"Why can I never tell what's real and fake with you?" I whisper.

"You can," Avery insists.

"No." I shake my head. "I can't."

"I'll tell you then."

She takes my hand and presses it to her cheek. A streak of dirt lines the side of her face. Set against her smudged features, Avery's golden eyes are striking. They stare into me, bare of deception, and my heart jumps in my chest. For the first time, I wonder if we will make it out of this alive. The thought tears me up inside, and not for me, but for Avery. She has to make it, and that means I have to make it.

Her expression falters and she let's go of my hand. "But I'm not telling you anything if you think you can find out information about me and then die on me."

"I feel fine, Avery, I swear."

"You're sure?"

"I'm sure," I answer evenly.

She scratches her arm. "It probably hasn't been long enough to know."

"Talk to me," I urge.

Sighing, Avery says, "I am Avery Eloise Scottam, born in Missoula, Montana on December 15th. I'm a Sagittarius. I am twenty-five years old. My favorite color is pink. My favorite subjects in school were Art and English. I love all unhealthy food and I especially love chocolate milk and hot chocolate."

I sit us up, shaking my head. "Those are facts. Those don't tell me who you are."

"You know me."

"I don't," I deny.

"Okay. Fine." She swallows. "I…feel like I always need the approval of others, and sometimes, I do stupid things because of it."

My jaw hurts and I realize I'm clenching it. "Like Duke?"

Avery's chest is flush with mine, her face close. She watches me for a moment before talking. "You know, I don't think you're upset as much by the kind of person you think I am as you are by the fact that it doesn't matter."

I narrow my eyes. "What do you mean?"

She pushes herself to her feet and speaks directly to my soul. "You still want me, whatever bad things I've done, and you hate that."

15
AVERY

I watch Ben until my eyeballs feel frozen in place, and I keep watching. It feels as if it's been days, but it's really only been hours since he ate the berry. If he dies, I don't know what I'll do, and not because I'll be lost alone in an endless forest surrounded by hateful nature. I can't do this without him. I don't want to do this without him.

Maybe I'm not his friend, but he's mine.

Ben sighs and lifts his eyes from the twig he spins between his fingers. "Would you quit staring at me like that? It's creepy."

"It feels like it's been forever since you ate the berry."

"With the way you're watching me, yes, it does." He has an interesting voice—part gravelly, part smooth, and altogether deep. It makes me think of rain and thunder. It's generally stormy when directed toward me. Right now, it's soothing rain after a day of hot, relentless sun. A balm to my eardrums. Because if he was suffering the effects of poisonous berries, he wouldn't be speaking so well. This means the berries are edible, and of course, that Ben won't die.

It seems to be the one form of good news out of this whole fiasco.

"How long do you think it's been?" My teeth feel gross. I long for a toothbrush—not even toothpaste—just the brush to clean them. A hot shower or bath. Or both! Blankets. I'd kill for some blankets. And a mattress. I sigh dejectedly. I miss home.

I'm endlessly hungry, and I fear I may be ill at some point from drinking that unpurified water. It's probably corroding my innards right now, bacteria growing all around my organs, disintegrating everything vital to being healthy.

Maybe that was Ben's plan all along: Get me to drink the contaminated water. Then if I die, he can't say it was intentional. He was trying to help. I'll be gone, and he won't have to worry about me anymore. He'll have Duke all to himself once again.

All will be right in Ben's world.

It isn't as if Ben would miss me anyway—or Duke, for that matter. I'm nothing to either one of them. My thoughts pulse with mistruth, and I guiltily sink lower to the prickly ground. Ben isn't trying to kill me. He's actually trying to help, against his instincts, I'm sure, but still. Plus, Ben drank the water too. And he also ate the berry to check to see if they're poisonous or not.

Ben answers, "I think it's been long enough, but I don't know that for sure."

The ache in my stomach has turned painful, but I've had more sustenance than Ben's had in a long while. He ate a berry, a single berry that may or may not be killing him right now. At least I had trail mix. I will never put it down again either.

I pace from one tree to another and back. "Just so you know, if you die on me, I will bring you back to life just to kill you."

His lips twitch. "Noted."

I grab a handful of berries. If Ben hasn't died by now, or shown signs of being poisoned, I'm sure they're fine. At any rate, I'm tired of being hungry. I lift them to my mouth, pausing when Ben speaks.

He warns, "Careful. If you eat too many at once, you could get sick from overdoing it. Your stomach hasn't had much in it the last few days."

I stick out my tongue and shove the berries in my mouth, chewing up the somewhat sweet, but mostly bitter, fruit.

"What are you going to do if you get diarrhea?"

I freeze, the berries a glob of mush in my mouth. To say that relieving ourselves in semi-privacy has been interesting is putting it mildly. If there was, so to say, an emergency of some kind? I cannot even fathom how that will pan out, nor do I want to. I swallow the berries, wondering if I've guaranteed myself future misery.

"Girls don't get diarrhea," I say, turning my face from Ben's view.

He snorts. "I have a sister. Believe me, girls do."

I smile, focusing on a butterfly as it flutters by. "I'm sure she'd appreciate you telling people that."

"Yeah, well, I'm generally not one to share secrets. That's you."

I am instantly furious, my face and body on fire with it. I thought we were on the path to being okay. I should have known better. I swing around to face Ben and shriek, "Why do you have to ruin everything?"

Face twisted, Ben lunges to a standing position, vibrating with retribution. "Because you ruined us before we really had a chance!"

I stumble back from the wrath of his tone. I clearly see the pain in his eyes. It's deep. He's so good at hiding his emotions that I never expected to see such hurt on his face. It stuns me speechless. It lets me know how much I could have meant to Ben—how much I might have already meant. Tears fall from my eyes before I have a chance to realize they even formed.

"Because I don't know what's real with you," he continues in a quieter voice.

My throat closes around any words I might want to say.

"Because…I see possibilities of what could be, and I don't know if they're all an illusion. Because I want this you to be real."

"Ben—" I lift out a hand beseechingly, wishing I could take away the hurt crushing his eyes with a brush of my hand.

"I was falling for you, Avery," he says in a choked voice. "Maybe I already had, because I can't imagine anything hurting as much as your betrayal did. And you acted like it was no big deal, like you couldn't understand my animosity. That's what pisses me off the most—you made me care about you and then you threw my emotions away, like they never mattered, like *I* never mattered. I thought you were special. Turns out I was an idiot."

A sob leaves me, my chest heavy with grief. "That's not true, Ben. I do care about you."

His eyes shine with sorrow; Ben's mouth is pulled down with it. "I don't know who you are, but what's even sadder than that is that you don't seem to know who you are."

I clasp my hands together beneath my chin, unconsciously begging him to listen to me, to hear me. To see me. "I'm trying to show you!"

"How can I believe anything you do or say?"

"You can't, not if you don't want to."

Ben lowers his head. "I guess I don't."

"I give up," I whisper, shaking my head.

His eyes clash with mine, something like fear in them, but I pretend I don't see it. When Ben says my name, I pretend I don't hear it. I've tried and tried to get Ben to see past my mistakes, and he can't, or won't. I'm tired of it all, and it's wearing me down. There is a point when enough is enough. I've reached it.

With jerky movements and muttered curses, I drop to the ground, curl up, and squeeze my eyes shut, blocking Ben from sight. I wish I could block him from my mind and heart as well.

BEN

I sit across from Avery, studying her. A full day spent with her and I don't know her any better. Or maybe I do, but I don't want to see it.

I give up.

The words echo through my consciousness, stabbing my heart each time. I cross my arms to keep from reaching for her. At this point, I'm fighting myself more than I am her. I already know I want her. I know I enjoy her company, quirks and all. I also know I would have to be some kind of stupid to open up to Avery any more than I have. Like I told her, she'll use it against me; she did before. We'll get back to civilization and she'll somehow profit from this ordeal, I know it.

I give up.

I grind my teeth together, hating those words, and that they came from her mouth. Avery doesn't give up. And yet, she is, on me. *It's what you want, isn't it?* If it is, why does it make me feel so shitty?

A bird cries in the distance and she jerks. Avery stills, but she never opens her eyes. I glance at the hunting knife near my boots, unease worming its way into my mind to pick and prod. I don't trust the sight of this weapon in the middle of nowhere. It shouldn't be here.

"Avery." I say her name softly, her eyes immediately opening. There's weariness in them. The need to protect her flares up, even if it's from me. I scoot closer, sitting beside her. Our arms touch, and she shifts away. "Talk to me."

"I don't want to." There is an edge to her tone, a warning.

I ignore it. "Do it anyway."

"Why?"

"Because it'll make us both feel better. Talk to me."

A crease forms between her eyebrows. "About what?"

I hold her gaze, her irises catching the light of the sun. It gives her an otherworldly aura. "Anything."

Again, Avery asks, "Why?"

Her question is valid. I know what she's thinking. Why would I want to know anything about her when all I do is try to push her away? "Why did you come to Illinois?"

"I told you—"

The look on my face halts her words.

Avery brings her knees to her chin, hooking her arms around her legs. "I was looking for something."

I don't release her gaze. "Did you find it?"

The air seems to grow hotter as we stare into each other's eyes.

"Yes..." she answers. "And no."

"Why no?"

Avery moves her hands to her face, sighing.

Despondency is etched into her pose, as if the weight of things she cannot change is too heavy for her. She is nothing like I thought she was, and I'm still not sure what she's like. I tell her, "You're a complex individual."

Avery drops her hands, looking at me as she laughs with exasperation. "Am I? I think I'm pretty simple."

"Really?"

She turns her head, looking into the trees.

"How so?" I press. *Tell me, Avery. Tell me you're nothing like I thought you were. Or tell me you're exactly as I thought.*

"I wish I could close my eyes, and when I opened them, we'd be back home," she whispers.

I have to agree with her. "What would you be doing right now, if you were at home?"

"Probably trying new ways of styling my hair, maybe online shopping, or something equally silly." She sniffles. "You?"

"Let's see." I tip my head back and look at the clouds. "It's Sunday. I would most likely be at The Wolves' Den on Marquette, playing pool with Bob."

"Do you like playing pool?" Avery asks.

"I do," I tell her. "They'll find us today. You can be home by tonight and do those silly things you like, all right? And I can play pool again on a Sunday afternoon to pass the time. Just a couple more hours out here. You can do it."

Avery spontaneously bursts into tears, hiding her face against her knees. Alarmed, I demand, "What's wrong?"

I thought I would enjoy seeing Avery beaten down. I don't. It's wrong, and I hate it. Nothing should make her feel this way. She's too strong, and stubborn, to let anything get to her.

"I don't have a razor," Avery wails. "I'm going to look like a Sasquatch before too long."

I choke back laughter, a funny sound escaping me as I do. Nothing about this maddening scene so far has made her cry, but the thought of being hairy does it.

"And what if I get my period before we're found?" she continues pitifully. My stomach lurches at the thought of Avery's blood running freely unto the land, any thought of laughter immediately wiped from existence.

"What am I going to do, put leaves in my underwear? Leaves are not absorbent!"

Shaking my head against an impromptu head rush, I look to the ground and watch shadows at play as the sun shifts. "When is it due?"

"Next week." Avery sniffles, wiping an arm across her face.

I exhale loudly. "That's good. We've got some time."

That makes her cry harder, to the point where she tries to speak and all that comes out are choked sounds.

"We won't still be here next week," I hasten to correct.

"How do you know?" Avery asks once she can produce intelligible words. She sniffles. "I wish I was home. I hate it here. I know I sound like a baby, but I really, really, really hate it out here."

"Have faith, Avery." I don't think I sound the least convincing, but I must to a certain degree, because she stops crying and looks at me.

"My mom used to say that faith is something no one can ever take from you," Avery supplies shakily.

"Your mom sounds like she knows what she's talking about."

Her face crumples and she cries harder.

Eyes trained on the woods around us, I skim the area for any approaching predators. I'm not good at the consoling thing, and yet, I want her to stop crying, and not because of the ear-splitting sobs that may attract all kinds of wild animals—or repel them. They could do that too, I suppose. Still, I don't like seeing her hurt. And that's a real kicker, because I've been on this self-righteous quest of vengeance against Avery, the perceived wrongdoer, for months. It seems ridiculous now, given the circumstances.

Therefore, I pull her against me, holding her shaking frame within my arms, and say, "Avery. Please don't cry."

She lifts her head, her eyes gemlike, her face flawless even while sunburned, scratched, and splotchy from tears. "You made me eat the rest of the trail mix."

It takes a moment for her words to sink in. "Okay?"

A wrinkle forms between her eyebrows. "You went without so I didn't have to."

I run a hand along the back of my neck and avert my face. "Yeah. So?"

"You don't hate me."

I turn my head to look at her and say with utmost sincerity, "I don't hate you, Avery. Not even a little."

"Then why do you try so hard to convince me you do?"

"I thought..." I rub my eyes. "I thought it would make things easier. It hasn't."

It makes her cry some more, but she's smiling when she lassoes her arms around my neck. Avery presses a kiss to my neck and whispers, "Thank you for being honest."

I lift my arms and wrap them around her midsection, holding her tight. I want to get past this vendetta I have against her; I need to get past it. I'm hurting myself along with Avery, and I'm missing out on something that could be awesome. Only, I don't know how to trust her, or if I should. I rest my head to hers and sigh deeply.

Avery pulls back and focuses on me. "Do you have two parents?"

I frown, finding the question odd. "Yes. Doesn't everyone?"

"I mean, they were both in your life growing up?"

"Yes. Were yours?" She's mentioned a mother, but never a father, and any time the conversation veered toward her mom, she quickly changed it.

"Tell me about yours," Avery urges, ignoring the question.

A memory hits me and I smile. "One day, I was walking down the street with my friends. I was twelve or thirteen. This car pulls up, bass so loud the street is vibrating from it, and the windows roll down to reveal my mom and dad. They saw me with my friends and purposely set out to embarrass me. I was so annoyed with them, but they laughed and drove off.

"When I got home and complained about it, my parents told me they're a set pair. It always stuck with me. They meant it to mean that if I was going to be embarrassed by one of them, I was going to get it from both of them. But for me, it meant I had security in knowing that, no matter what, my parents would be there for me, together. And they always have been."

Avery lets out a soft sigh. "That's nice, Ben, I like that."

"Yeah, my parents are pretty awesome. I'm lucky."

I think of my dad with his gruff laughter and my mom with her sweet smile and I hope to God I get to see them soon. I wonder if the authorities have been notified; I wonder if my parents have been told. I hope my sister *hasn't* been told. She'll overreact.

And I can just see my brief, but unforgettable childhood friend, Opal Allen, slanting an eyebrow at me and asking me how I managed to get lost in a national forest. I need to get in contact with her if I ever make it out of here. It's been too long. She and Avery would love each other. I freeze at the thought, wondering why in the hell that came to mind. As if Avery and I are a pair. No way in hell.

"Parents are always there for you, especially to embarrass you," Avery muses, a faraway look on her face.

"Don't steal it, all right?" I say half-jokingly. "I might want to use a quote from that story someday."

"I wouldn't," she protests, jumping to her feet.

My voice is even when I say, "You did."

Her face drops and Avery turns, hugging herself. "I didn't know it meant that much to you," she whispers.

I focus on the sky as a flock of birds sweep through the trees. "You should have."

It was Duke's birthday party. He planned it, because that was the only way it was going to be exactly what he wanted. A huge, luxurious yacht was rented for the evening, and his friends and employees were given their fill of food and drinks as it traveled up and down the length of the Chicago River. A band was hired, and fireworks filled the black sky with bursts of light and sound.

"You looked beautiful that night," I tell her now. I clearly picture her standing on the vessel with the moon as a backdrop. She shone. "Red dress, red shoes, red lipstick."

Avery slowly faces me, shadows playing with her features.

"But then, you always do, don't you?" Old bitterness enters my tone at my next words. "It's part of the illusion."

"I'm so sorry, Ben." A single tear falls down her smooth cheek.

I wonder if she really is sorry. It doesn't hurt as much now, but the feeling of betrayal when it happened was unconscionable. I didn't know I could feel that way. She tore out my heart and crushed it beneath her flaming red high heel.

Realizing that she could hurt me that deeply made me glad that it happened early, instead of later, when I was completely in love with her. I've done nothing but fight that feeling ever since, building the walls, shoving her out, convincing myself none of it was real. That I don't want her, and that I don't care about her. All I do is prove myself wrong, time after time.

"I told you something in confidence," I say quietly, my gaze locked with hers. "Something I'd never told another soul, and you exploited a moment I cherished for your own gain."

A faint sound of grief leaves Avery, and two more tears appear. Again, she says, "I didn't know."

"You didn't know me telling you about the last thing my grandmother ever said to me before she died would be priceless to me? Private?" I shake my head in disgust.

Avery lets out a sob, holding a hand to her mouth, the other palm to her stomach.

It's time to get it all out. No more bullshit, no more vague digs and lingering resentment. It's now or never. We need to sort this out.

"No more lies, Avery." I stare at her hard, willing her to tell the truth, to tell me everything. "No more games. We talk. Now."

She nods jerkily.

"All right." I take a deep breath. "You're right, you know. I guess you didn't do anything wrong, in the business aspect of it. You could say I didn't copyright my words, and you would be absolutely right. Legalities have nothing on morality though, Avery, and that's something you didn't seem to understand."

Avery's eyes shimmer with golden sorrow. "I didn't set out to hurt you. I know—I know it seems like I did, but I didn't."

Heat scalds my face as I shift my jaw. "You saw a way to advance yourself, and you took it, never caring about how it would affect me. You made money off my *grandmother's death.*" Even now, it's hard to believe. I look at her, and I still don't understand how she could do it.

"No! I didn't. That wasn't how—I never—I didn't mean to hurt you. I just…I knew Duke would be impressed and he put us on the spot and it was the first thing I thought of and—it's a terrible excuse. I know that. I *know* that."

Avery throws her hands up and gestures to herself, openly crying. "I got carried away with this image and I didn't know how to stop, and I got lost, Ben. I lost who I was. I'm sorry. I'm a million times sorry."

"Why did you do it?" I demand. I want to know. I have to know.

"I admire you, you know," Avery whispers, not answering me.

"I can tell," I scoff.

"I do. So much," she says with feeling, her hands clasped together as she stands distanced from me by instinct or premeditation.

I slowly stand, eyes locked on the woman who showed me how much I could be hurt. "Don't lie to me anymore, Avery."

"I'm not lying."

My hands fist and my neck muscles tighten. "Don't lie!"

"I'm not lying," she screeches.

"Then tell me why you did it!" I roar.

16
AVERY

"I don't know." I shake my head. How do I tell him my reasons when they seem so inconsequential now?

"You don't know," Ben repeats in disbelief.

"Let me fix this," I plead, clasping my hands together beneath my chin. "I can fix this."

"You can't," he says, his face darkened with pain. "I wish you could, I really do, but it's too late."

"I can, I swear I can."

"How?"

"I don't know," I wail. I drop to my knees before him, watching doubt flood his eyes. "But I can. Let me try, please, Ben, let me try."

"You sold my grandmother's last words to me, Avery. You sold them to a weight loss program!"

"I know, and it was a horrible thing to do without your permission, but they were beautiful words, and inspiring, and I did it and I'm sorry."

Two days after Duke's birthday party, Duke set up a meeting between his employees. He told us the organization, and he told us what they were looking for. Then he told us to wow him, and them. One by one, he took us into his office, and had us pitch a slogan to him.

I didn't think. Ben's grandmother's words popped into my head and I blurted them out. Horrified, realizing what I'd done, I wanted to melt into the floor. When Duke announced whose pitch he decided on, I looked at Ben. His eyes went blank, his face cold, and that was the end. It was too late. I wanted to take the words back, but Duke said yes before I could say no.

But would *you have said no?*

That's the question I can't seem to answer.

Now, yes. But then? I still don't know. My head was in a different place entirely.

I cover my face with my hands and inhale slowly, releasing the breath with my eyes closed.

Not that it makes it right, but Ben doesn't understand how the words have helped so many women. His grandmother's words are captioned on billboards and pamphlets and commercials. They are the one time I gave credit to a woman other than my mom, and it went to Hillary Stitzer. The money made off the sale is in a savings account in Ben's name. I never told him that. How could I?

"You are more than a number on a board."

Those are the words that gave Ben solace, me Duke's attention, and tore what could have been between Ben and me into what never would.

"She wanted me to remember that whatever I do in life, I am good enough, whether I fail or succeed. I've always thought I had to prove my worth, and she wanted me to know that I don't, that whether or not I think I succeed, I always do." Ben shifts his attention to me. "Why did you do it?"

I open my mouth. "I don't—I can't—"

Ben's eyes flash black. "Just answer the question!"

I cry, tears dripping down my face. "I wanted Duke to see me."

"See you?" he says derisively.

I nod, my throat so tight it hurts to speak. "I wanted him to look at me the way he looks at you."

"Like what?"

"Like I matter."

"Why?"

I helplessly shake my head, keeping the truth hidden.

Ben gets to his feet, striding toward the trees and back. He jabs a finger at me. "You wanted to manipulate him."

"No."

"You wanted to make yourself indispensable."

"No!" I shoot to my feet.

"You wanted to seduce him."

My stomach churns. "No, no, I swear, *no.*"

Ben looms over me, furious and hurt. "You wanted him to think you're more than you are."

I shake my head again. Maybe what Ben is saying is true and I can't admit it to myself.

"Admit it! You're a fraud."

"You're right," I shout, the dam holding my truths at bay finally breaking. Ben blinks at the volume of my words. I step closer and lower my voice. "I am a fraud, but not the way you think. That woman you think I am? That overly ambitious, sickeningly sweet person with a razorblade tongue and no conscience you think is the real me? She isn't. *That's* the act. I made her up. "I made myself who I thought I should be. I spent more money on clothes, my hair, makeup, and exfoliations and waxes, in the last couple of months than I had previously spent on any of that crap over the course of my entire life. I didn't even have my first manicure and pedicure until I moved to Illinois."

Once I start talking, I can't seem to talk. The words just come and don't stop coming. I am confessing it all, and

It

Feels

Divine.

"I made myself perfect, but as you can see, I'm far from it." I smile self-deprecatingly.

Ben watches me, not speaking.

"I like to read for fun. Yeah, that's what I do. Or I watch television. I spend hours in my room writing. An exciting night to me is watching reruns of *The Gilmore Girls* and eating a pizza—a whole pizza, not even kidding. God, I miss those things." I hit my chest with my palm. "*I'm* the boring one! That's right. Me. I used to hang out with my mom, and okay, so a lot of people would think that's strange, but if you ever met her—"

Pain slices through me and tears sting my eyes.

"If you ever had the chance to meet her, you would love her. Everyone loves—loved—her. *Everyone.* She's the special one, the amazing one, the strong one. The beautiful one who knows how to act and dress, who can say a sentence that is so impactful you just stop for a moment and digest it—and the best part about her is that she didn't give a shit what anyone thought. Me? I'm a copy, and a poor one at that. I care about what *everyone* thinks."

"Avery—"

"These nails?" Sniffling, I wave them in the air, barely noticing the wary look on Ben's face. "Are fake. The straight hair? Fake. I had to train myself how to walk in heels. It took days, and I *hate* wearing the things. I really and truly do. You're right: the Avery Scottam from the office is a fraud. Really, I don't even like her all that much."

Each breath is shallow and sharp, bringing me back to who I am. I'm disappointed in myself for changing my exterior, but I had my reasons, and at the time, they seemed good. What is most disappointing is that my mom always told me to be true to myself, and somewhere along the way, I forgot that.

"I don't like who I've become, Ben," I admit in a broken whisper. I set a hand to my chest. "I'm real, Ben. Me. I swear to you I am. This is me. The person you see now. I have wavy hair and freckles and customarily dress in jeans and t-shirts. I'm scared of the most ridiculous things and I used to hate all those things about me, but even more than that, I hate that I changed who I am. I hate that I thought I had to. I never thought I wasn't good enough the way I was until I lost..."

"You lost?" he prompts quietly.

I blink back tears and take a shuddering breath. "Everything changed this past year. I moved to Illinois and...I thought I had to be someone else to be seen."

"I saw you perfectly, Avery, and I couldn't understand the charade you were trying to pull off."

I reach for him and Ben moves back. Heart aching, I confess, "That night we hung out together was the most real I've ever been. The most seen I've ever felt."

Everything clicked the night of Duke's birthday party. It was the first time Ben and I really talked and there was so much to say to one another. I told him all the truths I could, and he told me more than he should. We were talking about the stars and how infinite the sky seemed. I asked what would happen to the sky if all the stars fell at once. Ben said stars were like souls: something that would always be. He looked into my eyes and I saw the wonder in mine reflected in his. I think I fell in love with him right then and there. We kissed under the fireworks, hidden from the rest of the party.

Doubt darken his eyes, along with something else. "And you ruined it."

"I know. I did." My chest squeezes and squeezes until it hurts to even swallow. "I'm sorry."

"Why did you do it?" Ben demands. "Why did you take what I told you in confidence, words I could never put a price tag on, and sell them?"

Frustration tightens my neck muscles. "Because I was stupid!"

"No." He shakes his head. "That isn't going to cut it. I want to know, Avery. I want to know the truth."

"You don't."

"I do!" Fury flashes through Ben's eyes.

"Because—" I falter, biting my lip. How do I tell him? I guess I just do. I take a deep breath I gesture helplessly. "Because Duke's my father."

The only thing that moves are his eyes as he blinks. "Come again?"

"Duke Renner is my father."

* * * *

"I don't believe you." The words come fast and brutal.
I shrug. "He is."
"But…" Ben steps toward me, studying my face. "How?"
I roll my eyes. "Well, you see, my mom and him had sex and—"
"Nope, we're good." Ben covers my mouth with his hand. He stares at
me, looking for truths in my face. He repeats slowly, "Duke is your father."
I nod weakly.
An instant later, realization dawns on him. "He doesn't know, does he?"
"No. I didn't even know, not until my…my mom basically gave me a
deathbed confession. She had cervical cancer and…well…she didn't make
it." I smile weakly against the pressure on my heart. I miss her so much. I
don't think I'll ever stop missing her.
Ben's eyes drop.
"Growing up, it was just the two of us. I never asked about my dad, but
I obviously knew I had one. I didn't want my mom to feel as if she wasn't
enough. She was…she was everything to me. She was everything I ever
wanted to be."
He looks up and he doesn't look away.
"But I think that it made her sad too, for me, that I only had her." I
swallow. "Before she died, she told me his name and she made me promise
to not have preconceived ideas on the kind of man he is. Nothing could have
prepared me for Duke Renner." I laugh, swiping at my eyes.
A faint smile lines Ben's face. "He's one of a kind."
"I honestly didn't think I'd get the job," I confess. "I figured he'd see
right through me. I just wanted to see Duke once. I couldn't say no to the
interview, and when I was offered the job, I was agreeing to relocate to
Illinois before I had a chance to really think about it."
"Duke can be persuasive," Ben says.
I take a deep breath and add another confession to my ever-growing list
of them. "When I saw how much you mean to Duke, it made me jealous.
I had to prove that I was good enough. I had to be important. I wanted to
be the best and it got to the point where that was all that mattered. It was
like poison was running through my veins and I couldn't make it stop. I'm
sorry, for everything, I really and truly am. It wasn't me. That's the only
excuse I have."
Ben's mouth presses into a line.

"I cared about you, Ben, and…I still do. I tried to convince myself that what I did would be okay, but I knew it wouldn't, not when I saw that look on your face…" I clap a hand to my mouth to keep a sob inside. That look of devastation on his face. That look that told me he couldn't believe what I'd done.

"I swear I didn't want to hurt you. I didn't think. Or I did, but…not about what was really important. Duke wanted something spectacular and the first words I thought of were your grandmother's. I was selfish and wrong, and I only thought of me, and I'm sorry.

"There's a hole, right here." I pat my chest. "And I don't know how to fill it. I thought if I came to Illinois and got to know my dad, maybe the hole would fill, but nothing's been how I thought it would be, not from the start."

I hold Ben's gaze. "You're the only one who's come even close to filling the hole, and I made you hate me. I can only apologize so much. I can't go back in time and erase the mistakes I've made. I wish I could, but I can't. I can't do anything but hope you'll see who I really am and want to get to know me better."

He looks at me for a long moment before jerking his head in an ungraceful nod. "I know who you are. Now. I didn't before."

I let out a sigh of relief, weak with the hint of forgiveness I heard in Ben's voice. Another chance. I get another chance.

"You have to tell him."

I turn my focus to a nearby patch of dirt and sticks. "I don't know if I can."

"Why not?"

One shoulder lifts and lowers. "This whole time I've pretended to be someone I'm not. What's he going to think when he finds out it was all a lie?"

"You'll explain. He'll listen. Duke isn't an unforgiving man."

I lift my eyes to his and ask the question that haunts me. "What if he doesn't want me?"

Ben cups my jaw with his hands and brings his face close to mine. His eyes are deep brown with emotion. His thumbs stroke my cheeks. "You are special, Avery. Even I saw that when I told myself I couldn't stand you. I still felt it. Duke sees it too, I know he does."

"You're just saying that." I pull back, wanting to move closer. "You don't really mean it. You don't even like me."

"I like you." Ben's eyes stare truth at me. "Here, this you, I like."

My stomach somersaults. I say softly, "I like you too, so much."

Ben gives me a smile, and he gives me all the light in the world with it.

I focus on the dirt beneath my fingernails that probably will never entirely leave. "I had this naive thought in my head that as soon as Duke saw me, he'd know who I was. I even put down my mom's name instead of mine for each slogan I pitched—they're all hers anyway, with a little tweaking from me. Another reason I'm a fraud. Most of what's mine that's sold has been a variation of something my mom told me at some point."

"Duke doesn't take care of a lot of the fine print details. I do."

I look up. "But you're a copywriter, like me."

"I am, yes, but I do more than that."

"You deserve a raise."

He grins. "I do, and most definitely after this. Be sure to tell Duke that."

"But you…are you still…" I don't finish the words, not wanting them to be true. Sanders and Sisters won't be right without Ben there.

The grim set of his face tells me Ben's still planning on leaving the company.

"Just because I'm not at Sanders and Sisters doesn't mean we won't see each other," Ben says quietly.

"Will we?"

"Will you want to?" He lifts his eyebrows as he waits.

"Yes." I grab his hand and squeeze it. "A million times yes."

He opens his mouth, and then pauses. Clarity filters through his eyes. "Wait. Cecily Scottam. That's your mom's name?"

My eyes fill at the sound of her name. "Yes."

"I thought maybe you went by your middle name, but…you're Avery."

"I'm Avery."

"Everything you did was for her and Duke—who is your father."

"Yes," I whisper.

Ben looks at me for forever, his eyes focused on mine. He slowly nods, the mask completely gone from his face. His features are softer, kinder. "I don't agree with how you went going about it, but I understand why you did it."

A wobbly smile overtakes my mouth, and I exhale deeply, relief taking a good chunk of weight from my bearing. "That's enough." I hesitate, shoving a lock of tangled hair behind my ear. "Did you…have you looked at the contract for A New You?"

"Not yet. Why?"

I look at my stained shoes and shrug. "I just wanted you to know that the words are accredited to Hillary Stitzer, and that the commission I made from it is in a savings account in your name. I wanted to at least do that for you, and her—"

Ben lurches forward, startling me quiet. I open my mouth to ask about the dangerous look in his eyes just as his lips descend on mine. With the flavor of berries on our tongues and heated lust our captors, the kiss is deep and erotic. I feel it all the way to my core, and I press close to him, wanting us skin on skin. Ben's fingers tangle in my hair, tugging my head back to better manipulate my mouth. This is the way every woman should be kissed. With unbridled passion, with the knowledge that they are wanted fiercely, desperately. I moan, low in my throat, drunk on sensations.

He jerks back, his pupils dilated. Ben threads his fingers through his hair and pulls. Ben paces in front of me, agitated and intense. I watch him, wondering if I'm already losing him. Is he coming to his senses? Am I the illogical choice? What is his head telling him? And why won't he instead listen to his heart?

If I'd listened to my head, I'd still be in Montana. I wouldn't know my father, however secretly. I wouldn't know Ben. Sometimes, you have to tell your head to shut up so that you can listen to your heart.

"This is madness, right?" He swings back, tight-jawed, speaking before I can utter a sound. "But I don't care. I don't care what you've done, or if this is wrong or right. I just want you."

My stomach dips and spins. I can't breathe, his words stealing the air from my lungs. I clear my throat and say hesitantly, "A wise person once said, take a chance on me."

Ben frowns. "Your mom?"

"ABBA."

His expression clears and he laughs. Ben steps closer, his stance stiff. Questions dance across his features. "Will you take a chance on me too? You weren't the only one at fault. I didn't have to be so hard on you."

I open my mouth to interrupt, but Ben shakes his head.

"I was an ass. I *know* I was an ass. But if you'll let me, I'll do better. I swear." Ben's eyes entreat; they tug at the center of my heart. Ben crosses the distance that separates us, grabbing my face, holding it. Drilling all the force of his being into my soul. "I want you and I'm tired of pretending I don't. God, Avery, if you say you want me too, I'll be yours. All you have to do is say it."

"I want you," I say in a steady voice. "I always, always want you—even when you're an ass."

Ben's face goes so completely blank that I wonder if I've somehow pissed him off. His eyes lower, and when they lift, they're filled with sparking, maddening, electricity. He's on me before I can inhale, his mouth like fire on mine. Burning me, scalding me where our lips touch. I taste heady desire. I want more.

The stubble of his face feels like ecstasy against my flesh. I lean into him, my fingers finding his hair. We're kissing and ripping the already ruined clothes from each other's bodies. His hands palm my backside and squeeze as he spins us around, pinning me to the rough bark of a nearby tree. I shift my hips, bringing his erection to the apex of my thighs.

I kiss Ben, feeling the moment he lets go, his taut body vibrating with need. The kiss deepens, his arms coming up around my back, his hands holding my head still as he puts all the other kisses I've ever received to shame. I explore his body with my hands. Each hard muscle, every divot. They are mine to touch and revere. Ben smells divine, like man and earth and a hint of sweat. Is this really happening? Finally, he is mine.

I pause, Ben pulling back to meet my gaze. *Are you mine?*

He smiles, a small, half smile that makes my stomach spin and tells me without a doubt that I am in love with him. *So* in love with him. His mouth is hot as it starts at the corner of my eye and kisses a path to my collarbone.

Under the heat of the sun, and maybe witnesses of the inhuman variety, Ben and I drop to the ground as one.

Where we are disappears.

Anything before this moment is inconsequential.

Whatever happens after this doesn't matter.

I'm lost in Ben, and I want to stay that way.

I touch him, the thickness, the heat, how unbelievably hard he is, driving me mad. Ben hisses, his hands shaking as they smooth hair from my face. The act is careful, tender. I kiss his palm. His expression is tight, his eyes glittering. With my hand around his erection, slowly moving up and down, Ben's fingers trace the most sensitive part of me, making me melt as they caress and tease. Need builds, becomes uncontrollable.

On my back, Ben hovers over me, looking arresting. It makes my heart drum a responding beat of instinctive need. He nips my neck; I dig my fingers into his back. Something niggles at the back of my head, a faint warning that I'm forgetting something, but I push it away. We look into each other's eyes, desire adding stars to his, and with our lips pressed together, Ben swiftly enters me. Both of us freeze, relishing in the feel of him inside me.

Eyes unwavering from each other's face, Ben moves, and I move with him.

"You're beautiful," he murmurs.

"You're beautiful," I murmur back with a smile.

I find a piece of heaven in Ben, in us. When the sky blazes bright from the fireworks we create, I think I would be okay anywhere, as long as I'm with Ben.

17
BEN

We didn't use protection.

Obviously, neither one of us had any and the best option would have been to keep my dick in my pants, but was I thinking with my brain? No. I take a deep breath, telling myself one time is not enough for Avery to become pregnant, even while knowing that's a bullshit, ignorant way of thinking. One time is all it takes. I run a hand along my face and stare at the sky framed by trees.

"It's okay, Ben. I'm on birth control pills."

I jerk at the sound of her voice, turning my head to the side to meet her gaze. "That isn't one hundred percent, and you've missed days."

"Whatever happens, it will be okay." Avery's eyes shine with resolution. "We'll figure it out."

I swallow hard, nodding. "I know we will, Avery."

She smiles and gives me a soft kiss.

I exhale and let the anxiety go, for now.

Locked in each other's arms, we lie on a bed of earth and look up at a sky full of swirling clouds. Other than where we are, everything is as it should be. Even being in Shawnee National Forest—or wherever we are—isn't all that bad. We've got this. We are going to make it.

"Tell me about the tattoo now," she whispers huskily.

I smile. "Reggie Redbird is the mascot for Illinois State University; twenty-two was my baseball jersey number."

"What did you play?"

"Catcher."

"That seems like a hard position."

I shrug the shoulder Avery isn't using as a pillow. "It kept me busy."

I want to savor this. Avery is in my arms, right where I've wanted her the whole time, subconsciously or otherwise. Have I ever felt this peaceful? Avery snuggles closer, her head tucked beneath my chin. She lost her mother. My arms tighten on Avery. She came so far to find her dad. I stroke her hair, pressing a kiss to the crown of her head. I don't think Avery knows how brave she is.

Finally, I understand her.

"Tell me about your life before Illinois. Tell me about the real Avery. Tell me everything." I press my lips to the side of her head. "Tell me about your mom."

Avery goes still, taking a shuddering breath.

"You don't have to," I quickly backtrack.

"No. I want to." She lifts her head to meet my eyes. "Talking about my mom helps; it makes me feel closer to her."

"Tell me one of your best memories."

She wrinkles up her nose before settling back against me. "Do you really want to know it?"

"I do."

"Okay." Avery breathes in and out. "She took me roller-skating for the first time when I was five. I kept falling, and it was to the point where I was ready to cry and give up. I was embarrassed and felt like everyone was watching me."

I fiddle with a lock of her hair as I wait for her to continue.

"My mom started falling with me. At first, I thought there was something wrong with her, but after a couple times of her magically losing her balance each time I did, I looked over and caught her smile. She turned it into a game, and each time we fell, we laughed." Avery's voice cracks. "My mom had this great way of showing me different ways to look at things."

I hold her as she quietly cries.

"I'm sorry," she says once the tears fade.

"For what?"

"Crying all over you."

I tighten my hold on Avery and brush the dampness from her face. "I don't mind. I can't imagine how it must feel."

She sits up and works at tearing away another piece of her shirt.

I propel to a sitting position, confused by her behavior. "What are—"

It sounds like a bullhorn splits the quiet. Even the insects go silent as Avery blows her nose with gusto.

I stare at her as she wipes her nose with her shirt remnant.

"What?" She looks at me as she drops the fabric to the ground. "I just..." I shake my head, laughing softly. "You're so much better than I thought."

"You like that I blew my nose on my shirt?" Avery asks, looking doubtful.

"I didn't have a lot of options."

"Hell, yeah, I do." Grinning, I reach for her, a heavy make-out session ensuing.

The sun is directly overhead and blazing hot when we finally pull away for air.

"I have to say, this is one of the better ways to spend time," I confess.

"Since we've been here? I hope so."

"No." I kiss her neck. "Ever."

"Yeah, it's not so bad." Avery's eyes twinkle when they land on me.

"What part is not so bad?" I narrow my eyes at Avery when she laughs. I dive for her, tickling her sides as she squeals. I laugh at the sounds she makes as she wiggles about, and tease, "Come on, Avery, tell me or I'll tickle you until the sun goes down."

"Okay, okay, *okay*! Stop and I'll tell you."

I give her one final tickle before ending the torment. Avery lies across my chest, gasping for air. Her hair is spread out like a wavy fan, tickling my chin. There is a rock beneath my head and a stick digging into the back of my thigh, but I don't want to move.

"Well?" I prompt.

"This is pretty perfect, considering."

"I never thought I'd say this, but I'm glad I got lost with you," I admit.

Avery lifts her head from my chest, her expression open and sweet. My stomach drops through the earth as I look at her. I find myself admitting something else. "The first time I saw you, I forgot how to breathe. You literally took my breath away."

She tilts her head, studying me. "I don't believe you."

"Remember how I made wheezing sounds and started coughing?"

"You said you had asthma."

"I couldn't breathe, Avery," I confess. "I looked at you and I just—I couldn't breathe. Even then, I felt it."

"Felt what?"

"That you were meant to mean something to me."

Avery goes to her elbow, peering down at me. "But I annoyed you and drove you crazy."

"No. Yes. I mean—you...you do drive me crazy." I rub my forehead, trying to make sense of us and not sure there is a way. "You played games and you pretended to be someone you're not, and I was always second guessing myself around you, and your intentions. But I think, finally, I understand."

"What?" she asks unevenly. "What do you think you understand?"

"You're scared."

"I'm not scared." Avery denies it, but she won't meet my eyes.

"You're scared the real you isn't enough, but she is. You are." A broken sound leaves her and her mouth wobbles. A tear slides down the side of her face and I quickly brush it away. Silent, we both look at the sky, watching as the clouds change shapes.

"Are you okay?" I whisper.

"I'm okay," she whispers back, squeezing my hand.

"Hey."

Avery waits.

"You're brave." I touch her cheek.

"You just said I'm scared."

I trace her lips. "The two aren't exclusive. You can be both at the same time. Trust me, you're brave." Not wanting to make Avery cry again, I decide to change the subject. "Best advice you'd give someone in four words."

"Be true to you," Avery responds immediately, a soft smile brightening her features. "You?"

"Do what you love."

She nods, sniffling as she regains composure. "Fitting. What else you got?"

I scratch at the scabbed over cut on my face and say, "Worst thing you ever ate."

"Liver."

"Sauerkraut," I return. Worst tasting thing in the world, although, at the moment, I'd heavily consider eating it. I might even enjoy it.

"Oh, yeah, that's bad too."

I turn to my side so that we're face to face, close enough that I can count her freckles. I say softly, "Best kiss you ever experienced."

Aver leans forward, smiling faintly, and tips her face toward mine. "All the ones shared with you."

"Good answer." I smile and kiss her.

"I like this. This is nice," she says a dozen kisses later.

Avery settles beside me, nuzzling my neck with her nose. I put my hands behind my head and watch the world move around us. I can't remember the last time I paused long enough to experience a sunrise or sunset, or even just watched the clouds go by. Everything moved with lightning speed until I got here and had no choice but to stop and reassess myself. I was stressed out and lackluster before this trip. All that is going to change when we get back. Some change is good.

"There never used to be enough time for stuff like this. It was always work and socializing and go—I was always on the go," I muse. "I want more of this."

Avery sits up, positioned just right so that the sun haloes her. Her expression is part sad, part resolved. She knows the direction of my thoughts before I voice them. But she only says, "We should get moving before your bear friend or some other creature decides to come find us."

"Like a goat?" I quirk an eyebrow. "Or a crow?"

She makes a face.

Other than ourselves and a snotty scrap of pink fabric we decide to leave, there isn't anything to gather up. We're on the move within minutes, filling our bellies with berries and creek water before taking on the sun and mountains. Avery holds my hand as we walk, and I steal kisses as we go.

My feet are sore, and although better, my ankle periodically gives an uncomfortable twinge. I don't resent being here anymore. It's strange how much I don't miss my cell phone or the television or any other device I've come to rely on. I appreciate the open skies and fresh air much more than I used to.

"How long are you going to carry around that knife?" Avery takes the lead as we trample through a narrow pathway of trees, letting a tree limb snap back toward me.

Unlike yesterday, I catch it this time. "Until we're found."

"Why?"

Because I don't trust its presence here. I say, "Protection."

"Against what?"

"Hopefully nothing. But just in case."

Avery spins around and blurts, "I lied, okay?"

"About what?" I ask cautiously. What confession am I going to get now, and am I ready for it?

She swats at a bug that has the audacity to land on her arm, flicking it away without even glancing at it. I set my hands on my hips, wondering if she realizes how bad-ass she's getting. A day ago the thought of a bug on her had her screaming and jumping. I can't fight the smile that comes at the recollection.

Avery says, "I am scared. Life scares me. Being without my mom scares me. Our lives go by so fast and they never really seem to be ours."

My throat tightens. All Avery had was her mom, and now she's gone. I can see how she'd feel lost, how she'd fight to find a place to belong, no matter the cost to herself or others. Her words hit me hard, because they make perfect sense to me. And I understand myself a little better as well. "You can't control life." I lift my hands, palms up. "You just can't." She drops her gaze.

"That's what makes it so special, so precious."

Avery looks at me, her eyebrows furrowed.

I shrug. "That's it. That's all I can tell you about life. It isn't yours to control, but it is yours to live to the fullest, while you have it. I know it sounds cliché, and I could probably sell it to someone and make some megabucks 'cause people love that sappy shit, but there you have it."

She gives me a shaky smile. "You're much better with words than me."

"I don't know about that."

We share a smile, hers growing and becoming stronger.

"Thank you for putting things into a different perspective."

"You got me to see what I couldn't on my own too. What you said... you're right. That's why I'm quitting Sanders and Sisters. I'm making my life mine. I want the sunsets and sunrises. I want to go slow instead of fast. I want to make more memories and less money. I want to *live*. Really live, not half-ass it like I am now." I realize how true the words are as soon as they leave my mouth.

Avery inhales raggedly, understanding flooding her features. She exhales, nodding. "You should do that then. You should go on adventures and experience amazing things."

I stare into luminous eyes of gold. *Come with me.* I can't get the words out. That would be selfish of me. It's my dream to travel, not hers. Avery has a father to get to know.

Instead, I say, "You can do the same."

"I can't. I'm not that brave yet," Avery says softly.

"Being brave isn't something you learn; it's something you *be*." I step closer, touching a lock of her limp hair. "You're already there, remember? You've made it days in the wild. I bet you never thought you'd say that, did you?"

"No." Her smile is small, but genuine.

"You moved across half the country to find your dad. That alone is amazing, but you also could have been in hundreds of car wrecks along the way, and you weren't."

She nods, her back straightening the more I talk.

"And…" I take a deep breath, holding her gaze. "You lost your mom, and yet here you are, standing, living, even smiling."

A sound, tiny but full of grief, leaves Avery. My heart aches in response. I smooth the wrinkles from her forehead, pressing a kiss to her brow. "You are so, so brave, Avery."

Her hands lift to my ribcage, sliding around to my back, and she falls into my arms, holding me hard, shaking. My arms enfold her, my head dipped to rest against hers. The scent of dirt, and faint but mighty, grapefruit, clings to Avery, and I smile.

Even nature can't fully dispel her essence. I like that about her. I like everything about her, even her duplicity. It had merit. We stand like this for a long time and still not long enough, breathing, living, being. It is with regret that I pull back, a kink forming in my neck the only reason I do.

I think over her words, needing her to really believe that I am no longer holding grudges. "You should know that there can always be second chances, Avery, if people are willing to allow them. I am."

Avery's eyes flood with emotion, her face slowly lighting up to steal the rays from the sun, one by one. "We're really okay?"

"We're really okay." I move another inch toward her. "You should also know that it's okay to be scared, but don't let that fear keep you from having the best possible life you can."

"I'm going to try," she says in a voice that wobbles.

I give her a fierce look. "Try hard."

Avery nods, swallowing. "Where will you go when you leave Sanders and Sisters?"

"I don't know."

"What will you do?"

I squint at the sun, glancing at Avery with a half-smile on my face. "Just focus on living. That's it."

She sighs beside me, a dreamy look on her face.

"What are you thinking about?" I ask, amused.

"You. You're inspiring, profound." Avery shakes her head. "And you have no idea, do you?"

Not really.

"I'd love to know all the ways I am profound and inspiring." I face her fully. "But first, we're going in the water."

Avery blanches, shooting to the side. "No. I'm not going in any more water unless it's clear, see-through water where I know what's around me and how deep it is. Do you see that anywhere around here? No? Me either. I'm fine right here, thank you."

"Okay. Fine. Let's go fishing." It isn't as if we have anything else to do. Avery blinks. "Fishing? How?" "We'll make spears." I doubt we'll catch anything, and if we do, who is going to gut the fish? Because I can't. But it might be fun. "Come on, we're already in the middle of an adventure; let's make it a fun one. You game?"

18
AVERY

Am I game?

I look around us, seeing the same scenery I've seen for days. What else is there to do, other than walk and walk and walk some more? "Yeah. Sure. Why not? Let's go fishing."

"Great." Ben stands there, looking around as if he's searching for something, but he isn't sure what.

I cross my arms. "Have you even fished before?"

"Yes, I know how to fish." Annoyance tightens his tone. "Just because I'm a city guy and don't know shit about surviving in the wild doesn't mean I don't know how to fish."

"I don't know, Ben, you seem to be doing okay so far."

Ben's eyes shoot to mine. "Thanks."

I shrug. "You're welcome."

"You're doing good too, Avery."

We share a moment where the air becomes electrical and sway toward each other. Before I'm fully aware what we're doing, we're undressed and I'm against a bumpy boulder and Ben's inside me. It's hard, fast. Primal. There's another warning in my head, a buzzing that tells me I'm tempting fate to tip in a certain direction with this kind of behavior, but then Ben moves just right, and I forget it as my body finds release and pulses around his. He joins me, pulling out at the last second, his face buried in my neck, one hand around his penis, the fingers of the other hand imprinted on my butt.

"I feel like I could do this with you every hour," Ben says in a raspy voice.

My insides swirl at his words. "Are you saying you can't get enough of me?"

He nuzzles my collarbone before straightening. "I'm saying you're irresistible."

"I only want to be irresistible to you," I whisper, meaning the words. I don't want anyone else. Just Ben. Whatever happens, wherever we go from here, it will be Ben.

He leans back to look into my eyes, the depths filled with nameless emotions that can only be shown, not told. Ben feels it too. He feels the something for me I feel for him. He caresses the side of my face and I close my eyes to better experience his touch.

When Ben starts to turn, I lock my arms around his waist and squeeze, resting my cheek on his chest to listen to the pounding beat of his heart. A breeze forms, warm and fragrant with wild blossoms. With the view of overlapping mountains in the distance and spindly, tall trees and us in each other's arms, I don't feel lost. Or scared. I do feel naked though, the reality of that creeping in as the wind cools and certain areas of my body react.

I pull away, Ben grudgingly letting go, and round up my clothes. I giggle when I realize we both left on our socks and shoes.

"What? What's funny?"

"Us. We forget to take off our shoes." I toss Ben's shirt and shorts to him and make my way to the nearest body of water.

I clean up with the cold water, shivering the whole time. The clothes I put back on are slowly being reduced to stained rags, but they are better than nothing. Pinpricks dance along the back of my neck. I carefully straighten and look over my shoulder. Ben's back is to me as he zips up his shorts. Frowning, I look for the source of uneasiness, but as far as I can tell, we are alone. I shake it off, deciding the idea of unseen creatures lurking about is getting to me.

"How are we going to catch the fish?" I ask when I reach Ben's side.

He rubs the back of his head. For the first time, I notice his nose is peeling and his lips are cracked. "I was thinking maybe I can make a spear out of a tree branch and stab one. It's worth a shot."

"How are you going to make a spear?"

Ben flicks open the pocketknife. "With this."

"What about the hunting knife? That would probably work better."

"That would probably slice off a hand along with the wood. We're not using that."

Ben's been very odd about the hunting knife we found.

"All right, so we make some spears and we stab some fish. Sounds fun."

Ben squints at me. "You don't sound like you mean that."

"Does stabbing fish sound like fun to you?" I return.

He swallows, his skin turning a little green. "Not especially."

Stabbing fish is not something I ever wanted to try, but I'll do it if it means we get to eat something other than leaves and berries. I refuse to fillet them or poke out their eyeballs or whatever else is required, but I will stab them. I'll stab the crap out of them, but not literally. Right? Literal crap will not come out of them when I stab them, will it? And we're back to fish poop. Ugh.

I shake myself from my worrisome musings and focus on Ben. "How will we cook them?"

He just looks at me.

"We're cooking them! I am not eating raw fish, no way."

A small smile captures and releases his mouth within a handful of seconds. "I'm thinking between the two of us, we should be able to get a couple fish and cook them over a fire."

"Well," I say briskly as I head for a particularly dead-looking tree. "Let's find some branches and turn them into spears."

I pause with my back to Ben, pretending to study the fallen tree branches. I need a moment to myself to savor that smile. There was a time, far too recently, where I never thought I'd see one of those on his face for me. It's amazing how quickly things can change.

BEN

It takes a little time, but we scrounge up some thicker tree branches and sharpen them as best as we can with my pocketknife. It seems like early afternoon by the time we've fashioned a dozen spears that may or may not catch us some fish. It's close to being a second night spent out here, cold and worried. I physically turn from the thought, wishing that put it out of my mind.

"Tonight, we feast," I joke, holding up a spear.

The labor has been done in quiet, but it hasn't been uncomfortable. Working in the shade of a large tree, we've exchanged nothing more than looks and an occasional grimace or smile. It's been almost peaceful—as peaceful as anything can be when you're lost and starving. Having purpose is good; it makes our situation seem less dismal, even if it really isn't any less dismal.

"What do you think? Will they work?" Avery stands with her hands on her hips, looking like a different person from the one I've come to know. I'm suddenly hit with the knowledge that Avery's right; I didn't know her at all. I like this unpolished, fresh-faced, surprisingly fearless Avery much more than the too-perfect office one.

I straighten from my crouched position, my knees cracking as I do. The swelling has gone down in my ankle. I'm grateful for that small respite. "I think we won't know if they work until we try them."

She swallows, turning her eyes to the water. "We have to go in it again, don't we?"

"If I remember right, leeches like stagnant, still water. If we stick to the faster moving parts, I think we'll be okay. Let's walk downstream until we find some."

"Do you know how to prepare the fish, if we happen to get any?" Avery asks as we collect our spears.

I break out in a sweat that has nothing to do with the hot sun and everything to do with the queasiness running rampant through my stomach. As we make our way through overgrown weeds and grass that stings upon impact, I reply, "I know how. I just don't like to do it."

"Will you be able to?" Avery turns her head and lifts a questioning eyebrow. She walks with an armful of our spears, looking as if she fits right in as an outdoorswoman.

I fall into step beside her with the remaining spears. I hope it's not a lie when I tell her, "Yes."

We stop walking once we reach the faster-paced water. The water is clearer here. I can see rocks and pebbles and the occasional fish scuttle by. A soothing sound forms as water collides with rock. We each grab a spear and put ourselves on the cusp of where land meets water, and carefully move into the water.

Our eyes hold.

"Are we really going to do this?" Avery questions.

"Do you want to eat something other than mint leaves and berries?" I ask with lifted eyebrows.

Determination threads her eyes with prisms of gold. "You bet I do."

We both look to the water.

After a moment, Avery asks, "What, exactly, do we do?"

"You know, I'm not really sure?" I rub the back of my head with my free hand and study the water. "I guess we're going to wing it and see what happens."

Avery glares at the water and sets her shoulders. "Wing it. You got it. I can wing it." She steps forward, her face set to ferocity. "Here I am, about to wing it."

I open my mouth to express caution, but Avery plows farther into the water before I can speak. As she shrieks and hops and makes a sound halfway between a laugh and a cry, I'm hit with intense awareness of her. Her presence, her exuberance. Her light, her fire. *Her.* Whether it's devious or commendable, Avery doesn't do anything half-ass. And she doesn't stay scared for long either.

Avery looks at me, her voice breaking my reverie. "Do I just jab at them?"

I take a stilted breath of air and meet her in the water. My boots are immediately heavy with water. At this point, I don't care. "I think the trick is to stab at them before they actually make it past you. Move sooner than you think you should. They're fast. And Avery?"

She looks up.

"Don't stab yourself—or me, okay?"

"Right. Don't stab myself."

"Or me," I remind her.

Her eyes dance. "Right. Or you."

On either side of the water are green-colored hills with taller, more robust mountains behind them. The sky is blue; the sun is bright. This is a picturesque scene—gorgeous really. If nothing else good can be said about this unwelcome journey, it cannot be argued that it isn't beautiful out here. It's breathtaking, smelling of fresh air and pinecones and nature.

Avery wobbles, eyes locked on the water around her ankles. I put out a hand to steady her, gently holding her elbow until she catches her balance. Almost a week ago, I couldn't stand her—or so I told myself. Today, I'm helping her stand. Literally.

She thrusts her arm down, and the flimsy weapon cracks and breaks, three quarters of it floating downstream. Avery laughs as she turns to me. "We are exceptional makers of weapons."

"We would definitely win any war with our flimsy tree spears."

Her laughter turns louder, almost sounding like a cackle, which makes me laugh. The sun radiates around her, making her seem like a sun god with her golden hair and eyes. When the laughter fades, it's just us, standing in water, staring at each other. Our faces are close, her eyes exceptionally pretty, and I want to kiss her. I can do that now. I can have the thought that I want to kiss her, or not even think it, and just do it.

"Be careful," I tell her. "If you get too deep, the current will pull you."

Her eyelids become heavy as she focuses on my mouth. "How much deeper am I allowed to go?"

My throat turns parched. She's talking about us.

"Maybe I want to be pulled by the current," Avery adds when I don't answer. "Sucked under, spun wildly about, submerged in...you."

I take a shallow breath. "Avery—"

She doesn't let me finish, grabbing my shoulders to yank me forward. Our lips graze a second before I slip on the rocks and crash into the water, taking Avery with me. It doesn't even reach our waists, but I've learned my lesson with water and Avery. Before there's time for Avery to freak out, I grasp her under her armpits and haul her out of the deeper water until we're both once again standing.

"It isn't deep enough for me to get upset," she informs me as she recovers the spear I dropped and stabs it into the water.

"Are you sure?"

Avery cringes. "Well, no, not really. Something just touched me."

I laugh.

I think Avery is more surprised than I am when she lifts the spear and there is a fish wiggling from the end of it with its mouth gaping. She squeals and drops the spear into the water. I hastily retrieve it, lassoing her wrist as we make our way to land. Disbelief turns to amazement as I stare at the speared fish. With its colorful skin, it looks like a rainbow trout, and is about the size of my hand. I set it on the ground.

"I didn't really think I'd get one," Avery says, sounding almost disappointed.

"What's the matter?" Eyes on the fish, my mouth goes dry as its tail moves side to side. The spear didn't go deep and falls out of it and to the ground. That means I'll have to do the rest—a thought that makes my palms damp.

Avery looks at the fish with sorrow in her eyes. "I feel bad for it."

Turns out Avery is as much of a softie as I am.

"I'll kill it as humanely as I can." Stomach churning at what I'm about to do, I take my pocketknife, tightly gripping it.

Avery looks from the knife in my hand to my face. "What are you going to do with that?"

"I'll explain in a minute."

With a grimace on my face, I hold the fish as steady as I can and forcefully stab it behind its eyes. Avery squeaks, but I don't look at her, determined to finish this. I twist the blade into its brain, making sure it does what it needs to do. Saliva forms in my mouth, bringing a bitter taste of bile. With my switchblade and a shaking hand, I gut the fish so that it can bleed out. That done, I sort of collapse to my knees, twisting away from the sight of the disfigured fish.

"Ben? Are you okay?"

I wordlessly shake my head, taking deep breaths as I fight to not vomit.

"I get that you know how, but I'm wondering if maybe you *shouldn't* fish," she says wryly.

I flip to my stomach, a short bark of sound leaving me. "I'll be fine. Just give me a minute."

Avery kneels beside me, rubbing circles into my back. Her touch is soothing. She gives me a sympathetic look when I lift my head and meet her eyes. I exhale slowly, wiping a hand across my perspiring forehead. Avery continues to rub my back, the nausea fading as she does.

"It's called spiking and bleeding out," I tell her once I can speak without my stomach clenching. "It's supposedly the kinder way to kill fish."

Avery offers, "I'll fillet it if you tell me how to do it."

"This is embarrassing," I mutter.

She shrugs one shoulder, offering a small smile. "I think it's kind of sweet."

19
AVERY

More often than not, I miss, but by the time Ben notices my exhaustion and calls it quits, the sky has transformed from blue to gray and we have a total of four fish. That's four more fish than we had hours ago. I look at the bled-out fish with pride, feeling more accomplished than I have in months. I caught those. First time fishing, with spears even, and I got four fish. It lets me know I am not as inept with this outdoor stuff as I thought.

"You're better at this than I am," Ben announces.

Ben wasn't able to spear any fish, and although he made a half-hearted effort, I don't think he's too upset by that. The spiking and bleeding out took its toll on him. Poor guy. He looked physically ill by the whole experience. And we still have to fillet them.

"It's probably because you lost your glasses and can't see well," I tell him teasingly.

"Right. That's it." He winks at me, his hair flopping over his forehead. He's sporting a thick stubble at this point and it gives him a wicked look that does funny things to my insides.

Ben views the four fish set out in a row, his expression troubled. "I'm glad it's almost over."

"I'll do the filleting, if you tell me how to do it," I tell him again, running a hand along his forearm.

Ben meets my eyes, his alight with something soft that makes it hard for me to breathe. "We'll do it together, how's that sound?"

"Sounds like a plan, partner." I give him a quick kiss and he lightly trails his fingers down my back and across my hipbone.

With the scent of fish heavy in the air, we work as a team, cutting the meat from the bone and skin with quick movements. Ben only gags once. I turn my head to hide a smile. That done, we get the fire going in time for dusk to blanket the world. Everything is done together, and efficiently. This odd sense of belonging overcomes me. I look at Ben as we cook the fish on sticks over the fire, knowing I've found something close to home. I don't want him to leave Sanders and Sisters. I don't want him to leave me.

"You're getting good at fires," I tell Ben, swallowing back my dreary thoughts so that I don't put them into words.

Bellies full for the first time in a while, we sit beside each other and watch the crackling, snapping fire. Crickets chirp along with some incessant buzzing sound that comes from the trees. Right now, it doesn't feel like we're trapped so much as on a camping expedition. When I don't think about everything bad that could happen, this is even enjoyable.

He shifts until he's behind me, one leg on either side of mine, and wraps his arms around my waist. Ben brushes my hair to the side, causing me to shiver, and marks me with his lips. "I better be with all the practice I'm getting."

"I wonder what everyone is thinking about us right now," I muse, drowsy from the food and Ben's fingers as they play with my hair. "Do you think they're still looking for us?"

"Duke won't give up until we're found." Confidence runs true in his tone and it makes me feel better that Ben has such solid hope, and that it's in my father.

"I never told my mom, but I always tried to envision what my dad looked like." I close my eyes, a smile on my face. "Most often, I pictured a tall, lean man with golden hair and eyes and a strong jaw. For some reason, he always wore a cowboy hat and boots. It wasn't clear what he did, but it had something to do with ranching."

I hear the smile in Ben's voice. "Other than the height and the jaw, that sounds nothing like Duke Renner."

"I imagined they had a torrid love affair, but he was promised to another. That it broke his heart that he couldn't be with us." I continue softly, "Or, I wondered if he'd died, and that's why he wasn't around, and that's why Mom wouldn't talk about him."

Ben's arms close around me more, his head near mine.

"I never thought it could be that he didn't know about me. I'm not sure why, but out of all the scenarios, that wasn't one of them."

I twist my head to meet Ben's eyes. As soon as I do, he lowers his mouth and gives me a sweet, lingering kiss that floods my body with bittersweet joy. We haven't talked about it, but what happens when we leave here? We can say we'll stay in each other's lives all we want, but how will that be possible with me in Illinois and Ben wherever Ben decides to go? *Maybe he won't go.* The thought floods me with guilt. I will not ask him to stay for me. That would be wrong. I push anything but now from my mind, Ben's fingers in my hair lulling me to slumber. This is wonderful. He's wonderful. And I *feel* wonderful.

"I'm happy," I announce softly, a hint of disbelief in my tone. The words seem out of place, given our circumstances.

"Good. So am I."

I smile and sink lower into Ben's arms.

One second I'm about to fall asleep on Ben's shoulder, and the next I'm shoved to my back on the ground with a hand clapped across my mouth. Ben's lying directly on top of me, his head lifted, his body taut and unmoving. I try to ask him what the hell he thinks he's doing, but unintelligible sounds are all I produce.

Ben's voice, low and thick with warning, feathers across my ear. "Shh."

When I try to wiggle out from beneath him, he tightens his hold and lowers his face to mine. I immediately slacken my body at the look on his face. It's menacing. "Don't move; don't talk."

My eyebrows dip in question.

"We are not alone."

"Wh—"

He squeezes my shoulder, slowly moving his head side to side.

I jerk my head in what is meant to be a nod of submission, my heartrate stuttering before shifting into overdrive. I want to ask him what he means by that, and what exactly is with us, and where. "Where" is an excellent question. Body still as stone, my eyes flicker around us, looking for whatever has Ben spooked. If we're about to be attacked, I have no idea from which direction. A rock sits in my stomach as I envision a lion or wolf, maybe a bear, dragging me off to eat. What if it's that alien-goat-thing come back with its clan to finish what it started?

I choke back a whimper.

Ben carefully lifts his body from mine, instantly chilling me, and crouches feet from me. He pauses as if listening for something only he can hear. With fast, noiseless movements, he removes all evidence of us and the fire. I think that's a great idea, until I wonder why he needs to do that if there is only an animal near us.

"What's going on?" I hiss, terror clawing at me from the inside out.

He turns to me. "When I tell you, you run. Got it?"

"Ben," I whimper.

"You run."

"Why? *Ben.*"

"I don't think we've been in Shawnee National Forest for quite some time, and that worries me. I saw a fire not far from here. We're being tracked. Anyone who doesn't want us to know they're near us is not someone we want to find us." Ferocity stares back at me. "I mean it, Avery. You *run.*"

"W-where?" comes out in a disjointed whisper. I remember the sensation of being watched today. Were we? My body shakes with cold and fear.

A rustling to the left of us spikes the tempo of my pulse and widens my eyes. I spring up, ready to run, and I don't care to where. I move in a circle, searching for a predator I can't see. It's like spinning around in a circle of madness.

Ben's hand clamps to my arm, halting my progress to nowhere. He freezes me in place with his eyes, wordlessly telling me to stay put. It's a wonder I can hear anything around the pounding of my heart, but when Ben's mouth forms the word "run", I do, without a backward glance.

Call it instinct, call it cowardice: I am gone.

Ben will be fine; he's a fast runner. He'll catch up in no time. Heart pounding, I run without direction. Through high weeds that grab and slice my legs and arms, I go and go. I watch the darkening skies as I run. I have to keep moving, and whatever is after us won't get me.

But Ben...Ben it might get.

I slow to a stop, knowing I have to go back. I can't leave him. Whatever happens, we're in this together. Always.

My shoulders spring back.

I am *not* a coward. I am *brave.*

An animal growls.

I jump, screaming when a hand clamps down on my shoulder and spins me around, another immediately slapping over my mouth to halt any further sound. I'm dragged to a tree with a vicelike grip on my wrists, a heavy weight pressed against me to ensure I can't escape.

BEN

"What are you doing?" I demand. Avery was running toward danger, not away from it. My heartbeat hasn't been right since I saw her heading straight to the strangers I want to avoid. It sent fear so profound I thought I was going to vomit spiraling through me, with fury quickly following it.

She slumps against me, and I loosen my grip on her. Without saying a word, Avery wraps her arms around my neck and presses her frame to mine, burrowing her face in my neck. I stand with my arms raised, hands out, and with a hard swallow, I embrace Avery. My arms tighten, gathering her closer, and my cheek drops to the crown of her head. My heartbeat won't steady, and my pulse is past malfunctioning.

Avery's okay, I tell myself, closing my eyes. *She's okay.*

"I was...I was trying to find you," she tells me in a voice that shakes as much as she is.

My throat tightens. "You were supposed to run."

Working in an office side by side with Avery for months was torture. Part of the time because she seemed to purposely try to outdo me at every opportunity. Then there was the night of Duke Renner's birthday party and the ensuing days after that royally screwed everything up. But the other part of the time it was because she was likable. Too likable. My head and heart have been on a merry-go-round of torment since she arrived at Sanders and Sisters. It was easier to dislike her than try to figure her out.

"I left you for the crows," Avery states. "I'm not leaving you again."

Now I don't have that shield to help protect me from my own emotions.

Because I know her heart, and it's as fragile as anyone else's.

Because every bad thing she did was for someone else.

Because she doesn't give up.

Because she came back for me, and a hundred other details I can't wrap my head around, even as they stare me in the face.

Because she said she's not leaving me again.

I take a deep breath and slowly release it.

"Do you hear that?" she whispers.

I nod, looking in the direction of faint voices. "Yeah," I say flatly.

"It sounds like people."

I nod again, pinpricks of unease dancing along my spine.

Avery keeps herself perfectly still. "Is that who we're trying to avoid?"

A third nod.

She moves back to see my eyes. "Why? It's people, the first we've seen since we've been out here. They can help us."

Avery takes a step toward them and my hand snatches out, gripping her wrist to halt her. "They're hunters."

She looks over her shoulder at me. "Okay?"

"And we might be on their land. Either way, I have a bad feeling about them."

Avery shifts closer to me, standing on her tiptoes to try to catch a glimpse of the men. Her face is directly beside mine, making it hard to focus on anything but her. "How many are there?"

Grimness coats the word as it leaves my mouth. "Four."

They're too close to where our fire was, and I know they know we're nearby. How long have they been tracking us? In my haste to get far from them, I forgot whatever scraps are left of the backpack, and anything else we had lying about. These men are dangerous, and we don't want to have anything to do with them.

"Ben?"

"Yeah?" I look at Avery, catching the determined set of her jaw.

"I need to know if you trust me." She straightens her spine as if steeling herself for whatever cruel words I'm about to sling at her.

I jerk my eyes to hers. "Does we have to discuss this now?"

"Yes."

Frustration sharpens my tone. "Why?"

"Because I don't know what's about to happen, and I have to know that whatever does or doesn't, you trust me."

"I trust you," I tell her firmly. "Now you have to trust me, all right?" Avery nods.

"Whatever happens, don't fight." *Don't let them touch you.*

She frowns at me.

"Do what they say." My palms shake, and I fist my hands. *Don't let them hurt you.*

A twig crackles under the weight of a boot, and I freeze, holding Avery's eyes. "Don't look away from me," I whisper. *Don't let them take you away from me.*

Her eyes begin to slide to the side.

I shake my head, gripping her shoulders. Her eyes flutter back to mine. "Look at me, Avery. That's right, just look at me. Don't look away." *Don't let me lose you.*

"Aw, isn't this sweet." A husky voice drawls from behind. "A little romantic time in the forest between two lovebirds."

Avery's face is filled with fear, her features pale and pinched. Still, she stands tall. I won't let anything happen to her. I swear it, to her and to me. A barely perceptible nod acknowledges what I silently promise. Unlike finding the lodge, this promise I plan to keep.

"Jim, check this out," he calls. "I think we found the campers."

Although her expression is fierce, Avery starts to visibly shake.

"Is that so?" a second voice booms. "Well, come on then, turn around and show your faces. We don't bite."

His words produce laughter from his comrades, but it isn't friendly. It's the kind that slithers down your spine with foreboding.

"You forgot to say much. We don't bite *much*," one adds.

"Well, now, that all depends on the person. How about you folks? Are you decent or do I need to get the can of whoop ass ready? Come on, be polite and turn around." Impatience slices through the words.

I take Avery's hand in mine and slowly turn to face the unknown men. Four stand spread out in a line that blocks us from going forward. Their faces are hidden by shadows. One is substantially taller than the rest, and wider too. As a unit, they step toward us, bringing their features into focus the closer they get. Hard-edged faces without a hint of empathy look back at us.

"I believe you have something of mine." It's the tallest one, complete with a handlebar mustache and safari hat. Interest glints in his eyes as they come to rest on Avery. He shifts his gaze to me. "I'll take my knife now."

"You can have the knife," I say with a voice that sounds like sandpaper.

"And the lady."

My blood vessels constrict, tightening to the point of physical pain. Avery flinches, her eyes shooting to mine. I carefully shake my head, never breaking eye contact with her. They cannot have her. I will not allow it. As the men continue to talk, it sounds like the adults in the Charlie Brown movies inside my head; a bunch of noise without much sense to it.

"Jenkins, why don't you escort this fine lady to our camp."

That I hear perfectly well.

Shoulders forward, I face the men. "You're not taking her."

The man tips his head and laughs. "You confiscated my knife—some could say you even stole it. I think asking the same of your lady friend is only fair. We're tired of looking at one another's ugly mugs. Need a change of scenery. We'll be nothing but the best of gentlemen, isn't that right, boys?"

A chorus of agreement rings out.

Needles prick my skull, stabbing at me from all directions. Combustible rage throbs inside me, wanting to get out. They will not touch her, not while I live. I pull Avery behind me, never releasing her wrist. Avery makes a funny sound. I briefly wonder if it's out of fear or discomfort from the ironclad grip I have on her.

My voice is cold as I announce, "I don't think so."

"Boys."

Three barrels are aimed at me within seconds.

I flinch.

Avery inhales sharply, her nails digging into my back.

He chuckles. "Oh, I do think so."

"You touch her," I rasp, fury filling my blood, singing sweet and deadly. "You die."

I don't know how, but I'll make it happen. I'll squeeze the life out of him with my hands around his thick neck if I have to.

The large man tips his head back and laughs, his gut moving as he does. When he's had his share of mirth, he focuses on me with lethal intent. All traces of humor are gone. "I'm afraid you don't get it. You're on private property. Trespassing, I'd say. And, you see, we're the ones with the guns."

He steps closer, a slight tilt to his head as he makes a slow, wide circle around us. We turn with him, never letting him out of sight. The hunter stops before me, close enough that I can see the black of his teeth when he speaks and smell smoke and sweat. "What do you have?"

I lunge forward without thought, intent on smashing in his face. But he's ready, swinging his fist into my jaw. I hear a crack as pain radiates down the side of my face. Avery screams, piercing and unending. Seconds later, the atmosphere is ravaged by an animalistic roar that sends chills down my back and tightens my throat.

It's as if the beast is responding to Avery's call of distress.

It comes again, closer, louder, and the three men with rifles scramble to get out of the charging bear's way as it barrels through shrubbery and directly at the hunters. The black bear, larger than all three men combined, gallops after them. I stand still, confused by what I'm seeing, as the bear chases each of the men, bellowing its displeasure with them.

"Shoot it," the man closest to us shouts, waving his arms.

Another tries to aim the gun, but a bird swoops at his head and he cries out, dropping the weapon.

"What in the absolute *hell*?" the lead hunter rages, striding toward the chaos playing out beside us.

The sky is obliterated with black flying objects and Avery shrieks and drops to the ground as an army of crows swoop into the fray, pecking at one of the hunter's shirts as he screams and flails his arms and tries to outrun them. One of the crows comes near enough that I can see it only has one eye.

"No fucking way," I whisper.

It flies toward Avery, cawing once before taking off. She covers her head and cowers. I stare at Avery, disbelieving what I'm seeing, even as I know it to be true.

I kneel beside Avery, touching her shaking shoulder. "Avery, get up."

With ungraceful motions, Avery straightens her contorted form and looks around us, fear and awe riveted to her features as she takes in the scene. As if tag teaming, the crows and bear take turns terrorizing the hunters. It would be funny, if this was a movie and not reality.

Already turning to go, she states, "I'm trying to be brave, but right now, I am failing."

"We can't go yet. Wait." I put a hand on her shoulder. We need to make a decision here.

Annoyance puckers her mouth when she turns back to me. "For them to remember us? No, thank you."

"Just let me think a second," I demand.

Avery sighs and gestures for me to get on with it.

I scowl at her.

She lifts her eyebrows.

I want to be irritated with her, but don't have time for that. Turning an analytical eye on the situation, I go through possible scenarios, looking for the best one. While the men are distracted, we could run for it, like Avery said, but that's only a temporary fix. They'd still be out here, and they'd find us again. My eyes land on one of the guns.

Before I can come to a decision, it's taken from me.

A higher, younger cry joins the bear's, drawing the leader's attention. His focus, along with the weapon in his hands, swings to the bear cub who decided to join its mother. The hunter with the gun is the closest to us. This fact doesn't seem all that significant, until Avery moves. With a shout, she throws herself before the cub and directly in front of the rifle.

The world stops, along with my heart, and then it comes back with speeding force.

I sprint toward Avery. The fear is consuming; it makes it hard to even move. Chest tight, breaths choked, I try to get to her in time. "Avery! Avery, no!"

She looks up, eyes on me, steady and strong.

I love her.

The thought hits me hard enough that I stumble forward, breaking stride, as a shot cracks the night into pieces.

20
AVERY

In another incident where I react without thinking, I again find myself running. This time, however, it's toward danger. That little bear cub is not going to die. It would break Ben's heart. Let's be real: it would break mine too. In a move either valiant or senseless, depending on the person, I put myself between the firearm and the bear cub.

"Stupid girl," the hunter mutters, shaking his head with an evil grin.

"I am not a girl," I tell him firmly.

He gives me a weird look and I realize I inadvertently called myself stupid.

I jump forward, intent on wrestling the weapon from him just as Ben rams into me with enough force to send me sailing sideways. I land on the ground, the wind knocked from me.

Everything pauses when the gun goes off. I open my eyes, going motionless, and watch as Ben plummets to the ground, face first. Tears, instant and brutal, swim to the surface. I crawl to Ben, knowing that if he dies, I might as well go with him.

"Ben," I croak, shaking his shoulder. I search for blood on him, and finding none, shake him some more. "Ben. Are you okay? Answer me!"

He gingerly lifts his head and spits out dirt and grass. "I'm fine. You?"

I help him sit up and then I cover his face in kisses, tasting dirt and sweat and not caring. "I'm fine. I'm fine. I'm fine," I whisper over and over, trying to convince myself it's true.

Ben hugs me to him, his grip hard but welcome. "The gun went off. Is anyone hurt?"

Growls and grunts grow in volume, and I shift my eyes to the side. The mama bear has the hunter's firearm in its mouth and it's shaking its head, intent on demolishing the weapon. The bear cub sits beside its mom, contentedly watching. My eyes move down, landing on a motionless man. My eyes go up, and find the other three hugging one another, a tight circle of crows keeping them from going anywhere. They caw in a song of warning, pecking at the men any time they move the slightest bit.

"No one's hurt. It must have gone off when the bear went for him." I nod toward the prone man.

Ben runs a hand over his face. "This is crazy. Now what?"

"Tie them up?" I suggest.

"In a minute. They aren't going anywhere." He drops his hand, eyeing me. "What you did was very stupid."

I narrow my eyes.

"And very heroic."

An odd wheezing sound leaves me, and I feel my face crumple a moment before I fling my arms around Ben and hold him with all my might. I will never let him go, not in my heart. I pull back enough to meet his questioning gaze. "You're right—I do need my father. But I need you too, Ben."

Ben drops his head, taking a shuddering breath. He lifts his gaze and gives me a sweet smile. "You always have me, no matter what. I think you always did." He takes my hand and sets it to his heart, the meaning clear.

I have his heart.

He has mine.

"Someone kill me already," one of the hunters groans, yelping as a crow counters his words with a jab of its beak to his ankle.

"Do you hear that?" Ben stiffens and cocks his head, listening.

I frown, straining my ears as a strange noise vibrates from above. Wind picks up, tousling my hair about my head. "What is that?"

"I think it's a—"

Ben's words are obliterated as lights and blades come closer. Elation flares inside my chest and blooms outward, warm and happy. I jump up and down, waving my arms in the air. "It's a helicopter! They found us!"

Finally. Finally, we can go home.

BEN

My heartrate spikes. I move at a slower pace, not nearly as excited as Avery. Relief at being found is trampled by the knowledge that once we go back, everything else will most likely go back to the way it was. I watch Avery, not even caring about the helicopter. She'll be someone I don't know again. If we hadn't gotten lost together, we never would have found the strongest versions of one another. We'd still be strangers. In a way, we'd still be lost.

Avery jogs forward toward the clearing in the distance, and then stops, turning to face me. Her smile fades as she looks at me. I try to smile, but fail. Golden eyes sparkle with sorrow. "Ben?"

I see on her face what I feel in my heart. Whatever we found in Shawnee National Forest won't last. I already feel it falling away, sliding back into the ground of impossibilities that somehow worked for a guy named Ben and a girl named Avery who were stuck in the woods together. She'll advance at Sanders and Sisters; she'll get to know the father she hadn't been allowed. And me? I'll get to know the world a little better, and maybe what I want from it as well. As for us, I don't know.

"Let's go," I say with a forced smile. I brush my fingers along the side of her hand as I reach her, and she takes my hand in hers.

Fingers locked with the woman I swore I'd never want and instead want more each hour, I head in the direction of where the helicopter landed. It takes a dozen minutes to crest the small hill and it takes none at all. The helicopter propellers slow to a stop at the same time we do, and out steps the infamous Duke Renner, who I now know to be Avery's father. That knowledge makes my stomach queasy—maybe because I'm in love with his daughter.

Duke's short black hair is windblown, his ice-blue eyes set on my face. There are hundreds of questions there, waiting to be voiced. Even now, on a rescue mission, in the middle of the country, he's dressed in a suit and tie.

Avery stops and then steps forward, stopping again. She sighs, not making another move to reach him. I squeeze her fingers, sensing her confliction. Duke's her dad, and he isn't.

Two people rush past him, first-aid kits at the ready. Another helicopter is nearby, sporting the insignia of law enforcement. There are some official-looking men who keep their distance as we're looked over; that must be their ride. I wonder what we look like to them. If the paleness of the woman's face who asks me to sit down is anything to go by, pretty bad.

Avery and I are literally pulled apart, but our eyes find each other's as we're examined and asked questions. I don't want to let her go. Her face says the same. We were shoved together and told to be a team. We're more than that now. We are connected in a way that only some form of disaster can create and never take away. We're bonded.

When it finally hits that we will soon be gone from this place, I drop my head to my knees and breathe. I feel numb. We thought we might die. We didn't know when we'd be rescued, if ever. We haven't properly bathed, or eaten, or had clean water, in days. Avery and I faced not only the weather, but wildlife, and criminals on top of that. We got through so much shit together.

I can look at the world now and demand: *What are you going to throw at me next?*

And I'll be ready for whatever it is.

"Are you all right?" are the first words my boss says to us, his chiseled features blank. I know the look well. It's his serious face. If Duke isn't grinning, then Duke means business. He's concerned, worried. I wonder if Avery can read his facial expressions like I can.

"Yes," Avery tells him with only a slight quiver in her voice.

I glance at her, expecting her to be looking at her father, but her gaze is set on me. Avery is pale beneath her sunburn, shadows lining her eyes. Yet, with the moon behind her, she shines. I pity the brush that tries to manage that wild mane of hair. I look down, take a sharp breath, and look up again. Those eyes haven't left my face. They speak to me. They tell me things Avery has never spoken.

"Ben?"

My focus shifts to Duke.

"You okay?"

I study him, looking for a sign of her in him. Maybe the full lips, the high cheekbones—definitely the doggedness of spirit. You tell Duke something he doesn't want to hear, and he gnaws at it like a bone until it becomes what he expects. I see that in Avery. She never gave up, even when she wanted, and she never gave up on me, even when she should have.

I give a short nod.

Duke clasps a hand to each of our shoulders. White teeth, some crowned for no other reason than to be esthetically pleasing, appear. "Good to see you two are all right. Damn, you had us shitting bricks. What the hell happened?"

Neither of us speak.

Duke looks between the two of us. "No pressure. Talk when you're ready."

Avery nods once. I do a poor imitation of the same.

"How did you find us?" I ask through a dry throat.

"We saw a fire back there." He hitches a thumb over his shoulder. "We thought it should be checked out. Was that yours?"

Avery nods toward the hunters. "It was probably theirs."

Duke looks around us, as if noticing the men and animals for the first time. "Who are they?"

"Bad men," Avery mutters.

Duke's eyes narrow. "What's been going on out here?"

I meet the gaze of one of the uniformed men. "They threatened to kidnap Avery; I also believe them to be illegally hunting on private property."

"And the animals?" the officer asks faintly.

I shrug. "I guess they helped us."

The man's eyebrows furrow.

With a bellow that causes Avery and I both to jump, the black bear and its cub meander across the land and over the side of a hill. Cawing, the crows bid their goodbye as well.

"You might want to notify someone to change the Shawnee National Forest's website. There *are* bears here," I tell the uniformed men, wryness in my tone.

"Let's get you two to the hospital." Duke puts an arm around both of us. His voice is low when he says, "I apologize to you both; this is the last thing I wanted to happen."

Duke moves us toward the helicopter, his hold not relinquishing until we're seated. Enigmatic blue eyes drill into mine. "You want to explain all that in better detail to me?"

Exhaustion hits me. I shake my head. "Not now. I will, but…not now."

Not one to take no for an answer, I'm surprised when Duke sits back and nods. "All right."

The ride is noisy and uncomfortable, but Avery and I are silent. The void grows; we both draw back into ourselves. It makes me feel sick. I catch her looking at me, sadness lining her shimmery eyes. With a lump in my throat, I look away, my fingers fisting in my lap. I want to hold her, but it feels as if I am not allowed. I know Avery would let me, and yet, I keep my distance.

Why does it feel as if I'm losing everything?

I feel Duke's eyes on us, probing and curious.

I say nothing, and maybe by doing so, I say a lot.

21
BEN

The television, although not that loud, grates on my eardrums. My parents refuse to leave the room unless the nurses order it, and even then, they sometimes put up a fight. All I can think about is Avery in the room across the hall, and how there's no one with her. It puts an ache in my chest and a sour taste in my mouth.

"You should sue them," my mother states.

I snap my eyes to her. She's about as tall as a middle schooler and has short brown hair. My mother is sweet, but get her mad and she turns into something scary. Hurt her kids in any way and it's go time. She views my recent predicament as an attack against my person.

"Mom, stop."

"That Extreme Retreat company and your boss too. What kind of people promote those kinds of heathen activities? This isn't the Stone Age."

"It's uncivilized, and dangerous, yes, but we all knew what we were getting into. Their belief is that throwing people into crazy scenarios is the most effective way to form authentic teamwork skills. It says it right on the pamphlet." Of course, it doesn't say to get lost. That was all us.

Sally Stitzer looks me in the eyes and says, "You're my son. I'm supposed to look out for you. If I don't, who will?"

I close my eyes. "I'm not suing anyone."

"If you won't sue the company he hired, then sue Duke Renner," she continues fiercely. "He never should have sent you on some insane wilderness expedition. It's barbaric."

"We all agreed to it. We even signed a waiver beforehand." I don't add that it was implied that if we didn't go through with it, we might lose our jobs. Opening my eyes, I meet my mom's angry, worried face, and say firmly, "I'm not suing anyone."

She makes a sound of pain. "Ben—"

"Sally," my dad says warningly. "This isn't the time."

"He could have died." The last word comes out choked.

I sigh. "Anyone can die at any time. I didn't. Let's focus on that."

"And that poor girl! What's her name again?"

"Avery. Mom—"

"Avery. That poor thing. She was almost kidnapped! Who knows what would have happened to her if they'd managed to get away with it?"

My skin heats up as I think about what could have happened to Avery. It isn't until I feel the ache in my joints that I notice my hands clenched around the sheet. I loosen my fingers, my eyes on the wall across the room. I feel bad about it, but I want them to leave. This room has been full of people off and on since I was admitted. I know it hasn't been the same for Avery. Her mother is gone, and her father doesn't know he's her father.

She's alone.

I don't want her to be alone.

"Sally, that's enough," my dad barks, noticing my agitation. "Let's take a walk. Ben needs to rest."

"Oh…I'm sorry, Ben. I don't mean to get worked up. You can't imagine how worried we were and it could have been so much worse. I keep thinking about that, even though I know I shouldn't." A warm hand brushes hair from my forehead. She sounds on the verge of tears as she asks, "Can you even see without your glasses?"

I smile and take her hand, squeezing her fingers. "Yes, Mom, I can see."

"Okay." She takes a deep breath, wipes her eyes, and looks at my dad. "Let's grab a bite to eat and come back in a couple hours."

"You don't have to come back tonight," I tell them quickly.

Her face pinches.

My dad puts a reassuring arm around my mom and looks at me through his wire-rimmed glasses. "We'll grab something to eat and go back to the hotel. How about we call around eight tonight?"

"That sounds fine."

"If you need anything at all, if you're lonely, or…" My mom appears unable to produce words.

"I'll talk to you tonight, and I'll see you in the morning," I reply gently but firmly.

Putting a hand to her mouth, my mother nods as my dad navigates her from the room. I let my head fall back and close my eyes.

"I always knew you were an attention seeker. Although, I never thought you'd go this far. Who orchestrates getting lost for a little media time?" My eyes pop open to the sight of an elfin woman with choppy reddish-brown hair and a wide smile. She wears a pink and red striped shirt and lime green shorts with boots. I haven't seen her for a couple years, but I'd know her style anywhere.

"Opal." The smile that bends my mouth is immediate and genuine.

"Bennie!" She lunges for me, wrapping her arms around me and squeezing to the point where I fear for my life. Opal Allen, my grade school friend, pulls back to meet my eyes. With a twinkle in hers, she declares, "I saw you on the news. Did you know you're famous?"

"Not as famous as you. Thanks for the comics you sent a while back. They're great."

Opal shrugs, rocking on her heels. She pats my shoulder, her gaze intent. "I'm glad you're not dead."

The smile grows. "I'm glad too." I shift on the bed until I'm sitting up more. "What are you doing in Illinois and how did you get here so quickly?"

"We flew out from North Dakota this morning. Primarily, I came to see you, but since I'm here, I've been showing off Blake to basically everyone." Opal turns, her body humming with anticipation.

"'Mr. Sunshine'," I murmur, for the first time noticing the man standing in the doorway, quiet and motionless. His eyes are glued to us, noting every look or smile we share.

"Yep. 'Mr. Sunshine' in the flesh. Isn't he hot?" Opal says huskily, her tone appreciative.

I lift an eyebrow at Blake at the same time he does. "Definitely."

Opal laughs at that; Blake scowls.

Blake steps into the room, his presence not exactly tense but definitely not comfortable. I would call him wary. Sporting ripped jeans, black boots, and a purple 'Skittles' T-shirt, he looks like a perfect match to Opal. His eyes are dark enough to look black in the low light. He nods. "Blake."

I point to myself. "Ben."

"Are you okay, really?" Opal asks quietly, grabbing my hand with both of hers.

"Yes."

Opal studies me, finally releasing my hand after a drawn-out pause. "You'll tell me about her when you're ready."

I flinch. "What?"

"Whoever's put that look in your eyes. You'll tell me about her when you're ready."

I turn my gaze to Blake, but he only shrugs. I meet Opal's eyes. "I will."

"All right, Ben." Opal smooths the lines from my forehead. "We're staying near Chicago for a few days. I'll call before we leave the city. Maybe we can do lunch somewhere?"

"You bet."

Blake reaches over, offering a calloused hand. We shake, and he nods again before moving toward the door.

Opal gives me one last hug. I enfold her frame in my arms, missing my friend even as she stands before me. It's been too long. I tell her that. Out of every friend I've had through the years, she is the best one I've had. She was a terror when we were younger, and we didn't even get to be friends all that long before she was sent to a different foster home in a new area. Even as she told outrageous tales even I knew to not believe and seemed to *want* to get into trouble, Opal was authentic.

"I know." Opal steps back. "Let's make more of an effort to see each other, all right?"

"Want to do some traveling?" I halfway joke.

Blake's eyes shoot to me.

"Maybe," Opal answers slowly. "You're not thinking Australia, are you?"

"No." I frown. "Why?"

"No reason. Okay, Blake, let's get some food. 'Bye, Ben, love you!" Opal pulls her boyfriend from the room.

It takes a couple minutes after Opal and Blake leave to get my head straight. I'm flooded with thoughts of Avery. I inhale and exhale slowly, suddenly nervous. It isn't long before I'm flinging off the sheet and tugging on a pair of athletic shorts under the hospital gown I was told I had to wear. Rolling my IV stand with me, I cross the room and enter the hallway.

A nurse stops on her way past, looking harried. "Can I help you?"

"I want to check on...my friend." Calling Avery a friend doesn't feel right, but nothing else does either. What is she to me? For a moment, she was my world, the center of my focus.

"You should be in bed," she scolds.

"I won't be long."

She doesn't budge.

"She's all alone in there. Please. I want to make sure she's okay," I beseech earnestly.

Expression softening, the nurse nods once. "Make it quick."

The door is open a crack and I knock before carefully pushing it the rest of the way open. My socks make a shuffling sound as I move toward the bed. "Avery?"

She slowly sits up and turns her head, silently watching me approach. Her face is clean, her freckles more noticeable than ever. The few scratches Avery has aren't deep and shouldn't scar. She has a similar IV bag attached to a tube with a needle in her hand. I almost passed out when they put the needle in the back of my hand and blood spurted out. I bet Avery took the whole thing much better than I did.

"Hi, Ben."

Her hair softly waves about her shoulders. She looks small, and young, and hesitant. I want to tell her I'm done with hiding what I feel. I want to tell her a lot of things I have no right voicing. There's something between us. There could be more. Yet, we're at a standstill. Avery's going in one direction with her life and I'm going in another.

I stop beside the bed. "Hi."

We meet each other's gaze and look away at the same time. Neither one of us seems to know what to say.

"How are you doing?" I ask, gripping the bedrail in an effort to steady my limbs. I feel shaky and hot and cold.

"Good." Avery picks at the blanket covering her legs. "Tired. You?"

"Same." I straighten and look toward the door. "I should let you re—"

"Please stay."

I swing my eyes to Avery.

"For a little while." She scoots to the side, patting the empty space beside her. Avery waits expectantly.

I climb into the bed, the side of my body pressed to hers. She smells good, and her being close to me sets my skin on fire with tantalizing images of what we shared in the forest. More than that, is the sensation of balance, rightness. I don't want to be anywhere but where I am.

Avery turns on the television, finds a random show, and rests her head on my shoulder. I let my eyes close, listening to the faint drone of the television.

"Would it sound weird if I said I kind of miss being lost?" she asks quietly.

"I'm not sure," I reply slowly. I turn my head until we're at eye level. "What do you miss about it?"

Avery shrugs. "I don't really know. Maybe because even though we didn't know what was going to happen to us and it was terrifying at some points, it was simple. We survived. That's all we had to focus on. Everything is complicated again now."

"Reality generally is."

"I know." She settles back against the pillow and shuts her eyes. "But I wish it wasn't."

I mimic her action, getting drowsier by the minute.

"Everything seems smaller, congested. Less important, even."

I agree. It does.

"Did you tell Duke?" she asks.

"Did you?" I counter.

Avery sighs. "No. I can't, not yet."

"When?"

"I don't know if I can, Ben." She sounds defeated.

"Avery."

She stills at the sound of my voice.

"If you don't tell him, you'll regret it. Often, the biggest regrets we have are the words we don't speak." I smile at the ceiling. "You can use that one, free of charge."

Avery snorts and laughs softly. "You're right, you know."

"I know." Because I'm living it. I haven't told her how much I admire her, or how talented she is, or how her never giving up when we were lost in the national forest made me stronger. I haven't told her that the thought of not seeing her on a daily basis puts a peculiar tightening sensation in my chest, or that I get anxious when I think of my future and know she won't be a part of it.

"Did you tell him?" she asks again after a couple minutes.

My pulse hikes. "I'm meeting with Duke tomorrow."

Avery lets out a ragged breath. "You're really doing it."

"I'm really doing it."

"It will be good for you," she says firmly after a lengthy pause.

I study the wall across the room, knowing she does the same.

"It's so noisy here...and busy," Avery says softly.

"I know. It doesn't feel right to have all these walls either." I gesture toward the ceiling. "Or that."

We turn our heads at the same time and lock eyes, our lips within kissing distance.

"Do you know where you'll go?"

"Alabama." Even as I answer, the beat of my heart quickens with something akin to anxiety.

She gives me a quizzical look. "What's in Alabama?"

"I don't know, and that's what I want. I'm going to all fifty states, starting with Alabama."

"Why is that your first stop?"

"If you alphabetize the states, it's the first one."

Avery laughs. "You're silly."

"Silly and alive, exactly how I want to be." My eyelids close, and I sink farther into the bed. "You're going to be okay, Avery. I know it." "Sure. But will you?"

I focus on my breathing, in and out, over and over. At the start of this, Avery symbolized everything I detested. Now? I think of her and I'm proud of the person she is. I truly believe she can do anything. I am in awe of her, again and again. Can I really leave her? Do I even want to?

"I will be," I reply evenly.

"I'm sorry for everything I did that hurt you," Avery says sleepily. She finds my hand, locking our fingers.

"I'm sorry too. I should have been better to you," I tell her, gently squeezing her fingers.

"It will be good for you, but not me," comes out in a whisper that about breaks my heart.

I turn my head, my eyes tracing the lines of her profile. Avery's eyes are closed, and as I watch, her breathing steadies. With a stilted breath, I shift until my forehead rests on her temple. I shut my eyes, falling asleep to the sound of her soft breathing.

AVERY

After I take a steaming hot bath that I stay in until the water turns cold, I dress in a long-sleeved pajama top and pants and wander around my apartment. We've been back in Chicago for five days. Everything seems unreal.

I am unable to eat or focus on anything. Sleep evades me. Brown eyes haunt me. For the first time in quite a while, I am lonely, but not for just anyone. I miss Ben. I spent every minute of multiple days with him. I slept beside him. I heard his voice so often that now I swear the echo of it hums through my mind.

I grab my cell phone with shaking fingers and bring up Ben's name and number, and I stare. He's a phone call away, and also a whole world. Duke apologized profusely and gave us each two weeks of paid time off, along with a therapist's phone number in case we needed to talk to someone. I told him all of that wasn't necessary, but he insisted.

I want to be busy so I don't have time to think. About who I recently was, and how to get back to who I used to be before my mother's death. I found the me I know and like in the Illinois wilderness; I want her to stay.

I thought meeting my father would be worth anything, but nothing is worth the loss of trueness to oneself. I'm scared to tell him who I am, even while knowing that if Duke can't accept me as I am, then he doesn't deserve to know me.

Ben is right; I have to tell Duke. The whole reason for me to adopt the polished Avery Scottam persona and relocate to a city that's bigger than any of my small-town dreams was to impress my dad. But it was all a lie—a lie I can no longer live.

I set down the phone and grab a blanket off the back of the couch. Eyes trained on the fireplace with no fire, I think of Ben's parting words to me when we left the hospital after our mandated twenty-four stay for observation. He didn't seem unfriendly, but Ben was distant. He looked torn. I know the feeling well.

Ben said to me: "If I had the chance to do it all over again, I'd want it to be exactly the same."

I didn't know how to take his words at first; I nodded and got in the cab that would take me to my apartment, desolate over the end of something that never really was. I've thought of them at least ten times a day since. I understand now. He does not regret me. He is grateful for the time we spent together.

Tears sting my eyes.

Duke is hosting a going-away party for Ben next week. I feel sick at the thought of Ben leaving and having no idea when he'll be back, or if he will. More than that, I wish him the best, even if it leaves me hurting. Because, really, how can I be sad that he's happy? That would be selfish, and although I've seemed exactly that at times, where Ben is concerned, I cannot be. Not now. We made no promises to each other. And yet...we did. Without words, but we did. We were a team. Partners. Friends. Lovers for a moment that felt blissful and infinite.

A tear trails down my cheek, and I hastily wipe it away when the doorbell rings.

My first thought is that it's Ben, and my heart races with nerves and anticipation. Reality crashes down on me as I cross the room, and right before I open the door, I know it won't be him. I also don't expect it to be Duke. Cologne, faint and expensive-smelling, touches my senses. I stare at his broad and symmetrical features, searching his face for traces of me, searching for the missing parts that make me who I am. His face is set in stone, a piece of paper crumpled in his large hand.

"Hello," I greet carefully.

Wordlessly, his arm shoots forward, the hand holding the paper halting directly before my nose.

I don't look at the paper, my gaze held by furious blue eyes. My throat drops to my stomach, making it hard to produce words. They come out ragged and shaken. "What is it?"

Other than a muscle jumping in his jaw, Duke doesn't move, and he doesn't respond.

I slowly reach up and tug the paper from his strong grip. My hand drops to my side. I don't even glance toward the paper. I already know what it is: one of the slogans I pitched with credit given to my mother. Somehow, Duke found it, or someone showed it to him. My thoughts crisscross to Ben, wondering if he would do such a thing. Maybe anything I thought he felt for me was a lie, and this whole thing has been a setup to get back at me, and this is the grand finale in his "Get Back at Avery" quest. I would deserve it.

And yet, I don't believe that.

What we shared, although brief, was true.

"Scottam isn't that common of a last name," he begins quietly. "I admit, when I saw it listed on your resume, it caught my attention. I thought it was a coincidence; I should have known better. There aren't a lot of those where I'm concerned."

My breathing picks up, short and shallow. Tingles of unease erupt along my skin. He knows I'm his daughter and he's not happy about it. I should have expected it, and maybe that's why it hurts so much—because I did. I don't know the details of the relationship between my mom and dad. I know they were together at some point. I know she didn't want me to know him, and I know that he's never been a part of my life. Whether or not that was by choice is a question I can't answer. My mouth trembles and I press my lips together in an attempt to hide it.

He looms above me, larger than the doorway. "Who are you? What game are you playing at?"

"Game?" I blink. "I'm not—"

Duke brushes past me, entering the apartment. "Where is she? Did she put you up to this?"

He strides the length of the apartment, opening and closing doors, looking for a person he'll never find. That rips a sob from me. I've done the same. Even knowing she's gone, I've still looked for my mom in rooms. The heart can't always accept what the mind already knows. Duke calls out for my mom, the sound of her name like a fresh slice through my heart, and he reappears before me, looking agitated.

"She's not here."

I shake my head.

"Is she your mother? You look like her. I don't know why I didn't see it sooner," he spits out, this detail seeming to infuriate him more. Duke slams his fists to his hips and glares at me. "Are you doing this for money? Is that it? I wasn't good enough for her then, but now that I have money, I am?"

Silent tears stream down my cheeks. I look at my father, my vision blurring as I try to make sense of his words.

"Say something!"

I flinch.

Duke watches me. In a contemplative tone, he questions softly, "Who are you? What is your connection to Cecily Scottam?"

"I'm—she's—" I gesture helplessly, my throat closing around another sob. I hold myself, wishing my arms were my mother's.

The paper falls from my hand, Duke's gaze following it before lifting to me. His skin pales, the harshness falling away to nothing. Slackness takes over his face and Duke stumbles back a couple steps, as if he's physically hit with overwhelming emotion. He holds his head and spins toward the door, bumping into the doorway as he hurries from the apartment.

I don't understand what's going on. Duke Renner looks as if his heart was ripped from his body. Numb, I follow, finding Duke sitting on the floor to the left of my front door, his head resting on the wall. Pain, deep and undeniable, holds his features hostage. I sink to the floor beside him, looking at the wall across the hallway.

"She's dead," he says. It isn't a question, the words as hollow as the hole in my chest.

"Yes," I whisper.

It's a long moment before Duke speaks again. "How?"

"Cancer."

His eyelids close; he takes a shuddering breath. "How long ago?"

I sniffle. "Almost a year."

"You're her daughter."

Again, it isn't a question, but I answer it anyway. "Yes."

I wait for Duke to ask who my father is, but he doesn't.

"I was married once."

"I know. Ben told me."

"It didn't last long. It wasn't the right person. I married someone to try to replace another, and it didn't work. She—your mother—couldn't be replaced." Duke turns his head toward me, his eyes stark with longing and sorrow.

"What…what happened?"

He looks forward. "Do you want her version, or mine?"

"I never got any version, so…both would be nice."

A faint smile lines his face. "She would tell you I wasn't mature enough, and much too selfish, to be a husband, that I was more worried about getting ahead in life than having an actual life." Duke pauses. "She would be right, to a point."

"What's your version?"

He shrugs one broad shoulder. "I asked Cecily to marry me; she said no. My pride was too strong to let me try to change her mind. I left, and I never saw her again. It didn't make me think of her any less. There have been times, more than I care to admit, that I wanted to look her up, but I never let myself give in. I'm stupidly stubborn that way. I've always wondered about her, where life took her, what she became, if I'd see her again."

Duke faces me, his knee touching mine. "Did she have a good life?"

The enormity of the situation blasts into me, making me weak with emotion. I'm sitting with my father, having a conversation about my mother. It makes it hard to not weep.

I give a wobbly smile. "She did. She laughed a lot; she was happy… even—even at the end, she was still smiling."

His eyes flicker. "She had a good husband? Your dad is a good man?"

"I think he is," I answer after a brief pause.

Duke exhales slowly. "Good. That's good."

I set my hand on his knee, holding his gaze, and emphasizing each word slowly, tell him, "I think you're a good man."

Confusion filters through his eyes before Duke goes unusually still. He looks at me as if he's seeing me for the first time, and I guess in a way, he is. I refuse to look away from his face as he processes what I said, and what it means. He studies me for endless moments. Duke gives his head the barest of shakes. His eyes trail over my features again and again, looking for something. I think, after a time, he finds it.

Duke straightens his back, blinking at me.

"Did you know about me?" I ask, my gaze finally dropping to where my hand still rests on his knee. I start to move my hand away and Duke grasps it in his, tightly squeezing it.

"Are you…you're mine?"

I meet his eyes, catching glimpses of me that I hadn't been able to see before. I have his mouth, and the shape of his eyes. "We can do bloodwork to verify it, but my mom told me…before she died…yes, I'm your daughter."

He then does something I will never forget. He lets out a choked sound, blindly reaching for me to gather me in his strong arms, and he softly cries. A tear drops to my cheek. I close my eyes, relishing in the feel of my father's arms around me for the first time as *my father*. My first dad-daughter hug, and at the age of twenty-five. I smile, both sad and happy.

"I didn't know. She didn't tell me. Cecily, why didn't you tell me?" he whispers against my head, hardening his hold on me.

My heart fills, and breaks. I hug my father, crying for my mom, and my dad, and everything I lost, and everything that could have been. I cry for the family I never had, and for the one I lost when my mom died. I also cry for the one I now have, with this man, my father, but with relief, with a feeling of peace. I wish I could have had my parents at the same time, instead of losing one to find another. It's a complex mix of pain and elation.

22

AVERY

"Do you know why she wouldn't have told you about me?" I ask as we sit at the high table in the dining nook beside the kitchen. The wall is made up of windows, showing a great view of the busy street, and beyond that, the river. Sunshine streams into the room, highlighting the side of Duke's face. Two cups of coffee sit before us, untouched.

Red-rimmed eyes settle on my face, raw emotion in them. "The same reason she didn't say yes when I asked her to marry me. She thought she knew me better than I knew myself, and I guess maybe she did." Duke looks at the palms of his hands, closing them and opening them.

"She didn't want to feel like a burden, and over time, I might have begun to look at her and you that way. I wanted to make something of myself and nothing I did was ever good enough. Every time I reached a goal, there was another to overcome. I had to continue to succeed."

He looks at me. "And she wanted the best for you. It isn't something I care to admit, but she probably did the right thing. I wouldn't have been the best, not then. But she also didn't have to do it on her own." Duke sighs and shakes his head. "I wish she would have told me."

"Mom was stubborn," I say with a smile. Using the past tense to describe the spark that was my mom's life seems wrong. Yes, she's gone, but she also lives in my heart, always. "And fierce. Independent."

"Bullheaded," Duke adds, half of his mouth lifting.

"That too."

We share a smile.

I state simply, "She was the best."

Pain fills Duke's eyes and he turns his face to the scene outside the window. "Definitely that."

"How did you see the paper?" The crumpled-up paper with the statement 'Don't ever give up on you' and Cecily Scottam's name.

"I was at the office, getting things ready for when Ben's gone, and I found it in a pile of material Ben said we should consider selling to one of our greeting card companies."

Ben. I'll see him in a handful of days and after that? Will I ever see him again? And if I don't, am I okay with that? I look down, locking my fingers in my lap. No. I'm not. I can't make him stay and I can't make him feel bad about going. Is this how my mother felt, when she let Duke go?

"She used to tell me that, you know."

I look up. Another piece of the past has been put in its place. "Did she?"

Duke nods, sadness claiming his eyes and thinning his mouth. "Cecily pushed me away, but she also pushed me to better myself."

There is so much I want to ask. I wonder how long they knew one another; I wonder how they were able to let go of each other. I wonder how my mom could give up that kind of love. And I see her, clear and bright, smiling inside my head as she says, "I didn't give up anything. There was no sacrifice, not for you."

I briefly close my eyes, taking a deep breath. Everything I knew growing up wasn't quite right; my childhood was filled with gaps where another person should be. Two people made me, but I only knew one. I was split in half, but my mom tried her mightiest to make me feel whole.

I am okay—or, at least, I will be, I whisper to her from the recesses of my mind.

"What really happened..." Duke begins slowly. "With you and Ben when you were lost?"

I stare at the table, my shoulders lifting and lowering with each breath I take. I finally look up, holding my father's curious and somewhat wary gaze. "We saved each other."

His eyes narrow. "That's it?"

"That's it." That's so not it, but I'm not sharing more. It's personal.

After a strained minute, Duke nods. "Will you stay at Sanders and Sisters?"

I search my father's face, seeing only sincerity. "Would you like it if I did?"

"Yes," he answers right away. "I would."

I start to tell him I'll stay, but I hesitate. Something holds me back from making that kind of commitment. Not even sure why, I say to Duke, "I don't know."

Duke's shoulders drop. "I just got you."

I touch his shoulder. "Even if I don't stay there, I'll stay a part of your life—if you want me to be."

"You *will* be a part of my life," he states firmly. "You are. You're my daughter."

My throat closes around another set of tears, but these are good ones.

At the sight of my tears, Duke stands and enfolds me in his arms once more. Serenity comes with the embrace. I have a father.

"I'm never letting you go, Avery. I promise you that," he quietly vows. "You're aren't getting rid of me. I'm here, to stay."

I burrow my face in the crook between his shoulder and neck, hugging my dad with all my strength. I have years of hugs to stock up on. Years of stories to tell, memories to make, and laughter to share.

I grew up in Montana and that was my home. But now, here, in my dad's arms, I also feel home. Mingling with the scent of my dad's cologne is a softer, sweeter scent, like a hello and goodbye from my mom came through an unopened window. Peacefulness descends, and I can breathe a little easier.

BEN

Oblivious to my presence, my coworkers interact with one another as I keep company with the shadows. The party is outside, on the spacious second floor deck of Duke's studio apartment. Strings of lights cover the railing, soft music playing from the stereo system that costs more than I make in months. I'm not generally antisocial, but it's interesting to watch the people I work with laugh and talk with one another, completely at ease and having fun. These people are my friends; some I consider close to family. It will be strange not seeing them almost every day. This is a bittersweet event and I'm the guest of honor.

The person I have yet to see is Avery; she's the one I want to see the most.

I run a hand across my face, disrupting the new black glasses I purchased on my return. Blinking my eyes into focus, I straighten from the wall, my heart slamming into the barriers around it as my gaze latches on to a golden-haired beauty dressed in creamy lace that molds to her breasts and flares from her hips in a tantalizing dance of seduction. The demureness of her dress contrasting with the curves of her body makes my throat dry and puts an ache in my groin. She didn't straighten her hair, letting it fall naturally around her bare shoulders in waves. The world fades, sounds mute, and it's only Avery and me when she turns and notices me. Funny, no one else did, but she sees me right away. Avery smiles and the sky tips.

I try to breathe and find I can't, and I think, air is overrated. Her eyes shine like golden pools as she walks toward me. Vivid and inimitable, Avery lives in the light that makes up the sun. The sound of voices picks up, the music seems to blare, it all raging through my head in a cacophony of heightened awareness. Avery looks happy, at ease in a way she hadn't before we got lost together.

I meet her in the middle of the deck, fisting my hands to keep from threading my fingers through her hair and kissing the hell out of her luscious mouth. I can see her freckles, the sight of the adorable markings tipping my mouth up at the corners. I think she knows who she is now, and she is one bad-ass, sweet, complex, compelling, silly, smart, brave woman. She's everything.

"Hello, Avery." My voice is uneven and raspy.

"Hello, Ben," Avery replies, her features soft, welcoming.

One more touch, a part of me begs. Just one more touch and I can let her go. It's a lie, but I've told it to myself daily since we came back from Shawnee National Forest. I stayed away after the hospital, thinking it was best for her if we didn't interact. I was going to cut the ties, make a clean break, and whatever other cliché one can think up to explain keeping their distance from something they want and shouldn't. .

I'm looking at the woman who uprooted my life and all I can think about is how glad I am that she did.

"This is a nice party," she continues.

"Is it?" I haven't participated; I don't know if it is or isn't.

Avery laughs. "It is."

I nod. "Good. I'm glad."

Avery steps closer, her voice low when she tells me, "You don't have to worry about me being pregnant. I got my period."

Relief hits me, but there's something else that comes with it, something faint, and maybe a little sad. Something I wasn't expecting. I look into golden eyes, all shutters taken down from my heart. *One day. I can see that with you one day.*

"Good," I say with a parched throat. "That's good."

She gives me a quizzical look. "Are you feeling okay?"

"No," I say abruptly.

"What's wrong?" Avery steps closer, bringing that citrus scent I love with her.

"I, uh..." I rub the back of my neck. It's best to get it all out there. That way, there can be no regrets from my end. "The thing is, I..."

A hand grabs my biceps, unusually hard, and I look into glacial eyes. "Ben," is all Duke says, my name on his lips sounding like a death sentence.

My stomach plummets to my feet.

He knows.

"Hey, Duke." I look at where his fingers are squeezing my arm, the knuckles of his fingers tight. I lift my gaze back to his, trying not to flinch at the look in his eyes. "Thanks for the party."

"Tell me you aren't looking at my daughter the way I think you are," comes out in growl.

Now is not the time to be a smart-ass, and yet I ask, "What way would that be?"

Duke's jaw goes taut. "The way *I* look at a woman."

"Dad," Avery moans. "Please don't turn into an overprotective, control-freak."

"You're just a child!"

"I'm twenty-five!"

He swings around to face his daughter, jabbing a finger of his free hand at her. "I just got you. As far as I'm concerned, you're still a baby!"

"Duke, come on," I try to reason, stunned by this fatherly side I didn't think he had. "I think you're looking into the situation way more than is warranted."

Duke turns hard eyes on me. "What situation?"

"No situation," I hasten to assure him. "It's a figure of speech."

"I asked you what happened in the forest," he says to Avery. "You said nothing."

Avery's face goes red. "I didn't say that; I said we saved each other."

In spite of my arm being slowly amputated by Duke's grip, my body warms at Avery's words. I meet her eyes, and she smiles weakly.

"You implied that nothing happened!"

"Dad, stop already," she moans, sounding exactly as an exasperated daughter should.

"Is everything all right over here?" Carrie Marx asks, appearing next to us, her green eyes moving from one face to the next. She's a phenomenal artist and savvy with social media, her talents taking the company to places it otherwise wouldn't go without her.

"Duke's giving me a proper goodbye, right, Duke?" I jerk my arm in an attempt to dislodge his grip and he finally releases me.

Duke smooths a hand over his black and silver hair. "Right."

Carrie tugs at the end of her braided red hair, looking unconvinced. "Well, if you're done, maybe we can get back to having a party—or start having one." She lifts her eyebrows.

I look around, noting all eyes are on us. It's a small group, and we're pretty close. A kink in the balance and everyone is affected. Duke's present mood has those around him uneasy. Even with being a hard-ass to the end, he's generally a level-headed individual.

"You're fired," he tells me.

I said generally.

"I'm not an employee of yours anymore, remember?" I cross my arms and meet my former boss's lethal gaze. He's being an ass. Yes, he just learned that Avery is his daughter. She's also an adult. "I gave my notice as soon as we got back."

"Did you?"

I gesture around us. "This is my going-away party."

Duke rubs his jaw. "Hmm."

I roll my eyes. "That you're hosting."

"Good." He drops his hand. "Then I won't have to fire you."

I make a sound of disbelief, shaking my head at Duke's behavior. "What exactly are you so pissed about?"

As far as I know, he doesn't know what went on between us. Then again, maybe that's why he's so pissed—because he doesn't know.

He opens his mouth, looking ready to tear me a new one, and then he stops. In a bemused tone, Duke tells me, "None of your damn business."

"This is supposed to be a goodbye party for Ben," Avery says softly, taking her dad's hand to tug him around to face her. "Can we try to make it a good one?"

Duke drops his gaze. "Avery, I—"

"Let's talk about it later—or not at all," she adds, glancing at me.

"But—"

"Please." Avery widens her eyes, using one of her innocent looks that used to make my teeth clench and had all the other men like putty in her hands.

It works.

Duke nods brusquely, sending one last glare my way before striding toward the outside bar, complete with a hired bartender.

Avery gives me an apologetic look when our eyes meet, but I can't even be upset. She is who she is, and I want her exactly as she is. I will never go back to pretending I don't care for her. With pressure in my chest and a weird emotion I can't name swirling through me, I give her a small smile and she returns it.

23
BEN

"What's up with him?" Carrie asks, following Duke with her eyes.

Avery takes a deep breath and blurts, "He found out I'm his daughter and he's having a difficult time adjusting."

The redhead blinks and then slowly nods. "Oh. Well, okay then. Understandable. You'll have to explain that all to me one day."

Avery laughs softly. "I will certainly try."

Carrie tilts her head and studies Avery. "You seem...different."

"Oh?" Avery's eyes shoot to mine. "How so?"

"I don't know, but you do. More carefree, maybe? I'm not sure." She shakes her head and looks at me. "It's still hard to believe that you two were lost out there for days. That must have been scary."

I look at Avery, not saying anything. I haven't said much about our experience to anyone; I doubt she has either. However terrifying it was at times, it was ours. We shared it. And it turned out to be something special. Life-altering.

"What happened to the men who harassed you?" Carrie continues.

My eyes don't move from Avery's face. "We had to give the police a statement about what happened. The men are facing criminal charges and jail time, probably large fines too."

Carrie shakes her head. "That's so crazy. I'm glad you're both okay."

Out of everything we faced, the scariest moment was when she was almost taken. Even now, my heart squeezes, remembering the look on her face—as if half of her wondered if I'd be able to save her. I swallow thickly and look down. *She's safe*, I remind myself. *She's here, and she's safe.*

Again, I fight the need to take her in my arms. Sweat breaks out on my skin and I swipe a hand over my damp forehead.

"It's so weird how lost you guys got. You ended up on private land, right? Completely out of the designated area," Carrie muses.

"It was the crows," Avery comments.

Carrie blinks. "Crows?"

"Yes." Avery nods and offers no further information.

I fight a grin and shove my hands in my pockets, enjoying the flummoxed look on our coworker's face.

"It isn't hard to believe that you were the first one back," Avery says after a pause.

Carrie and Anne found the lodge in a couple hours. It's no wonder; Carrie is a natural athlete who enjoys hiking, kayaking, hunting, and any other thing you can think of that has to do with outside.

"Trust me, it wasn't easy. Anne whined the whole time. The only reason she made any effort to get back was because she knew she wouldn't get her phone until she did."

I spot Anne Dobson, dressed in her usual black clothing, standing alone near the railing, texting on her cell phone.

"It looks like Nate and Juan mended their relationship," Avery states, continually glancing at me as she provides small talk to cover up my sudden muteness.

Although it was nothing like what happened with Avery and me, Nate Fields and Juan Martinez had a small mishap on the mountains. A snake found them, or they found a snake. Either way, it didn't end in the best of ways.

"Sucking the venom from someone's butt can do that to you, I guess." Carrie clears her throat to keep a laugh inside.

"I guess the retreat worked then, didn't it? We're all better for it. Only a couple of us had bad experiences. Well worth the pain." Derision clings to my words.

No one says anything for a dozen heartbeats.

"Duke said he recommended that you both—or any of us if we like—speak with a counselor in case there is any post-traumatic stress." Carrie's eyes are on me.

"Do you wish it hadn't happened?" Avery asks softly, ignoring Carrie.

I take in the image she portrays, hope and doubt clashing in her eyes, and I step closer.

"I'll just…" Carrie jabs a thumb over her shoulder and hastily exits our sides.

"No," I tell her in a low voice, reaching up to touch a lock of Avery's hair. It slides through my fingers, and I move another step toward her, until our faces are side by side, our fronts inches apart.

I turn my head the slightest amount to the side and rub my cheek against her hair. A small sound leaves Avery, her hands coming to rest on my arms. Her palms tremble against my skin. I squeeze my eyes shut, wanting her with me today, and tomorrow, and forever.

I jerk back at the direction of my thoughts, staring down at Avery. I breathe raggedly, the words stilted when I say, "Come with me."

"Hey, Ben! Are you going to actually tell anyone goodbye tonight, or just hang out in a corner with Avery?" Bob Bellamy calls from across the deck, grinning and saluting us with a beer.

"Not that we blame you," Nate adds, wiggling his thick eyebrows.

I meet Avery's gaze, drinking in the flummoxed look that's taken over her features, the way her chest moves fast with her breaths. I say it again, with more feeling and firmness. "Come with me."

"Calling Ben Stitzer, now a former employee of Sanders and Sisters, to the center of the deck for unforgettable farewell shenanigans," Juan shouts, his accented voice larger than his five-foot-five frame.

Nate chants my name, gaining an irritated look from me. The rest of the guys join in, until all I hear is the drone of "Ben." When I don't join them fast enough, they come to me, pulling me toward the bar. Even Mike Schooner, the quiet one out of the Sanders and Sisters' employees, gets into it, thumping me on the back.

I look at him, surprised by his behavior. He smiles and shrugs. The guy rarely speaks, let alone partakes in anything involving a group. I guess we've all changed since the Extreme Retreat experience. And, I suppose, for the better. Some of my resentment toward Duke's unconventional actions fades, with stress on the word "some."

"Drink up, buttercup," Nate urges, shoving a beer in my face.

"I'm not really in the drinking mood."

"Fuck that shit," is Nate's response, his hold on the beer never wavering. He's got a body like a tank and a personality to match. Brutish and massive.

"Your mission tonight is to get completely shit-faced. No exceptions," Bob states, a stern look on his bearded face. His spiked hair sticks up at least four inches from his head, reminding me of a porcupine.

"To the point where you're either puking sick, or so hungover in the morning that you'll vow to never, ever drink again." Juan clinks his beer bottle to Nate's.

With a sigh, I grab the beer and take a swig of it. The guys cheer. I shake my head at their antics, but there's a smile on my lips.

I spend the next couple of hours being berated into drinking, but whenever I can, I look for Avery. She talks with Carrie and Anne, meeting my gaze more times than I can count. With a one-way ticket, I leave for Alabama in a few, short days.

She didn't answer me.

I asked her to come with me and she didn't answer.

"Let's do shots," Carrie exclaims, her arm shooting up, a bottle of cinnamon whiskey in her hand. She dances in a circle, laughing as those nearest her whistle and clap. Before long, Bob is dancing with her, his spikes never once budging. Bob's always had a thing for Carrie. I never could figure out if it was reciprocated, which made me think it wasn't. The way she's looking at him now tells me something may have changed.

"Miss." The bartender hurries from around the bar, reaching for the bottle. His scholarly face looks panicked and completely out of place for his line of work. Stereotypes and all that. "Miss, please, let me pour that for you."

Carrie spins around to face the bartender, her eyes dancing. "You have to dance with me first."

The bartender's hands fall to his sides. "But, I…"

"It's fine, Lawrence, the bottle's on me," Duke tells the man, clapping him on the shoulder with enough exuberance to send him stumbling forward a couple feet.

Duke's gaze turns to me, the message clear: *None for you though.*

Hands on my hips, I look to the stars. God help me if Avery and I do end up together. Duke will hold a grudge against me for eternity.

My eyes find Avery, a weird calmness and determination descending, and my response to Duke is just as clear: *I don't give a shit.*

He scowls at me, snagging the bottle of liquor from Carrie and taking a few large swallows before giving it back.

"This song is for you, Ben and Avery," Nate hollers, whooping as "Hungry Like the Wolf" starts.

Carrie grabs my wrist and pulls, motioning for Avery to join us. "Come on, guys, don't just stand around! It's time to have fun." She leaves us to corral the others. "That means everyone here!"

"This really isn't something I can dance to," Avery tells me.

"What if I dance with you?"

She narrows her eyes. "You can dance?"

I lift my eyebrows, adapting a serious expression. "I don't want to alarm you, but…prepare to be amazed."

Avery grins and crosses her arms. "I'm waiting."

"Next song," I promise.

It's my luck that the next song to come on is by Justin Bieber. I groan; Avery laughs.

She cups her mouth and shouts, "Show me your moves!" To the delight of the Sanders and Sisters' employees, I moonwalk across the deck. I stop before I hit the railing and look at Avery. "Well?"

She taps her chin and shrugs, calling, "Not bad. Got anything else?"

I nod to her. "You first."

A mischievous glint enters her eyes just before Avery leaps into the air, does some contortionist move, and lands facing me, out of breath and with a wide grin on her face. After that, everyone gets involved, doing some crazy move in an attempt to outshine the previous participant. Mike has us all beat with his breakdance moves. There are laughs, and even more laughs, when Nate splits his pants.

"That's why dudes don't wear skinny pants, man," Juan informs him, chortling around his words.

"Suck my—"

Juan puts his hand out. "Just stop right there. There will be no sucking of any of your extremities. Been there, done that already. Never a-fucking-gain." He shudders and chugs half a bottle of beer as if he needs to erase the memory from his mind.

Anne, who hasn't said or done much besides interact with her phone, lowers it and looks at Juan. She laughs, loud and hard, as if she's surprised to find anything around her funny.

We all stare.

Anne doesn't laugh, or smile, or really talk at all. Juan blinks at her, and he laughs with her, his laughter growing in volume. Anne actually puts her phone in her pocket, a miracle in itself, and moves to stand by Juan.

More beers are drank; more songs play. Duke even removes the stick up his ass long enough to do a group slow dance and flourishing rendition of "Never Tear Us Apart" by INXS. This is the comradery I'll miss. All of us, together, having fun. I look at Avery standing across from me, her arms around Carrie and Mike. Her face is flushed, her eyes shining, and damn if she doesn't make my heart skip a beat.

I'll miss her the most.

* * * *

Ed Sheeran plays next, and as if on cue, the lights dim and the unofficial dance floor clears. Pulled by an invisible force, Avery and I end up face to face. I reach for her, cupping her cheek, running my thumbs across either side of her face. Her eyes close; my throat tightens.

Not caring if Duke decides to kick my ass because of it, I brush my lips along the corners of hers. I capture her mouth with mine when she tips her head back. A backdrop to our powerful emotions, we sway to the music of one Mr. Ed Sheeran. The guy gets it.

I hold her loosely, as if she is glass and able to break. She isn't, I know that, but she is something to treasure. I know that now too.

"I forgive you. I think I forgave you almost as soon as it happened," I say against her cheek, feeling her stiffen in my arms. "I just didn't want to admit it."

Her hand sweeps across my back, compassionate and true. Avery whispers, "I never should have done it, Ben. I will forever be sorry."

"I didn't have to treat you so badly, and I'm sorry. I didn't know, Avery." I pause, the words like lumps in my throat. "I didn't know how to deal with the way I felt. I was stupid, and immature, and…"

Avery pulls back, her eyes lightning, and she shuts me up with a hard kiss that melts my bones. I pull her closer, until the only thing between us is mere clothing that can easily be removed—it won't be, of course, but it could. Reiteration on "easily" and "could". I thread my fingers through her silky hair and kiss her with all the passion in my soul, all the fire in my blood. I kiss her with everything I have.

It isn't until the jeers and catcalls reach our ears that we pull away. The slow song has been replaced by a fast one, and Duke stands nearby, seething.

"Your dad is not doing well with the idea of you and me."

Avery stares at me. "Is there a you and me?"

My pulse picks up; everything but the woman standing before me disappears. "Do you want there to be?"

Large, gold eyes, study me. "Do you? You're leaving, and I don't even know if you're coming back."

"I asked you to come with me," I remind her.

"But what does that mean? Is that all you're asking me, or are you asking me more?" Avery swallows, stepping back. "Do you want me for now, or do you…do you want me forever?"

The music becomes deafening, and my heartbeat along with it. My skin is flushed, wet with sweat, and nausea makes an unwanted appearance. What is she asking me? Seconds tick on and I don't reply. It isn't that I don't have an answer—it's that my answer scares the shit out of me.

Disappointment flitters across her face.

I step forward, not sure how to make her understand something I don't entirely understand. "Avery, I—"

"Avery, come inside with me a moment; there's something I want to show you." Duke puts a hand to his daughter's elbow, coercing her from me. Her eyes haven't left my face. "Can it wait, Dad?"

"It can't. It has to do with your mother."

I shift my gaze to him, staring him down. Duke knows Avery won't say no to that. He's manipulating her.

Duke's face is impassive, but a hint of arrogance is in his bearing.

Seeming torn, Avery shoots me a look full of questions, and lets her dad take her into his swanky living quarters. This version of Avery is another I don't know, and another I know isn't her. Where's the fiery woman? Hell, where's the antagonistic one? I want to tell her to stop trying to be what she thinks everyone wants her to be, and just *be*.

You're never happy in life unless you're you. I found the real Avery in the mountains of Shawnee National Forest. No way should coming back to Chicago be able to take that away—not even her dad should be able to take that away. I have to remind her; I have to be able to be alone with her long enough to get all the words out.

Watching them walk inside feels as if I've already left; I'm already gone. Only they're the ones leaving.

If it comes to me and her dad, Avery will choose him. I expect her to. I want her to, when I think with my head and not my heart—the heart I said I'd have to be stupid to give to Avery. I don't even think I gave it to her; I think I threw it at her. And that's what scares me: I am in love with Avery Scottam. Was I ever not? Even when we're fighting, I feel more alive, more energized, than at any other point in my existence.

I sigh, getting drawn into a conversation about baseball with Bob.

As the night progresses, Duke is never far from Avery, watching her with a faint look of wonder on his face, and wrath each time he catches me near his daughter. I think Duke senses what I feel for Avery; he wants to protect her, but he also doesn't want to lose her, not to me, not now. And Avery just got her dad.

They have years of catching up to do, and endless details to share with each other. They don't know each other that well, and I see the yearning on each of their faces to connect with a link to who they are. Maybe it's unfair of me to ask her to leave him. I finish my beer, turning from the sight of Avery. It is unfair of me.

But if she says yes, I won't look back.

24
BEN

It's close to one in the morning by the time the party breaks up.

I hurry to where Avery is, quiet as she tells Carrie good night. Before she realizes I'm beside her, I touch her arm, causing her to jump. "Avery? Can we go somewhere and talk?"

Shadows cling to her eyes, and they're not all from the night around us. "It's late, Ben. Can we talk tomorrow?"

I move in front of her, blocking the exit. "What did Duke show you?"

Avery shifts her eyes to the side, something like grief hovering over her. There is the faintest crack in her voice when she says, "I'm tired. Please, can we talk another time?"

I step to the side, confused and worried by her behavior. "Yeah. Sure. Have a good night."

Avery nods, her head bowed. As she passes, she trails her fingers down my arm. "Good night, Ben."

I turn as she walks toward the door that leads down the stairs and outside. "Avery."

She pauses, her back to me.

"Remember who you are, not who you think you need to be."

Her shoulders lift as she takes a deep breath, and Avery walks from the studio apartment.

I stare after her long after she's gone before I shift my jaw and go in search of Duke. I storm onto the deck, scanning the premises. The bartender cleaned up quick and left. The only sounds are that of the wind, and the people and cars below. My hands open and close at my sides, ready to punch something. Preferably Duke Renner. I can do that. He isn't my boss anymore. I scowl when a voice reminds me that he's still Avery's dad.

I rest my elbows on the railing and stare at the river, its depths dark and deep as it slowly undulates.

His words reach me first, alerting me to his presence. "Do you really think you're worthy of her?"

I glance at Duke, a cool breeze ruffling my hair. "What did you say to her?"

His jaw hardens. "Answer with care. If you think you're worthy of her, then you're not. If you don't think you are, then you're not."

"So, basically, either way, I'm screwed." I straighten, so over Duke's self-portrayed superiority. Anger vibrates through my words. "What did you say to her?"

Duke grips the railing between his hands, facing the city of lights and people. "As an employee, I've always thought highly of you...but as someone interested in my daughter, that is one *hell no.*"

One corner of my mouth hikes before falling back into a line. "I sort of already got that impression."

"I want what's best for you, Ben, and yes, I hate to see you go. You're great at what you do." Duke turns his head, nailing me with his sparking eyes. "But if it comes down to what's best for you, or Avery, I'm going to look out for my daughter."

I look away. "Are you saying that as a person, or as a dad?"

A low growl can be heard with his words. "Does it matter?"

I turn back to Duke, a muscle bunching in my jaw. "Yeah, it does. As a father, no one is going to be good enough for your daughter. So, I need to know, are you saying that as a person who knows me, or as a father who just learned of his daughter's existence?"

Crevices form around his eyes and mouth. "What do you want from her? You hated Avery a couple weeks ago, and now, what? You want to date her?"

"I don't want to date her."

A hand bunches around the fabric of my shirt and twists, Duke's face inches from mine. "Then what the hell do you want with Avery?"

"I want to..." I look into furious blue eyes and speak from the heart. "I want to marry her."

His grip slackens, his face pales. Duke steps back. A layer of ice surrounds us, quick and deadly. "You must be drunk to say something like that to me."

I feel lost without her, lost in a way I can't stand. Around the fierce beating of my heart, I speak. "I want to marry Avery. Maybe not now, but some day. When I think of what I want to do with the rest of my life, none of it seems right unless she's with me."

Duke examines me as if he thinks he can see my soul if he stares long enough.

I stand straight and proud, my eyes never leaving his. "She thinks she has to be a certain way so you'll be proud of her, so you'll want her. When she first came to Illinois, she was a completely different person than she is now. You have to remember what she was like. She did that for you. Avery thought she had to impress you, and because of that, she made bad choices."

He watches me.

A frustrated sound is ripped from me. "She's losing herself, and if you don't let her live the way she wants, before long, she won't know who she is. Tonight, even, she was different."

"And you think that's with you? That you're what she needs? Maybe you don't know her as well as you think you do."

I jab a finger toward the general direction of the front door. "I know the woman who just walked through that door isn't the Avery I was lost in the woods with."

"What makes you think you know her at all?" Duke asks slowly.

"I was with her in the wilderness," I state with grim firmness. "I know her better than anyone else alive right now."

Neither of us speak as Duke digests my words; there is not even the barest flicker of emotion on his face.

"You're leaving," Duke says after a time, as if to remind me.

"I am."

"You think she wants to go with you."

I shake my head. "I don't know."

"But you want her to go with you."

"I do."

"Why are you leaving?"

"I need a change. I want to explore the world around me."

His shoulders slump, a curious brightness coating his eyes. "I just got her." A note of pleading accompanies Duke's words. "Don't take her away."

I close my eyes and drop my head. "It doesn't matter what I want; I asked her and she never answered me. That's as good as saying no."

"Where are you going?"

"Alabama."

Duke narrows his eyes. "Why Alabama?"

"It seems like a good place to start." I shrug when his scrutinizing look doesn't abate. "I want to see all fifty states."

"When do you leave?"

"August 23rd."

Grimness takes over his face. Duke walks past me, his parting words, "August 23rd can't come soon enough. I hope you enjoyed your going-away party."

"Thanks," I mutter, running a hand across my face. I'm tired, and slightly drunk. Duke Renner, the man I've always looked up to, can't wait until I'm gone, and the person I ache for, is not with me.

AVERY

The first day back to work is a blur.

I walk in a fog, unable to concentrate, forcing smile after smile. Something is missing. Something big. I stop before the closed door to what used to be Ben's office, the office that is now mine. The office I don't deserve. It should still be Ben's and he should be here and he's not and it makes my eyes sting and my throat tight.

Ben and I were supposed to be the creative team here, but we never, or rather, I never, got the grasp of that. I wanted to be better than him, and I was, but the cost wasn't worth it. Funny how that hindsight thing works.

I move on, settling into a chair in one of the rooms and opening a folder that holds important information on Elliot Accessories. I stare at the words, not really seeing them. Nothing about this feels right. The rooms are too small and I feel constricted; I can't get enough air.

"Avery."

I look up from the contract between Sanders and Sisters and the makeup company with which I used parts of my mom's words to cement a deal. Mike looks at me with quizzical blue eyes, his shirt misbuttoned and one side of his hair sticking up while the rest is smoothed down. He reminds me of an absentminded genius scientist, which is pretty spot on. He talks about things I can't even guess at involving space and time and alternate worlds. He's also good with numbers and oversees our account financing and planning, with help from Duke when needed.

Being the owner and main operator, Duke knows all the roles in the agency, delegating duties as he sees fit.

"What are you doing out here?"

I shrug and look around the gray-and-brown-toned room with flourishing green plants and lots of natural light from the many windows. "Just looking over some papers."

"It's the reception area," Mike states in case I forgot.

Anne glares at me from her spot behind the desk, one hand on her cell phone. "She's been out here all morning, and frankly, it's distracting me from my work."

"You're working?" I widen my eyes. "Wow. I'm so sorry. I thought you were on Facebook."

Her phone dings that she has a notification at the exact same time Anne says she isn't on Facebook. She gives me a look and shoves her phone into a desk drawer, snapping it shut. Anne yanks the telephone from the receiver, muttering, "I'm ordering lunch."

"Duke gave you the keys to your new office, right?" Mike asks.

I sit up straighter, eyes on the now closed folder on my lap. "Mm-hmm."

"You know you can use it…right?"

It feels as if Duke gave me the office more because I'm his daughter than because of any talent. That isn't what I want.

What do you want? a voice in my mind asks. It sounds like Ben.

You, I silently answer.

"It's Ben's," I say softly to Mike.

"Ben's gone."

My eyes fly to Mike's. "Not gone-gone, right? Just gone from here?"

"Right." Mike tilts his head, scrutinizing me. "He no longer works here."

I set a hand to my pounding heart. "Oh. Okay. Right. Good."

"Are you okay?" Mike asks.

"Yeah. No. I'm not sure." I shake my head. I feel weird, out of place, almost numb. I made a choice; I have to stick with it. I'm choosing my dad. Leaving with Ben would be taking a chance I can't afford. My mom chose me over Duke; I'm choosing family over love as well. Another voice insists: *But was she glad she made that choice? Was it the right one?*

I look out the nearest window, watching as vehicles speed by.

Why can't I have both?

"If you need to talk…" Mike waits.

"Oh, my God," Anne mutters. "If I wanted office drama, I'd watch TV."

"Anne, shut up." I jump to my feet and stride from the waiting room.

Anne snorts. "What's her problem?"

"Anne, shut up," Mike answers.

I walk down the hallway of framed magazine articles regaling the many successes of Sanders and Sisters. It shows an impressive line of business savviness that made Sanders and Sisters a well-known name, along with Duke Renner. I stop at the door that leads to my new office, pausing with my hand on the doorknob. I step into the room with snowy white walls, feeling Ben's presence.

It's bare of his baseball stuff. The family picture of Ben with his parents and sister is gone as well. I walk to the center of the room with its lone window, high and small behind the desk, and close my eyes. I breathe in, smelling the lingering scent I associate with Ben—fresh soap and man—and I walk briskly to the desk, setting down the folder and taking a seat in the chair.

A rectangular box wrapped in gold foil with a folded piece of white paper beside it greets me, resting perfectly centered on the desk. With fingers that tremble, and dread and anticipation in my heart, I open up the paper. A single sentence takes up the space with bold, black ink.

To the woman I got lost with in order to find myself: live like you never know what's going to happen next—because you don't.

The paper drops from my fingers, confusion and questions putting a wrinkle in my forehead.

Hands shaking, I move for the gold-wrapped item.

A firm knock sounds on the door a second before it opens, revealing my father. I set my trembling hands in my lap. Dressed in a navy-blue suit with a gold tie, he beams at me. "Avery! Just the woman I was looking for. Have lunch with me and a representative from Applebee Coffee?"

"Why?"

Duke blinks at the inquiry. I am not normally one to question anything. "Because we want them to use us for their new advertisement and I request it of you."

"That's fine. I just want to know, why me?"

He looks behind him before stepping into the room. Duke closes the door and stares me down with his icy-blue eyes. "I don't understand what you're asking."

I stand on legs that shake and steady myself by gripping the back of the chair. Ben's parting words the night of the party have been turning around over and over in my head. *Remember who you are.* I am not weak. I am not timid. I am not a pushover. I am strong. I take a deep breath. "Carrie could go, or Bob or Nate. Why do you want *me* to go?"

"Because you're part of my creative team."

"I'm not the only one," I press. "Why me, specifically?"

"Because you're my daughter."

The answer hits me hard, and I take another breath around the sting. "Then the answer is no."

His eyes narrow. "You didn't let me finish."

Mouth dry, I wait.

"But even if you weren't, I'd still want you there. You're beautiful, smart, and charismatic. People naturally gravitate toward you. You have flare, Avery, and you get things done. You make an excellent figurehead for Sanders and Sisters. I want you to be the official face of the organization, and one day, many years in the future, I want you to take it over. When people think of Sanders and Sisters, they'll envision you."

"That…sounds like a lot of power." Duke's words are flattering, but they don't wow me like they would have in the past. His vision is not my vision.

"Yes." His eyes gleam. "It does."

"I don't need that."

Duke steps farther into the room, turning his focus to the cufflinks of his suit jacket. "You might, in time."

"What does that mean?"

His voice is low when he says, "Life disappoints. Sometimes all we have to keep us going is our work."

The words come out before I can halt them, frank and accusing. "You could have fought harder to keep her."

Pain, faint and brief, sweeps across Duke's face. "I could have, but I didn't."

I think of my mom, how she worked hard to make every day wonderful, but always also carried that hint of sadness. I thought it was for me, but now I see that it was for Duke—or maybe it was for all of us. My dad carries it as well. Is that what I want, to live with regret for a person I too easily let go?

"Ben didn't see any of that," I choke out.

He lifts his gaze to me, one dark eyebrow cocked. "Any of what?"

"He didn't see me as some kind of—of trophy, something nice to look at, but that's about all its worth."

Anger flashes across his face. "I'm not saying that at all. You misinterpret my words."

"I don't know what you want from me," I whisper. The hollowness inside stems from that feeling of worthlessness. My mom knew. She knew Duke is the kind of person who has an insatiable drive always pushing them forward. She tried to warn me. "I think you want me to be something I'm not."

"That's not true," Duke cuts in.

"I'm not like Cecily. She wasn't afraid of anything, and she wasn't afraid to be herself." Tears burn my eyes. "I'm afraid all the time."

Duke studies me, cool and efficient. "Take the rest of the week off, Avery. You're not ready to come back."

I look into my dad's eyes and speak my biggest fear. "You're disappointed in me."

"I'm not—" Duke lowers his voice with his next words. "I am not disappointed in you. I could never be disappointed in you. Go home, get some rest. Come back next Monday if you feel up to it."

"And if I don't?" I feel torn in separate directions, and once again, I know what it is to feel like my life is not my own.

Duke runs a hand over his face, looking tired and older than his years. "Go home, Avery."

I snatch Ben's note from the drawer, take the unopened item in the gold wrapping paper, and hurry past my dad, flinging open the door to multiple faces hovering in doorways. I stop, looking from Carrie to Nate to Juan to Bob.

"We were..." Nate ducks back into his office and slams his door, and the others follow sheepishly.

I shake my head and grab my jacket and purse from the closet, not bothering to tell Anne goodbye. Her eyes are glued to something in her lap, and I'm betting it's her cell phone.

It's a mile walk to my place; something I would never consider before our team-building excursion. Too much work, and I'd ruin my hair and makeup. Without hesitating, I turn in the right direction and go, looking straight ahead, tuning out the sights and sounds around me.

I thought it would be easier being here after the truth was out. But then, I never thought I'd have to come back without Ben. I stop as pain pierces my chest. I was scared, and I still am, but Ben is the one thing that doesn't scare me. I would go anywhere with him. I would face anything with him. But here I am, avoiding him. How do I tell him that I want nothing more than to say yes, but I can't because I don't want to fail my father?

The night of Ben's going-away party, Duke showed me a picture of him and my mom together, young and beautiful and in love. I am a part of each of them.

Shaking my head, I pick up the pace, jogging across the street before someone gets pedal happy and smokes me. This city has a high crime rate, something that terrified me when I first moved here. I don't even care anymore. It seems insignificant. Leeches, crows, goats, bears, unknown watery depths and hunters with guns—they're all insignificant. I don't stop moving until I reach my apartment building. I go still, staring at the massive brick structure that's made of vintage brownstone mixed with cutting renovations. I love this place.

A buzzing sound beside me turns my skin clammy. I never saw a single bee in the wilderness, but of course, now I do. I've gone my whole life so far without getting stung. I could be allergic and not even know. I could die. I shift my eyes, trying to find the flying insect before it gets a chance to sting me.

Don't run, I tell myself, because that is exactly what I want to do. *Hold still, and it won't sting you.*

But it lands on my forehead and I freak out, swatting a hand to my head and effectively receiving a stinger to my palm in the process. I scream in surprise, the sound high and short. Chest heaving, I stare at the rapidly growing welt, waiting for the real pain, waiting for my hand to get swollen up to the point where it spreads throughout my body and my throat closes and I can't breathe. I watch until my vision blurs and I see double, but the welt doesn't change, and my throat doesn't close up, and I don't die. And really, it doesn't hurt as much as I thought it would.

I frown. *That's it? This is what I've been afraid of?*

I let out a long breath, drop my hand, look around for any potential witnesses to my small bout of madness, and laugh. That wasn't so bad. Maybe I can stop being scared about the things I don't understand. Another buzzing sound takes over the first, my eyes widen, and I sprint toward the haven of my home. Or not. Being stung once in my lifetime is quite enough. For all I know, the bee could be on a quest for vengeance to honor its now dead bee buddy.

25
BEN

I spend the week pacing my apartment when I should be getting my stuff ready.

I pick up the phone a hundred times with the intention of calling Avery to demand that she talk with me, but I always set it back down without contacting her. I left the ball in her court, and she left it there too. I run my fingers through my hair so often I'm surprised there's any left, and I do it again now. I could go back to my old claim of duplicity on her part and chalk this up to another one of her games, and maybe feel justified in being angry at her for a while, but that isn't what this is.

I also want to call Avery to hear her voice. I want to tell her I've slept on the balcony of my apartment every night since we got back, because sleeping inside, alone in my bed, feels lonelier than being outside with the elements. I miss her scent, her touch, the way I feel when I'm with her, as if I can't breathe and exasperated out of my mind and on fire.

Avery Scottam is the one piece of my life I know with surety I can't live without.

I grab a piece of luggage from my bedroom closet and haul it to the bed, unzipping it and tossing stuff in.

The person I least expect a phone call from is Duke, but I get it anyway. Glaring at the cell phone, I slam my finger on the answer button and bring it to my ear. "What?"

"When are you leaving?" he asks gruffly.

"Friday, same as the last time you asked." I throw a shirt at the pile of clothes.

"What time?"

"Why? You planning on showing up at the airport to make sure I go?"

"What time, smart ass?"

"Ten," I answer shortly.

"What's the airline?"

I shift my jaw. "Delta. Anything else?"

It's a long time before Duke speaks again, his voice oddly hitched. "Yeah, one more thing. What you said about Avery at the party...you meant it?"

I debate on not answering, but find myself doing so, with honesty. "With all my heart."

The asshole doesn't bother saying goodbye, just ends the phone call on me without another word. I shake my head, finding the whole thing sketchy, and finish packing my bag.

AVERY

I look up crows on the internet. I figure it's harder to fear something when you understand it. I mean, I hope. I sip hot cocoa and read with my computer on my lap, fascinated by what I find. According to the website, crows don't forget a face, and when they encounter a mean human, they will teach other crows how to identify the human.

A group of crows is called a murder, which I find odd but also cool. When a crow dies, the murder will surround the dead bird and have a funeral of sorts. Like detectives, they gather to find out who killed the other crow. Then, the murder will form a group and chase predators in a behavior called mobbing.

I pause, thinking back to their behavior that last night in the forest. Had the hunters killed one of theirs? Is that what the crows terrorizing them had been, and we'd just been lucky to have it benefit us? Whatever it was, I'm grateful for them, something I never thought I'd think.

Crows are much smarter and loyal than I realized.

The panic grows the closer it gets to Ben's departure time; a sense of wrongness following me around like a dark shadow. He's leaving tomorrow. I stare at the cell phone; I carry it around with me everywhere. I want to call Ben. I want to tell him: *Yes, I will go with you! I will go with you anywhere!* Instead, I order takeout I don't eat and stare at the wall.

The phone rings, my dad's greeting words: "You're fired."

I jerk back from the receiver, almost falling off the couch. "What?"

"You no longer work for Sanders and Sisters, effective immediately. If at some point in the future, you'd like to resume your employment with the company, you may contact me to see if there is a position open, but not for many, many months from now. I didn't want to do this over the phone, but..."

"Then why are you?" I tightly grip the phone to my ear, stunned and hurt. Duke sighs, the sound ragged and worn. "Because I can't tell you goodbye to your face. Because I want you to have a better life than your mom or me. Because I know you love Ben and Ben loves you. Because I won't be responsible for your unhappiness, damn it!"

I stare unseeingly, breathing fast, mind spinning.

"I love you, Avery, and I want you to be happy. However unfortunate it may be, Ben makes you happy."

I snort, wiping my arm across suddenly weepy eyes. "Come on, Dad, admit that Ben's a pretty great guy."

"He is," he allows after a long pause. "Be safe, take care of yourself, and call me often. If Ben hurts you in any way, I will hunt him down and castrate him. Be sure you tell him that."

"Dad, I can't—I don't know if—" I am unable to choke out the words, too much emotion pressing on me from all sides.

"You do know," he interrupts gently. "His plane leaves at ten tomorrow."

I focus on my breathing, my vision blurred by tears.

"Avery? You got all that?"

"Okay, Dad," I whisper. "Thank you."

After ending the call, I take the gift I have yet to open, laughing until tears come to my eyes when I see it's a DVD of *Stand by Me*. I should have known. Ben was adamant that I watch this someday. Tonight is as good a time as any.

* * * *

The next morning, I dress and race to the airport, pushing past people as I search the main terminal for Ben. The airport is packed, but I barely notice. I ignore everything but the need to find Ben before he steps onto a plane and out of my life. I rush up a flight of stairs and veer to the right. I scan the screens, more confused the longer I search. There are so many flights. Frustrated, I decide to walk. This place is a madness, but I press on, determined to find Ben.

I see him standing near a set of stairs that lead to a security checkpoint, staring out a window. He looks contemplative, and as I watch, determined. Ben's dark hair is shorter than the last time I saw him, his face clean of facial hair, dressed in jeans and a black T-shirt. Adrenaline spikes through me, along with heady relief.

"Ben," I call as I rush toward him, my voice breathless and high.

He turns from the stairwell, disbelief lining his face. "Avery. What are you doing here?"

"I got stung by a bee."

Ben's eyebrows lower. "I see."

I try to catch my breath, continuing on. "And...it made me realize that being stung isn't that bad. Like all the other things I'm scared of, and I somehow manage to overcome. Like everything we got through together when we were lost. I didn't think I could do any of that, and I did. You make me stronger—or being near you makes me stronger."

I'm not making sense, but my heart knows what I need to say, so I keep talking. "I don't want to not do things because I'm afraid of being stung, or—or whatever." I shake my head and try again. "I read about crows too, and really, they don't seem all that bad, as long as you're nice to them. I found out that it's easy to be scared of something you don't understand, but I understand them better, and now they're not so scary. I was shutting myself in a box before even attempting to get out of it."

Ben doesn't say anything, his eyes steady on my face. I can tell the healing cut on his left cheek is going to scar, adding mystery and character to his features.

I take a deep breath. "The point is that I don't want to live my life with regrets, and letting you go to Alabama without me, well, that would be an astronomical regret."

Time ticks by, our reality paused even as the rest of the world rushes around us.

I shift my feet nervously. "What are you thinking?"

Ben smiles, crinkles forming around his eyes. "That's interesting."

I swallow. "It is?"

"It is." He nods, looking to the side. "You see, the thing is, Avery, I decided something too."

Fear takes over my pulse, spinning it out of sync. "You did?"

"I did." Ben turns his lightning gaze on me.

"What?" I whisper. "What was it?"

"I decided that it wouldn't be worth it."

Ben steps closer, bringing his scent, bringing his fire, directly into my hemisphere. I close my eyes. I've missed the feeling of him being near. I didn't realize I could miss a sensation that much. Ben brings meaning to what is otherwise senseless to me, and I feel incomplete without him.

His fingers are cool upon my cheek, forging a trail to my lips. "Any adventure I might go on, without you, isn't worth it. I'd still be lost, Avery. Because you're what I'd be trying to find, and you're already here."

Ben swallows. "You lied about being scared, Avery, but I lied too. The thought of not being with you—it *terrifies* me. I'd rather fight with you every day, than have boring orderliness in your absence."

My eyes pop open.

"I was leaving," Ben says.

"I know—"

"No, you don't." Ben shakes his head, piercing me with his intense eyes. "I was leaving the airport to come find you."

"But your trip. Alabama…"

"I don't need to be anywhere but with you. I'm staying in Chicago."

"You're willing to give up your trip for me?" It's a beautiful sentiment. I sniffle and blink, releasing tears. "You can't do that, Ben."

Confusion mars his face. "Isn't that what you want? Isn't that why you're here?"

"No. I want to be with you, but I also want you to do what you planned. I want you to go to Alabama." I cup his jaw, feeling the prickles of stubble against my skin. "And I want to go with you."

Hope dares to lighten his eyes, but then Ben goes still, his voice particularly deadened when he asks, "What about your dad?"

"My dad fired me from Sanders and Sisters last night," I tell him, laughing.

Ben jerks back, anger reddening his face. "What the hell? Why would he do that?"

"Because he didn't want me to end up like him and my mom. He wants me to be happy." I swallow thickly. "And Ben, he knows I love you."

He goes still, his eyes shooting to mine. His nostrils flare as he takes in a breath, holds it, and releases it.

"I love you, Ben."

Ben briefly sets his forehead to mine. With shaking palms, he pushes hair from my face and looks into my eyes. "I love you too, Avery, so much."

Something light swirls in my stomach, something I can only ascertain as to be jubilation. We had a rocky path, but here we are, choosing to be with each other, whatever may come.

Ben's voice is rough with emotion when he says, "He told me to stay away from you."

"And he saw how miserable I was with you gone," I answer.

Wariness lingers on his face. "You're sure?"

I laugh. "Yes. I'm sure."

As I watch, his expression transforms, and it's so sweetly happy that my heart stutters in my chest.

"I watched the movie you sent me. I love that movie. It's a great movie."

"I told you."

I wrinkle my nose at him.

Ben laughs, pulling me in for a kiss, electrocuting my nerve endings. The bustle of the airport fades away; the only people here are Ben and me. I want to do this every day. I *can* do this every day. The kiss goes on and on, until the point where I have to pull away to get any air into my lungs. I smile so widely at Ben that my cheeks hurt, and he returns it, looking boyishly handsome.

He takes a deep breath, briefly resting his forehead to mine. "Avery."

"What is it?"

Ben steps back, shaking his head. "I can't do it."

I frown. "Can't do what?"

He runs fingers through his hair. "I can't let you leave your dad, although, with the way he's treated me since finding out how I feel about you, I kind of feel like being a dick to him. Which I can be. Here. In Chicago. With you close to him."

My pulse picks up. "What are you saying?"

"We're going to be together." Ben threads his fingers through mine. "You said you need me, but you need your dad too. I'm not going to take you away from him or force you to choose."

"You'll stay?" I whisper, my pulse ricocheting with joy.

Ben squeezes my fingers. "I want to be where you are, Avery. You're my adventure."

"What about traveling, seeing the United States?"

He shrugs. "We can do that together, in small spurts. We'll be pros at mini-vacations. Maybe we can even go camping."

I pause, taking in Ben's twinkling eyes. "Maybe. Eventually. In a camper."

Ben laughs.

My chest fills, my face stretched wide with a smile. "I am so unbelievably in love with you. Just, um, one thing before we start all this adventuring." I hold up a finger, giving him an imploring look.

"What's that?"

I gnaw my lower lip with my teeth. "Would you mind terribly if we go to Rosa's, like, right now? I didn't have breakfast and I'm *starving*. Plus, as you know, we both are due a major pig-out session."

Humor dances in his eyes as Ben tugs me close for another kiss. "Anything for Queen Avery."

Keep reading for a special excerpt of *THE MAP TO YOU*, by *USA TODAY* Bestselling author, Lindy Zart.

They both had secrets that could drive people apart—or bring them together forever...

Keeping his inner demons at bay means Blake Malone has more than enough trouble on his plate. He doesn't need any extra complications. But that's exactly what he gets when, on his way to North Dakota, he leaves his truck unattended—and returns to find a beautiful woman sleeping in the front seat.

Opal Allen seems to have a knack for attracting trouble. Which is why she isn't about to tell her new road trip companion the real reason she needs to hightail it out of town. But Blake has a way of seeing right through her, which is both terrifying and exhilarating. Now her biggest problem is figuring out how to resist their undeniable attraction. Because once this road trip is over, she plans on never seeing Blake again.

But the best adventures don't go according to plan.

Look for* The Map to You, *on sale now.

1
Blake

Last I checked, I was traveling alone.

I walk to my grandfather's truck, a 1987 Ford F-series pickup in blue and white, and blink at the small form curled up on the seat.

Under the darkened dome of the sky, it's hard to discern anything other than the size of the thing inside my truck, and that it has dark hair. It could be a man, a woman—even a kid. I quickly scan the parking lot, searching for any accomplices to a premeditated crime involving yours truly.

It's the end of August, and the days can be wicked humid and hot, but the same can't be said for the nights. I have on a light jacket to help keep the chill off my skin. I glance into the cab of the truck. Small as this person is, they have to be feeling the cold.

The night is still and quiet, only two other vehicles taking up parking spaces of the 24-hour convenience store. It's after midnight on a Wednesday. Most sane people are home and in bed. I focus on the stranger in my truck. Whatever they're up to, it's bound to be nefarious. I like my share of nefarious dealings, as long as I'm the one doing them.

Muttering to myself and craving a cigarette, I carefully set down the plastic bag of chips, beef jerky, and orange juice I purchased to curb the hunger gnawing at my gut. I rub the stubble along my jaw, head cocked, as I come to a decision. It's an easy one—whoever they are, they can't stay in my truck.

Hands out, palms down, I soundlessly skulk around the front of the truck and toward the passenger side. My eyes shift from side to side in pursuit of any possible friends of theirs hoping to make my night especially spectacular with a blunt object to the back of the head. I feel ridiculous, sure I look like the Pink Panther slinking around in the dark.

My boot kicks a piece of gravel and it pings against the side of the truck my mother secretly kept in a storage unit all these years for me. I didn't even know the truck was still around until my brother Graham unknowingly drove it from North Dakota to Wisconsin my last week in the Cheesehead state. I just about cried when I saw it. Just about, but not quite—because crying would be bad for my image. My throat burned from keeping it in, though, and when Kennedy, Graham's girlfriend, commented on the redness of my eyes, I told her it was a reaction to whatever perfume she'd doused herself in.

Smooth, that's me.

I wince, hoping the rock didn't do any damage to the truck. This is one of the last pieces I have of the man who never judged me in all the years he was alive. Good thing for my grandfather's untarnished view of me that my life didn't completely fall to shit until after he died.

A head snaps up, and large, dark eyes slam into mine. I freeze against the unexpected jolt of them. The woman appears youngish, her face pointy and elfin. Her features are interesting, like it couldn't be decided whether to make her look exotic or plain. We study one another for one charged moment, and then whatever had her immobile collapses. Her mouth opens in a piercing scream, and she scrambles to the middle of the cab. I jerk back, her reaction startling me.

"What the hell kind of a person creeps up on someone like that?" she accuses. Her voice is breathless, but there is an undertone of huskiness that brings my nerve endings to attention.

I open my mouth with the intention of apologizing, and then realize what I'm about to do. Scowl taking over my features, I grip the door handle and pull. She scoots across the seat with her back to the driver's side door and, wide-eyed, looks back at me.

"Get out…of my truck," I say slowly, setting my palms on the worn and torn vinyl upholstery to lean forward menacingly.

"You left the doors unlocked. And the windows down," she adds, like that makes it acceptable for anyone to commandeer my vehicle.

I nod. "A clear welcome to all vagrants far and wide."

"I'm not a vagrant," she insists, tightening her arms around herself.

Something in her tone gives me pause, and I sweep my gaze over her. Her hair looks dark brown or black and is styled choppily around her face and jaw. The woman's chin juts forward as our eyes connect, silently rebellious. There are dark splotches beneath her eyes and she's holding herself protectively. Under the cropped jean jacket and jeans, her figure appears slight. She reminds me of a terrier, tiny and fierce with more boldness than common sense.

"Who are you and what are you doing in my truck?"

"I was contemplating hotwiring it and selling it, but then I wondered if it would actually start."

"It starts." Usually.

When she doesn't answer the first question, I lambaste her with my eyes, refusing to be the first to break the stare. Her mouth is small and pursed with annoyance, like I'm bothering *her* by wanting to know what she's doing in my truck. Under the heat of my gaze, she makes a face and looks away, showing me her profile. Her nose is long and slim, her chin sharp and stubborn. It feels like a small victory that she was the one to break eye contact. Something tells me she isn't one to easily give in.

"Conversations generally work best when you talk," I say shortly.

Sighing, the woman regards me as she sits up straighter. "I fell asleep," she mumbles, her mouth twisting at the confession.

I squint my eyes as I straighten, peering over the hood of the truck. We appear to be alone, but that doesn't make me relax any. Appearances are commonly shit and not to be trusted.

My shoulders pop as I rotate them, and I level my gaze once more on the stranger. "I want to make sure I'm understanding this right—you picked a random truck in a gas station parking lot to fall asleep in?"

"No." She picks at the hem of her jacket, a shiver going through her small frame. "I watched you go into the store." Almond-shaped eyes latch onto me. "You seemed harmless enough."

I lock my fingers behind my head and look at the star-strewn sky. This is an insanity I cannot be a part of. An urge to laugh hits me and I repress it, knowing it won't sound in any way normal. I don't need this right now. I have enough problems without this, whatever *this* is.

I stride around the truck and grasp the door handle at the same time she propels herself in the other direction. My blood ignites, and with a stiff jaw, I reach into the truck, grab her tiny wrist, and pull, my eyes refusing to let go of hers. Anger flashes through her eyes and contorts her features. She doesn't look quite as innocent now. She looks vicious, and mighty—for a munchkin. Calling me an assortment of colorful names, she fights to get free of my grip, and I only tighten it, swinging her down from the cab. She lands awkwardly, stumbling into me, and then she savagely kicks my shin with a booted foot. I grunt and twist her around, her back to my front, and barricade her with my arms.

"Let go of me!"

She squirms against my shackled arms, her head barely reaching my chest. Her body is a compact heat source, singeing me where it connects with mine. She's tiny, proportioned more to that of a teenager than a young woman. There's too little of her, and yet her rambunctious attitude seems to make up for it. I put my mouth close to her ear and feel the pulse pick up in her wrist I hold. The pose would be erotic, if not for the hellion in my arms.

"Start talking. Now. Or the police get involved." I am loath to involve law enforcement in anything that pertains to me, but she doesn't know that.

Her body goes limp, tremors having their way with her form. "Please, no. No cops," she beseeches, her small voice twinging my conscience.

Has she been in trouble with the law? Has her past been so twisted with corruption, like mine, that she sees any authority figure as an enemy?

With a frustrated growl, I release her.

She spins around, a triumphant look on her face, and dives to the left. I move with her, blocking her. Her eyes narrow as she calculates her next move. She feints right and goes left again, but I am right there with her. She's fast and sneaky, but I am a professional at games, no matter that I retired from them years ago. There was a time when I spent most of my days either getting in trouble or trying to get out of it.

One word leaves me and it is coated with warning. "Talk."

The woman's shoulders curve inward and the bravado drops from her face, making her look young and scared. "People are after me," she whispers.

Interesting. I cross my arms and widen my stance. "Who?"

"I don't know who." She drops her eyes and resumes her pathetic look, hands clasped before her. "They've been following me for days and... when I saw that your truck was *unlocked*, and *unattended*"—I frown as her voice loses its softness and turns sardonic—"I took cover until they left. But they'll be back. I know they will."

She grabs the front of my jacket and yanks me forward, her eyes enormous and pleading. She is stronger than I would have guessed. "Please, wherever you're going, please take me with you. Before they come back for me. Who knows what they plan on doing with me, but I'm sure it's something bad."

"You've been outwitting and outrunning unknown assailants for days?"

"Yes." She nods vehemently.

"On foot?"

Her hands drop from my jacket and she steps back. "What?"

I gesture around the mostly barren parking lot. "Where's your mode of transportation? How exactly are they following you? How many are there? What do they look like? And if they're so gung ho on apprehending you, what made them take off?"

"I don't—I don't know. I wasn't paying attention. I've been too busy trying to stay alive." As if knowing I don't believe a word she's saying, her eyebrows lower, and she hides her eyes from mine.

The whole situation is mad, and I'd have to be mad as well to even contemplate having her as a travel mate. And yet...free entertainment. Because if she is nothing else, she is certainly amusing. Something niggles at my brain. Something annoying. Knowing it's my conscience, I could ignore it, or I could face it. There is a reason she is so desperate to leave with me, and I'm pretty sure that at some future time I'll wonder what I was thinking to agree to this, but...

"I'm going to North Dakota," I tell her slowly, never once looking from her.

Hope brightens her eyes. "North Dakota sounds great. Perfect, really. Exactly where I was hoping to go."

I step closer, and she steps back. We do this until her back is flush with the truck box and there is no escape. Her throat bobs as she swallows, and though trepidation runs across her face, she doesn't look away. I set a hand on either side of her, trapping her within my arms as the cool metal of the truck box freezes my palms.

"I have an idea who you are," I say conversationally. I let those words sink in; I watch a million thoughts race across her features.

"Y-you do?" she squeaks.

I focus on her lips. They glisten under the light of the moon, soft and inviting. "How old are you?" I ask absently, my voice a low hum.

"Twenty-three."

Truth.

"How old are you?" she shoots back.

"Twenty-six. What's your name?"

She fidgets, and as if realizing she is, goes still. The pulse at the base of her neck flutters like it wants to fly away. "Piper."

Lie.

But I'll let her have it, for now.

"Piper," I say softly, bringing my face dangerously close to hers. "You... are a liar."

She swallows, her lips parting. The motion is done without thought, a nervous gesture, and yet I fight to straighten from her, to put space between us. To step back. It's either that or kiss her. I can do without knowing what the lips of a con artist taste like.

"Let's go." My tone is rough, strained with unwanted attraction for a duplicitous stranger.

She doesn't move from the side of the truck, and with a hand braced on the door, I turn to her. "Are you coming or not?"

"But you...you said..."

"That you're a liar? Yes. I recall. It wasn't that long ago."

"But..." She hesitantly moves away from the truck.

"You went to great lengths to procure a ride with me." I look her up and down, wondering what secrets she has trapped inside that imaginative brain. "Who am I to deny a damsel in distress?"

Her eyes narrow at my tone as she angles her body toward the passenger's side of the truck. She knows the kind of person she is, but she has no idea who I am. The look she shoots me before she gets in the Ford tells me she's having second thoughts. I wonder if I should tell her to get out while she can. A slow smile, hidden in the dark, claims my face.

* * * *

Opal

He's an alternative rock boy. That I am not surprised by. He's got the look—dark unkempt hair, derisive cast to his sharp features. The black bomber jacket with the upturned collar, the straight-legged jeans covering black boots. I bet beneath that jacket he has on a shirt sporting a band name. His vibe screams rebel and bad boy and loner and any other thing most mothers warn their daughters against. My fingernails dig into my palms, wondering if my mom would have done the same.

All he needs is a cigarette dangling from a corner of his mouth and he could be the quintessential man a woman's heart should always avoid. I've met his kind before. I've even dated them. Never for long, and never without wishing I hadn't.

This guy looks and smells like trouble. And his voice—it isn't smooth or all that appealing. In fact, it sounds like broken glass. Grating and sharp. Nothing about him cries "love of my life" material. Which is just as well. I don't need trouble right now.

"Why are you going to North Dakota?" I ask to fill the silence. My eyes want to close and I slide my fingers under the crisp denim fabric of my jacket and pinch the skin near my wrist. Hard. The resulting throb keeps my brain occupied and slumber out of reach.

A good portion of me thinks I will end up regretting my insistence on pairing up with the sullen man with the easily accessible truck. It was a spontaneous decision, brought on by lack of sleep, hunger, and being ditched by my ride when I slapped a roving hand from my thigh. I saw the North Dakota license plates on his ancient truck, and I figured that was a good sign he was heading in that direction. North Dakota is one state over from Montana—my destination.

"What's your real name?" he counters.

"Jackie," I fib, turning my head to look out the passenger window. Shadows and indecipherable shapes meet my eyes.

"We should make it to North Dakota in a day or two, depending on how far I can get before needing sleep," he comments, after a prolonged pause in which he silently called me a liar. Again.

"You never told me your name either," I say, staring at the headlights marking a narrow path on the freeway. Other than us, the road is empty. It's eerie, and makes me think of alternate realities and apocalypses.

"I didn't want you to feel left out with your mysterious persona." He fiddles with the radio, finds repeated static, and then turns it off. "Let's do it this way—you tell me yours, and I'll tell you mine."

"I can't tell you my real name. It's safer for you if you don't know."

The responding snort tells me what he thinks of that.

People usually at least try to believe me before assuming everything that comes out of my mouth is a lie. Which, most of it is. I don't know why I lie, especially now, when I sound like I'm from a cluster of bad action movies that use the same lines. It's habitual, an old form of self-soothing I never outgrew.

I clutch my scuffed and dirt-kissed pink backpack to my chest, my meager belongings inside telling a sad tale of a drifter with no anchors to anything but herself.

"If you know, then they can use that knowledge to hunt me down. They'd torture you, and let's face it, we both know you'd break."

His eyes snap to mine and back to the road.

I'm starting over, reinventing myself. I don't know how, but I am. I figure I'll know who I want to be when I catch a glimpse of her.

"Others have died for knowing it," I continue.

The man shakes his dark head, amusement adding lines to the side of his face I can see. "Really? Do tell."

I uncross my arms and sit up straighter, a spark of excitement entering my voice. "I'm an undercover agent on a top secret mission. That's all you can know."

"Does this mission include pink elephants and machetes?"

"How'd you know?" I swallow back laughter at the look he gives me.

His eyes flicker my way and down. "What's in the bag?"

I protectively pull the bag tighter to my frame. "Machetes and mace. A few stuffed pink elephants. Necessities for my mission."

"What's your mission, to ruin some kid's day by massacring stuffed animals in front of them?"

I freeze, my breaths as immobile as me. *Did I ruin her day, or her week, or maybe a couple months? Did I ruin her life?*

He glances at me, a slice of dark eyes that can shred and rebuild with a single look. "It was a joke."

"Best joke I ever heard," I mutter. I relax against the hard seat, feigning calm that left me with his words.

The man's hands flex on the steering wheel. He expels a loud breath. "You had a shitty childhood."

It isn't a question, and I don't answer. He thinks this is about me, but it isn't.

He swears, loudly and viciously enough that I jump, and I quickly tell him, "Yes, okay? I had a shitty childhood. You don't have to get mad. I mean, it wasn't all bad."

"No—I left the bag at the gas station."

I instinctively look at my backpack on my lap and the black duffel bag on the floor near my feet I was tempted to scavenge through while he was in the store. Lucky for him, I haven't yet added theft to my list of crimes.

I turn to him. "What bag?"

"The bag with food in it. The whole reason I stopped at that store."

"But you picked up something better than food, didn't you?" I chirp.

He scowls. "I need a cigarette."

My stomach constricts and gurgles as if to commiserate with him over the lack of food. When did I last eat? I think back over the many hours since I started this impulsive road trip. This morning—I had a granola bar this morning. Talking and thinking about food reminds me of how hungry I am. I have a total of one apple and three granola bars to last me until I can find a way to come up with more money or let go of the sparse supply I carry.

"Cigarettes are bad for your health."

"So is mentioning that to people who smoke."

That effectively shuts me up.

He uses one hand to roughly rub his face, his aura fraught with agitation. His movements are jerky as he flips on a blinker and takes the next exit.

I brace myself with a hand on the door when the Ford abruptly decelerates and merges sharply to the right. "Where are we going?"

"Hell comes to mind as an eventual destination, but for now, there." He points a finger at a beat-up red sign that has a cartoon chef with a white hat and a wide grin that reads "Chucky's Diner: Open All Hours. Come hungry, leave happy."

"Sounds like sophisticated dining. I feel underdressed."

The truck rolls to a stop at the intersection and the dark-haired man turns to look at me. I can't see his eye color, but that isn't necessary to feel the heat of his gaze as it strips me bare. His eyes feel like they are directly on my skin, burning me, seeing into me, revealing everything I don't want him to see. I don't understand why he is scrutinizing me, or what he thinks he'll find.

The breath I take is shaky, and the sound of it ends whatever spell he has me under. He blinks and faces forward, his motions stiff as the truck accelerates. Silence alive with pinpricks of unnamed sensation travels with us as he drives to the diner. I don't notice my legs are weak until I almost fall as I hop from the truck, gravel spitting under the pressure of my boots as I fight for balance. I shoot upright and pat down my layered waves of hair that take much joy in their constant mutiny. I try to appear nonchalant, even as my pulse dips and sputters and veers in dizzying directions.

He meets me at the front of the old Ford, his head angled to the side as he watches me approach. I think I prefer sound of any kind to his quiet, so I hum to myself as we walk through the partially filled parking lot, the dark building's windows filled with light and people. I hug my backpack to my chest, unwilling to leave it out of sight. A metal sign on top of the roof hangs sideways, swaying and creaking as a cool breeze goes by. I hurry past it, not wanting to be beneath the sign should it decide it wants to come down.

Before we reach the door, the scent of fried food teases my nostrils and I press an arm to my aching stomach as I step inside. I won't be able to order much, and I'll have to eat slowly to trick myself into thinking it is enough, but any food is better than the emptiness I presently feel. I am not a stranger to hunger, but it hasn't ever gotten better just because I got used to feeling it.

The handful of people seated at booths pause in their conversations and shift their attention to me and the man behind me. I inhale and hold it, paranoia telling me to turn around and walk right back out of this place. I scan the faces of the occupants, knowing it's unlikely I'll see anyone I know from my home state but searching all the same.

"I'm all about enjoying the scenery, but we'll get to a table faster if you move your legs," a deep, prickly voice informs me.

I clench my jaw and step forward, heading for a booth straight ahead across the green and white decorated room. With the various fake plants and flowers in pots and on window ledges, it looks like a floral shop threw up in here. Under a ceiling of megawatt-strength light bulbs, I get my first real look at the man I'm traveling with. We slide onto the booth seats, facing one another. His skin is bleached of color, making the blackness of his rumpled hair that much more obvious. The eyebrows are thick and low, giving him a perpetual displeased look. His nose is hawkish and arrogant, and there is a dimple in his chin. He's not handsome, but his eyes are deep, and the character of his features demands notice.

I look into his piercing gray eyes and my stomach spins, and the room spins, and everything but him is spinning. My fingers itch to cast his unsmiling features onto the fibers of a single sheet of paper, but I only have so much paper left, and my charcoal pencils are down to stubs. I can't draw anyone unless it's financially advantageous. His eyes are thunderstorms, lightning, and every natural disaster wrapped up in an iris. The man is unmoving, untouched, as the atmosphere pivots and straightens. Looking at me like he is not all surprised to find me intrigued by his features.

"Like what you see? I don't blame you. Most women do."

I swallow, my mouth dry. "Not especially, but it isn't like I can do anything about it."

His eyebrows shoot up, one corner of his mouth lifting and lowering.

I'm sure I look a fright. Other than sponge bathing from gas station and restaurant sinks, I haven't bathed in days. My hair feels heavy with dirt and the need to be washed, and what I wouldn't give for a proper bath. One I could sink into, with steaming hot water and scented oils and salts. I almost sigh at the thought. I left Illinois in a hurry, and other than the few clothes I tossed in my bag and other necessities, I am without most of my possessions. Possessions are just that, though, and it didn't make sense to take more than me and what I can't live without.

Two clear glasses of water thump to the table and my eyes snap up to the purple-haired waitress with a barbell through each eyebrow. She has a tired smile on her faintly lined face as she hands a laminated menu to me and my acquaintance. "Hi, I'm Vicky. Can I get you two anything to drink?"

"Just water," I say. What I really want to order is an unending supply of sweet, carbonated, caffeinated beverages.

"Coffee, please," he tells her, holding my gaze.

"All right. I'll be right back with that." She takes off, leaving the fragrance of apples in her wake.

He steeples his fingers beneath his dimpled chin and levels soulful eyes on me. "So, Piper-Jackie, did you commit a crime of some kind?"

"Why would you ask that?"

"Me, I like to plan for things." He straightens and shrugs off his jacket. I was wrong about the band name—it's a red Mr. Kool-Aid T-shirt. "If there's a chance I'm going to be viewed as an accomplice, and subsequently arrested, I want to make sure my schedule is free. You know..." he says in a bored tone. "Details."

His coffee is set before him, interrupting the conversation I'd rather not have.

"Are you guys ready to order?"

"No," he says at the same time I say, "Yes."

She divides her gaze between us, a small notepad and pen in hand. "Okay," she replies slowly.

"Toast," I blurt. "I'll take two slices of white toast."

The woman waits, finally asking, "Anything else?"

I chug the glass of water, hoping it will help fill the void in my stomach, and push the empty cup toward her. "More water, please."

Eyeing me, my dining companion orders white toast, two hard-boiled eggs, bacon, and pancakes. My mouth is salivating like crazy by the time he lists the last food item. We hand over our menus to the waitress, and the tension is in full force again. I pick at a loose pink thread on my bag and hope I'll suddenly become invisible and he'll stop examining me like he is. His eyes are like a hot touch as they lay claim to me.

"Is there anything I need to know before we get any further into our little adventure?" he presses.

"No," I respond. Nothing too bad. Nothing it would benefit him to know.

He pauses, turning his head to show me his prominent profile. The sound of his fingertips tapping on the tabletop is the only noise. He stops, looks at me. "You're either running to something, or away from it. I think I know which it is for you."

I don't reply, focusing on the salt and pepper shakers to the left of me. It's a little of both.

Our food is brought, mine small and lacking. I shove a piece of toast in my mouth before putting any butter or jelly on it, and his hand freezes around an egg. I bite off another chunk, swallowing before properly chewing. It's dry and flavorless, but it's sustenance. So much for my plan to take my time eating.

He slowly lowers his hand, and then sets the egg on my plate, his eyes turning to slits when I open my mouth to protest. Next, two pieces of bacon are plopped on the plate. When he moves to add a pancake to the growing pile of food, I snatch the plate away and shake my head. I don't want to be in debt to him.

I tear my gaze from the pancake, in this singular instance really wishing I had less pride, because if I did that pancake would be mine. A slice of bacon teeters on the edge of the plate and I sweep it up and into my mouth before it can fall to the floor and no longer be edible. Although, I'd be tempted to still eat it if it did.

"No more," I command around the crunchy, crispy bits of meat I have yet to swallow.

A barely perceptible nod is the only acknowledgment I get.

I eat everything on my plate before he makes it through his pancakes. I don't care about manners—not that anyone really ever taught me any. Stomach full, I sit back, content and sleepy. My mouth twisting against the words, I thank him.

"I'm not going to be able to last much longer on the road. I'll find the closest hotel and get us a room," he says quietly, adding salt and pepper to his egg before taking a bite.

"I don't need a room." My words are sharp. I don't have money for that. I'll sleep in the truck if he insists on getting one.

Exhaustion slumps his broad shoulders and he trains his tornadic eyes on me. He suddenly looks worn out by life, and it humanizes him, removes a layer of edges from his severe personality. "Where are you trying to get to?"

"Home," I answer immediately, my pulse thrumming at the thought. It is my biggest quest to have a place to call that, for once, finally. When I find it, I'm never letting it go.

"And where is home?"

"I'll know when I see it." I smile, knowing sorrow leaks out through the curve of it.

A frown takes over the space between his eyebrows. Crinkles form around his eyes as he squints at me, and he leans forward, resting his elbows on the table. His dark head tilts, reminding me of a raven as he wordlessly prods and deciphers, looks more into my words than I like.

"Truth," he murmurs, and I don't even ask what he's referencing, because I somehow already know.

About the Author

Lindy Zart has been writing since she was a child. Luckily for readers, her writing has improved since then. She is the author of *Roomies*, a *USA Today* bestseller. She lives in Wisconsin with her family. Lindy loves hearing from people who enjoy her work. She also has a completely natural obsession with the following: coffee, pizza, peanut butter, Bloody Marys, and wine. Learn more at www.lindyzart.com

Printed in the United States
by Baker & Taylor Publisher Services